THE ANTITHESIS

HYMN OF THE MULTIVERSE 2

SHATTER STAR PRESS
ISBN 9781794571501

TWO

HONOR

'Lo the Wrath

'Lo the wrath of Sanctum's Savior
The Nehelian who feasts upon the blood of his own kind;
Hear the laughter of his malice bellow,
Upon the highest spires of Eroqam.

'Lo the wrath of Sanctum's Savior
The Nehelian who drinks upon the souls of his own kind;
Hear the cries of his people echo,
As the flames of Sanctum rise.

'Lo the wrath of Sanctum's Savior
The Nehelian who yearns for the death of his own kind;
Hear the whispers of his victims tremble,
As the ruins fall from the sky.

'Lo the wrath of Sanctum's Savior
The Nehelian who is freed from his own kind;
Hear the screams of his pain and sorrow,
As the smoke clears in his demise.

'Lo the wrath of Sanctum's Savior
The Nehelian who is no more;
Hear the Angels shout in communion,
As light in Heaven is restored.

O

RUN

(The Enforcers have found you)

THE ANGEL FLED IN TERROR.

The sounds of screams and gunfire echoed through the darkness as her feet pounded over tiles. Bursting through the doors and past the genocide, fear blinded her, and she slid on a pool of blood. It was fresh; still warm.

She fell, cracking the side of her face against the floor. She felt a *crunch*, and knew something was broken. Her jaw tingled, and she couldn't feel her tongue. But that wasn't important right now. She needed to get away. Scrambling to her feet with a desperate sob, she continued to flee.

It was all wrong; she shouldn't have signed up. The infiltrations were never successful and even *if* she survived she'd have to face her family empty-handed. The rations were all but gone, and anarchy rose through starvation. The last of the supplies were held in safe-keeping by rebel groups.

No one *wanted* to do this. They just wanted to eat.

She had never thought her life would lead up to this very moment: running through a supplies facility in Sanctum, soaked in the blood of her friends. She didn't want to hurt anyone, and the Enforcers shouldn't have arrived so quickly. But then again, they *always* did.

Only seventy years ago she was attending school and studying to be an engineer. She dreamed of working at the Plexus when she graduated. But then the food ran out, and the sky went dark. There was no light, so everything began to die. She didn't even understand what happened. One day everything was fine, the next it was *gone*. She still remembered her world fading into the distance of the cosmos as their ship drifted away, floating toward a terrifying unknown. As far as she was concerned, her life had ended then.

She heard screams in the next room and slid to a stop at the door.

Keep running, said her instinct, but she had to see what was behind that grimy, circular window.

Two Enforcers were brutalizing another girl; she didn't know her name but had talked to her on the trip here. Too young to legally work, forced to do the rebels' bidding so that she might have a week of food.

Eventually the screams died, and their victim stopped moving. They kicked her battered, violated body to the side with the rest of the pile, laughing. Nausea crept up her throat, but this was something she'd seen before. The Nehel were vile and immoral; there was no atrocity too beneath them.

"Status," she heard a voice announce. It came from their radios.

"All clear," one of them answered through their masks.

The Enforcers dressed differently than the Sanctum militia; black armor and buzzard masks, with gleaming red eyes. Their belts were decorated with killing machinery—rifles, knives, and everything in between. They tried to look like monsters, but they didn't need costumes. *Savages,* filthy and barbaric.

"How many?"

"Fourteen."

"The Eye of Akul said there were fifteen."

"We only found fourteen, Commandant."

"I don't care how many you've found, Ara. They said there were fifteen, so you're missing one."

Her heart skipped a beat. She bolted down the hall, blood pounding in her ears.

She was going to die!

They were going to catch her!

She was going to end up like that girl!

Breathe, breathe, breathe…

Her eyes widened as an unguarded exit came into view at the end of the hall. She was only one hundred feet away from freedom. Hope gave her a boost of adrenaline, and her wings released as she ran even faster. The hall erupted with the sounds of tearing cloth and feathers beating air as she burst through the door.

Sanctum's evening light shined on her face and she closed her eyes, taking flight. Against all odds, she had escaped. She was *free!* She was—

BANG.

I
CROWN OF THORNS

Sᴀɴᴄᴛᴜᴍ ᴡᴀs ᴜɴᴜsᴜᴀʟʟʏ ǫᴜɪᴇᴛ.

At this hour, the streets were typically packed with traffic. Instead, a single aero-craft drifted by every five minutes. Fog had taken to the air, leaving the spires of my city as caliginous black outlines. I found the scenery fitting.

I waited in the opened doors of an Enforcer military craft, surveying the grain supply factory below. In the wake of gunfire, explosions and screams, my frown was apathetic.

Fucking angels; they *deserved* it.

My pilot, Lakash, looked over his shoulder. "They're taking too long, Commandant."

"Give them another minute. It sounds like they're cleaning up."

"Sir."

I crossed my arms, huddling into my coat. It was cold, as usual, but the weather was fine for us. All that sunny, sweaty crap in the top layers was for the *whites*. I didn't understand how they endured it.

Okay, Lakash was right; they were taking way too long. We only had a fifteen minute window. After that, the press would arrive, and I didn't think they'd like what they would find. But hey, *someone* needed to take care of this mess.

The sound of media aero-crafts echoed through the clouds. Lakash and I turned to the noise, sharing dismal looks. "Get some guards down here to fend them off. Arrest them if you have to."

"I wonder what your father would think?" he asked.

I rolled my eyes. Lakash and I had known each other since we were boys. He often mistook our friendship for permission to overstep his boundaries on the job. "What my father would think is none of your business. Get those guards down here, *now*."

Right about now my father was probably drunk in his study, drooling on the pages of a poetry book. Like *he* fucking cared what was going on anymore.

Lakash reached for his radio, while I leapt from the craft and flew to the vacant lot. When I landed my wings folded into my back, and I removed my radio from my belt.

"Status," I ordered into it.

There was a moment of silence.

"All clear."

I sighed in relief. "How many?"

"Fourteen."

Nope, that was wrong. "The Eye of Akul said there were fifteen."

"We only found fourteen, Commandant."

My jaw clenched as I tried to keep my cool. My brother was being lazy, and this wasn't the time for it. "I don't care how many you *found*, Ara. They said there were fifteen, so you're missing one."

There came a sigh. *"We'll find them, Qaira."*

The crafts were getting louder, *nearer*. Ten minutes had passed, and we still needed to clean up the mess. If we didn't find that last white soon, I was going to have to pull some serious bureaucratic shit. Maybe an arms deal gone wrong or something. All I had to do was get rid of the—

A door burst open behind me. I reached for my gun.

And just as the angel took off, I shot her in the back of the head. From such a close range, half of her cranium exploded and she fell from the sky in a trail of white feathers. When she collapsed, the remaining globs of her brain spilled across the pavement.

I put the radio to my lips, watching her bleed.

"Never mind; we're done. Get the bodies out of there."

* * *

"Hey," Ara said, removing his mask, "that was a nice shot."

We were landing at Eroqam, Sanctum's military headquarters and also my home. It rose higher than the tallest buildings of the inner city, sculpted from black *coua*. Coua was expensive to build with, because it was difficult to mine. Only the most important places in Sanctum were coua-composed, as it took forever to erode and was hardy against harsh climates. To attest to this, Eroqam stood long before the rest of Sanctum.

I watched the lines of armed guards awaiting our landing on the circular roof below us.

"She could have gotten away," I responded after a two minute delay, one in which I'd spent debating whether or not to punch my brother in the face for the headache he'd given me.

Ara scoffed. "Not with *you* standing there."

Our craft touched down and the thirteen of us walked in single file toward the Commons. My men would get unsuited and go home. I would go to my room and make a break for the stash of malay in my dresser. I began to itch a little while ago; it was far past due for another dose.

My brother followed me to the living quarters, a good fifteen minute walk from where we landed. Almost every trip from the Commons to the living quarters consisted of Ara talking my head off, while I (barely) listened. But this time, both of us were quiet as we traversed the long, dark walkway. It was after dinner, so most of our staff was gone.

"You alright?" I asked after we'd reached the halfway point.

He shrugged. "I don't know why we're waiting for *them* to attack us all the time."

I shoved my hands into my pockets. "I'm working on that. You know how the Council is."

"Ceram said grocers are running out of food in the lower districts. We can't stop every supply factory from being destroyed."

Ceram was my brother's girlfriend who, despite his previous statement, had everything delivered to her on a silver platter. That was the lifestyle of a woman promised to one of the Regent's sons. But he was right; Sanctum couldn't hold the fort forever. Eventually we'd become as weak and starved as the Archaeans.

"Patience, please," I muttered. "And while you wait, why don't you work on getting your priorities straight?"

He lifted a brow. We looked similar whenever he did that. *"Excuse me?"*

"What's more important, Ara? Eliminating all fifteen targets or getting your dick wet?" When he only glared at me, I elaborated. "I saw the bodies. You could at least *try* some subtlety."

"I didn't fuck any of them. Garan and Uless did."

I stared ahead. The dim light of our quarters could be seen across the hallway. "From now on, get the job done and get out. Do you understand? You don't need to *beat* the angels to death. That takes too much time. Just shoot them in the back of the head and move on to the next."

I blocked his path with an intimidating look. I wanted to make sure he understood that I meant business.

He looked away, sheepishly. "Right."

Ara's malice wasn't what upset me. I understood what happened to my soldiers on the field. Why *wouldn't* they want to tear the heads from their enemies? The Enforcers' brutality toward the Archaeans symbolized their hatred. They needed that hate to win the battle. I didn't respect the life of any angel, so I didn't care if one of my men put a bullet in an angel's head and then fucked the gunshot wound. I just didn't want them doing that when it compromised our operation.

Civility was useless against the Archaean Forces; my father had tried that for years. Our actions kept them scared. It made their soldiers question whether they *really* wanted to blow up one of our buildings if the chances of getting tortured, raped and shot were high enough. We kept their morale crushed beneath Sanctum's heel.

At the end of the hall we stopped at a sealed metal door. I punched some numbers into the keypad on our right, and it slid open.

The smell of food wafted through the air. Ara and I walked up the carpeted steps of our estate to the sound of strings music. Tae was cooking again.

As I put my briefcase down in the lounge and loosened my tie, my sister pranced through the doors, holding up a plate of bread and wearing an ugly, flowery apron.

"Just in time!" she chimed.

"Yeah, I'll be there in a minute." My hands were shaking.

My brother expressed much more enthusiasm about dinner and followed Tae into the dining area. I darted to the west wing, toward my room. Once there, I scrambled to my desk and grabbed a container of purple liquid from my drawer. I filled a syringe with it. I sat on the edge of the bed and rolled up my sleeve, injecting the contents of the container into my arm. The rush came near-instantaneously, and I closed my eyes.

Along with the other three fourths of the Nehel population, I was a malay addict.

At first the drug was legally distributed as a form of performance enhancement. It made us more alert, and although our strength probably didn't change, it sure felt like it. Aside from that, it gave off a euphoric effect for a while after administration. That was what I got addicted to.

After only two decades, studies at the Sanctum Research Center found that malay was highly addictive if used too frequently, and the withdrawals were almost *always* fatal. Unfortunately, that was long after nearly everyone in Sanctum already took it daily. The Council made malay distribution illegal, but looked the other way for our military. While thousands of people died from malay withdrawals and others became practically homeless trying to buy it from black market street merchants, we received as much of it as we liked. Eroqam couldn't have their soldiers dying off, after all.

Sometimes I wondered what the public would think if they knew the face of Sanctum, the oldest son of the Nehelian Regent, was really a junkie. The thought brought a twisted smile to my lips as I sat there with the needle still in my arm. Curling my fingers into a fist, I let out a long sigh as my stress escaped into the open air. *All better.*

Now it was time for the circus.

Everyone was already seated when I returned to the dining room. I frowned at my father, who sat with a napkin tucked around his collar like a toddler. I felt a certain sadness whenever I watched him. I still remembered the man he used to be; the one who taught me everything I knew. His rapid decline depressed me. Even strong, great men withered and waned at the end of it all.

I took my seat next to Ara and looked down at my plate. Tae didn't have much to do during the day, so she tried to perfect being a homemaker. I didn't really understand why, considering she was just going to be the mate of some wealthy Nehelian one day. Tae would never have to cook again after that. She didn't even have to cook *now*.

I pushed food around with my fork to make it look like I was eating. The malay made me a little nauseous.

"Qaira knows what I mean," Ara continued a conversation from before I'd arrived, and I glanced at him in question.

Tae shook her head, cutting up her food. "I think all of those places should be shut down. The filth they dredge up only makes Sanctum even more dangerous."

"Uh, what are we talking about?" I asked.

"Sapyr."

"You'd talk about that at the dinner table, in front of our *father?*" I almost shouted, casting my younger siblings a disgusted look.

Tae rolled her eyes at me. I didn't intimidate her at all. "As if Dad cares."

My father waved a hand, having finished his meal and now drinking a glass of wine. "I don't. Naked women bring in some of Sanctum's top revenue."

"This is fantastic," I muttered. "A family discussion about brothels."

"You act as if you don't go there as often as your brother," my sister chided. She turned to our father. "Use your napkin, Dad. There's food all over your face."

I didn't respond. I wasn't going to converse over my trips to Sapyr. I was a man; enough said.

Tae and Ara continued to talk about other nonsense, and I just sat there picking at my plate. My father wiped his face with his napkin, and then blew his nose. I grimaced. Any appetite I'd had was officially gone. I'd only taken about four bites before I stood.

"You've barely eaten!" cried Tae.

"It was gross."

She looked at her plate, stung.

I hadn't meant to say that; it wasn't gross, but it was either that or argue with her for fifteen minutes, and my time was priceless. My father and brother stared at me, their disdain mutual. I left the dining room without another word.

* * *

I spent the night in my room trying to devise a plan to get the Council to agree to search the Archaean refugee camp. I was certain that that was how the rebels got their intel. Someone in that camp was sending information to the Archaean base ship orbiting our gravitational field. Tonight's raid on our grain supply facility said it all.

About seventy years ago, the Archaeans showed up on The Atrium seemingly from out of nowhere. Their home world, *Felor*, had been destroyed and there were over a million angels on board looking for a new home. Their leader, an angel named Lucifer Raith, demanded that we let them stay.

My father spent almost fifty years trying to negotiate with them. At first he ignored their demands, arguing that we couldn't hold so many and sustain our world's resources. That was true. The Atrium wasn't a huge planet. But the Archaeans didn't leave, and eventually wore my father down with unrelenting pleas. He reserved a place in the upper layers for them to take refuge. It wasn't much, and it could only hold about fifty thousand, but that was fifty thousand angels able to eat.

The Atrium was only supposed to be a way station until they figured out what they were going to do. Yet to this day they hovered over us, demanding that more and more angels migrate to our world.

My father went crazy, and I took over. After years of passive defense methods of keeping the Archaeans from taking over, I was more than ready for a conflict. On my first day as stand-in Regent, I declared war on the angels. I also declared that there would be no more migrations, and the refugees could either go back to their ship, or stay while the rest of them found greener pastures.

Needless to say, Commander Raith didn't like me much. Their entire plan from day one was to force migration on us over time. However, the moment my soft, soul-loving father cleared out his desk, their plan went to shit. We'd spent the subsequent years at war.

Currently the Archaeans were trying to destroy our storage facilities so that we'd suffer food shortages. I wasn't able to retaliate because we couldn't reach their ship. Their technology was staggering, and from what I'd heard, it was what destroyed Felor in the first place.

We needed to raid their refugee camp. If anything, it would clog enemy communication for a while. A raid would also let Raith and his forces know that any time they felt like coming down to Sanctum, we were ready for a showdown.

The angels scarcely faced Nehel in physical combat. They feared our strength. We were warriors; they were scientists. Most of Archaean military training revolved around how to evade and defend against us. Trying any sort of offense was a death wish, and they knew it. Despite our superiority in combat, the fact of the matter still remained: we were stuck.

So there I was, writing down arguments that I'd use on the Council tomorrow. I couldn't believe I even had to *convince* them that we needed to engage. But, like my father, they felt civility was best. The only thing civility gave us was the early symptoms of famine. We could sit here and twiddle our thumbs all day; Lucifer Raith wouldn't stop until The Atrium was his.

And I wouldn't stop until he was dead.

There was a knock on my door, and I looked up. "Yes?"

My father came in and I glanced away, trying not to roll my eyes. I didn't have time for him.

My father's name was Qalam Eltruan. Until twenty years ago, he'd been the Regent of Sanctum. To the public, he still was, but I'd taken most of his roles behind the scenes. I played the good son and let him keep his face on bulletin boards so long as he didn't become a blabbering idiot. It was getting really close to that point, though.

But it seemed tonight he was lucid. He didn't have that familiar, clueless look about him that signified he'd wandered off for the thousandth time.

"How did it go today?" he asked, sitting down on a chair across from my bed. Physically, he appeared like an older version of me. All of his children looked like him, with brown hair and slender noses. But Tae, Ara and he all possessed green eyes. Mine were silver, like my mother's. Perhaps that was why I'd always been his favorite.

He wore a suit every day, even though he hadn't been to his office in ten years. He showed up at Council meetings and spoke to the press, but he hadn't made a military or political decision since his physician diagnosed him with *dementia*. I often wondered if the same would happen to me one day, since dementia was genetic. Personally, I'd rather a bullet in the brain.

"Not good," I sighed. "This was the fourth attempted bombing this month. It can only get worse from here."

My father frowned, emphasizing the wrinkles on his weathered face. He said nothing, however. It seemed he was just as useless as everyone else. Eventually, he nodded toward the pad of paper on my knees. "What are you working on?"

"I'm going to stand before the Council tomorrow and argue the right to raid Crylle." I might as well tell him; he was going to find out tomorrow anyway. Besides, he probably wouldn't even remember what I said two hours from now.

"The refugee camp? Whatever for?"

"The Archaeans know of places and people that they couldn't possibly have learned from their ship."

"The media will spin it as a hate crime. Some of our citizens want us to let the Archaeans in."

"Yeah, and some of our citizens haven't a fucking clue, Dad. *Where* are we going to put them?"

"Profanity, son. Can't you tone it down in front of your old man?"

"Sorry, but still."

He sighed. "I don't have the power to make those decisions anymore." He stood and put his hand on my shoulder. I looked up at him. "I know you'll do the right thing."

His words made me shiver. My father thought I was such a good boy. It'd crush him if he knew about the things I'd done, all in the name of Sanctum. There was no such thing as doing *right*. For the Regent, or at least the guy playing the part, the only decisions I ever faced were bad, or *worse*.

I returned to my work as he left. "Are you going to be okay finding your way back?"

"I'll manage. Have a good night, and don't stay up too late."

I smirked while he closed the door. I missed his fatherly guidance sometimes.

But I couldn't dwell on the past; not right now, anyway. I had to finish this proposal before the morning. At this rate, it would probably take me all night. Oh well.

No rest for the wicked.

II

THE STRENGTH THAT BINDS

"IN THEORY, IT SEEMS BEST IF we move our resources closer together, where they can be guarded by the Enforcers. I'm afraid it's gotten to this point, Commandant."

Shev Serro had been in front of the room for over an hour. He was one of the seven members that made up the Eye of Akul, which was the council that served Sanctum's Regent. However they tended to argue with me more than anything; elderly politicians never wanted to listen to the Regent's *son*.

Shev also liked to talk. Needless to say, I was dying of boredom. Perhaps he'd noticed my distant gaze, because I heard, "What do you think, Commandant?"

I leaned into a palm. "That sounds fine, but my men aren't going to like it."

"We'll rotate their shifts, that way they aren't sleep deprived. With over two hundred enforcers in Sanctum, I don't think it will be a problem."

"I don't really see why we have to use my soldiers. Sanctum guards could do the job just as well. It'd be a waste."

Enforcers were a private sect of the Nehelian military. Their jobs were handling Archaean conflicts and apprehending terrorists. *Angel exterminators.*

"Sanctum guards can't defend against angel rebels, Qaira. We've already tried that."

"Where are we moving the supplies?" I inquired, unable to think of a counterargument.

Shev frowned in thought. "Perhaps near the Aeroway? That will put them further from where the angels are slipping through, giving us more time to respond."

Well, at least the Council was good for something today. "Fair enough. We'll discuss the specifics after the meeting, Shev. But right now I'd like to address another issue."

Shev took his seat. "Yes, Commandant."

My legs wobbled as I moved to the front of the room. I didn't get any sleep last night and I was fucking exhausted. I'd downed five cups of coffee this morning and was pretty wired until Shev had opened his mouth.

My eyes slid over each face stationed at the semi-circular table in front of me. I cleared my throat, and then began:

"Last evening there was an attack on the grain supply facility in Lower Sanctum. The angels managed to bypass security codes and exterminate the armed guards at the entrances. When I examined their bodies, there were no signs of a struggle, so I'm guessing the angels used stealth to kill. That also means they knew of their positions beforehand."

The council shared a look.

"We have an insurgent," I announced.

Kanar Venta was the first to speak. "That's a rather bold statement. Are you sure you have enough evidence to back it?"

"What I saw last night was evidence enough," I snapped. "And I'm going so far as to say that the insurgent is communicating with someone in Crylle, and they in turn are sending that information to the Archaean ship."

"What do you suppose we do about it?" Shev asked.

I took the list from my breast pocket. "We're going to cut communication lines from Crylle and their base ship. Being able to talk to one another was a luxury. I also want to send a team of twelve enforcers, including myself, into Crylle for interrogation."

My father conveniently awoke from his mid-day nap. Up until now we'd ignored the fact that he was passed out and snoring all morning.

"The media will see it as a hate crime, Qaira," he stated.

"Dad, you said that yesterday."

My father paused, momentarily confused. "Did I? Oh, yes; I sure did. But the fact remains, son."

I crossed my arms. "I don't care *how* the media sees it. The general public does not dictate Eroqam's actions."

"The power is in the people, Commandant," Kanar reminded me.

"No, the power is in Eroqam. It's been too long that we've let our subjects run the show. Look at where that's gotten us. Where are we? Are we in a state of *permanent stability?*"

The council said nothing, sharing another look.

"Sanctum is collapsing and I can't stand by anymore. We're acting in our people's best interest, and I don't care what you have to do to keep it confidential; our raid is happening."

Isa Forr, the only female member of the Council, rose from her seat. I waited for the quip. She opposed me for the sheer entertainment of it. "Qaira Eltruan, are you suggesting we take an armed unit of enforcers into a *civilian* refugee camp with the intention of causing violence and fear?"

My eyes narrowed. "That is *exactly* what I'm suggesting."

"The Archaeans will retaliate far worse than before if we do. We don't even know what kind of weapons they have. We haven't seen the whole picture here."

"Is the Eye of Akul afraid of the angels?" I demanded.

"It's *rational* fear if we don't know—"

"The Archaeans won't even know what happened," I interjected. "We're cutting communications with their base ship, remember? The refugee camp will be isolated, and if we can keep the press from crawling up our asses, there's no way that Commander Raith could find out. At least until we leave."

Isa opened her mouth to respond, but an explosion shook the room.

The members of the Council gave startled cries, and I looked out the window. An enormous debris cloud rose around the south wing of Eroqam, painting the sky black. My eyes widened.

In an act of desperation, I punched the window out. I stepped over the sill as my wings released, shredding my suit. I hadn't expected to fly today, and now my favorite shirt was ruined.

The Council cleared out of the room and scrambled into the hallway, but my father stayed behind, watching me with a terrified gaze.

"*Get to the main level!*" I shouted. Before he could reply, I dove from the window.

The streets were in chaos. Screams of panic rode in with the wind. I let myself drop until I almost hit the ground; then my wings tilted and I shot toward the pillars of smoke like a speeding bullet.

A few Enforcer aero-crafts were already traversing the debris cloud. We were trained to respond quickly. As I approached the one in front, my soldiers saw me coming and slid open the door. I rolled in.

"*Ara! Where is he?*"

"He's in the craft behind us," said Uless.

I relaxed, reaching for a rifle on the rack.

"Sir, what the fuck is happening?" Uless asked as I loaded my weapon. "Why are the Archaeans attacking us in *broad daylight?*"

"Good question," I muttered. After loading the chamber, I attached a blade beneath the barrel. Our assault rifles were a combination of machine guns and bayonets. It made the weapon somewhat useful at close range. "I guess we're about to find out.

Gunfire erupted through the sky.

"*Hang right!*" I screamed at our pilot as bullets *plinked* against our craft. As the craft tilted, we all nearly lost our footing. I snatched the radio from Uless' belt, seeing as I didn't have my own.

"Do *not* leave the smoke!" I ordered the other teams. "I repeat, do *not* engage; we'll bring them to you!"

It was the first time that I'd ever seen an Archaean fighter craft. Like the rest of their technology, it far surpassed ours. They moved faster and more fluidly than we ever could, and as of right now we were monumentally fucked.

I had no idea how I was going to get the whites to follow us into a trap, so I switched the radio to a different channel. "This is Commandant Qaira Eltruan. I am requesting *immediate* Sanctum airstrike backup."

Another explosion; this time a clothing store half a block away. An Archaean jet was closing in.

Plink plink plink plink

A bullet penetrated our aero-craft. It tore through the face of an Enforcer beside me. Blood and flesh splattered our suits.

"*Fuck! Tela, get them off of us!*"

"I can't!" he shouted. "Sir, they're too fast!"

Someone finally responded over the radio, *"Commandant Eltruan, what's your status?"*

"*About-to-fucking-die!*" The radio was so close to my mouth that I was practically swallowing it. *"We have Archaean crafts obliterating* Upper Sanctum! I need a strike team yesterday!"

"Airstrike team has been dispatched, Sir."

Another enemy jet appeared in front of us. It opened fire on our windshield, killing Tela. Our now-pilotless craft spun out of control.

I dove for the seat, throwing Tela's body aside. I swerved past the new enemy vessel and sped for the smoke. They thought I was retreating and followed. The angels took the bait.

I could barely see without a windshield. Gusts of freezing wind and debris violently beat against my face. My teeth gnashed together as I held on for dear life.

I ripped through the center of our waiting army, and they fired at the pursuing Archaean crafts. Both erupted into balls of fire seconds later. Some of my soldiers on-board cheered in celebration over the fact that we were still alive.

But that had been *too* close.

"Sir!" someone shouted through my radio. It was Ara. *"Archaeans are on foot near the Agora!"*

Shit.

A couple of enemy vessels were left. There was no way I'd be able to reach the Agora without getting shot out of the sky. This was such a fucking mess.

Thankfully, over a dozen Sanctum aero-crafts appeared.

"Requesting orders, Commandant."

I nearly dropped my radio trying to respond. Flying with one hand wasn't exactly a walk in the park. "All units commence a full-on offensive. Make sure you keep them busy."

"Roger."

Our task force roared by us. Gunfire ensued. That was my cue.

I steered my craft north, toward the Agora. It was time to take out the rest of the trash.

Five whites were skirting the rooftop of a restaurant. One of them was holding a rocket launcher. This didn't look good already.

I steered away, deciding to land out of range. I was pretty sure our craft wouldn't survive a rocket, since it didn't even have a windshield. The craft touched down and I grabbed an armored vest. "Get ready," I ordered to my team, but they were already way ahead of me.

I slid open the door and stepped onto the middle of the evacuated main street. My team followed suit. My wings unfolded and I took to the sky, chasing down the angels who'd seen us and fled. They must have had a craft nearby. What were they even doing here?

I closed in on them in a matter of minutes, aiming my rifle at the girl carrying the rocket launcher, but she managed to swerve out of the way and I shot the white beside her. As the dead Archaean plummeted to the ground below, the girl spun and returned fire. The rocket barreled toward me in a streamline of blue phosphorescence.

I rolled mid-air as it whirred by. It hit a grocery store instead, setting the Agora on fire.

Great.

And then I was right in front of her. I swung my rifle, cleaving her head from her shoulders. Before she fell, I swiped the rocket launcher, and my men took down her friends.

I found their deserted ride about four blocks away, atop Yema Theater. While my men secured the perimeter, I studied the alien craft. It was smooth and shiny, like liquid silver. I ran my fingers over the surface, whistling quietly. This thing was incredible. How did it fly so seamlessly?

I grabbed the radio I had stolen from Uless.

"Status."

"All clear, Commandant."

"Good. I need two crafts for a pick-up at Yema Theater. The whites left us a parting gift."

Ara responded this time. *"On my way, Qaira."*

I dropped the radio and sank to my knees, ripping off my vest and chucking it aside. Sanctum had prevailed again, but her damage was heavy. Black smoke and debris slithered into the horizon, billowing over dozens of ruined buildings. There were probably a hundred casualties, maybe more. This couldn't keep happening.

My lip curled with indignation as I watched the militia fight the fires. *Fucking vermin;* they attacked my home. Now it was personal.

Crowds of nosy people flocked the streets, photographing the carnage. I listened to their cries of outrage with a growing smile. The attack had actually worked to my advantage. The Council would have no choice but to allow the Enforcers to raid Crylle. And now we had an Archaean specimen—one that could reveal the secrets behind their alien technology. I was one step closer to killing Lucifer Raith. One step closer to freedom.

I could almost *taste* it.

III

NEEDLES BEFORE THE PRAYER

As EXPECTED, THE EYE OF AKUL ruled in favor of raiding Crylle.

We had suffered two hundred civilian casualties, along with millions in lost revenue from repairs to the Agora and Eroqam. We also lost five aero-crafts and fifteen of my men.

The raid was scheduled to take place in a week. Kanar and I agreed to pull the plug on Archaean communications several hours before we went in. I'd have two hundred enforcers on standby around Sanctum should Raith's forces appear in my absence. I wouldn't be stupid twice.

The vessel I'd recovered was being analyzed by our defense team scientists. I was told there was a lot about the craft that was completely beyond our comprehension.

While the Sanctum Weapons Research facility spent all evening uncovering the Archaeans' military secrets, I was at Sapyr with my brother and a few of our friends. We were celebrating the progress over the last several days.

Sapyr had been Ara's choice (it always was) and I was bored. Entertainment of this sort only thrilled adolescents and the sex-deprived. And my brother. Yet oddly enough he wasn't even paying attention to the dancers tonight. He, Garan and Uless were reminiscing about near-death experiences in the Sanctum army.

My attention was drawn to a young girl on stage who had made her way over to me. The stage was a less a stage and more a narrow catwalk between the bar, and I was sitting at the bar,

23

waiting for our drinks. The peeler saw my face. Now she was going to bother me until I gave her money, since she knew I had a ton of it.

She bent down and spread her legs. I watched her dance, her lids half-mast in well-practiced lust. With a resigned sigh, I handed her twenty usos so she'd get lost.

Sapyr had been in business for over five hundred years. It was the apex nightlife for young males (and females, weirdly enough) who wanted a place to dance, drink and enjoy more devious pleasures should they have enough money for it. It was always dark save for the stage, where fluorescent lights flashed across women who, for some reason, found this to be a satisfying career. Most of them were junkies, supplied with all the malay their sore, tired veins could carry in return for their services. They didn't even try to cover the tracks on their arms.

I didn't like coming here; it reminded me of all the things that were wrong with Sanctum. All the things I couldn't fix because I was no better than the filth that surrounded me.

The tender brought my drinks and I grabbed the tray, carrying it over to our table. I sat down and Ara nudged me.

"You want in on this round?" he asked, gesturing to the shot glasses.

"No thanks." I didn't like Cardinal; it tasted like antiseptic.

My brother frowned. "Stop being such a vagina."

I glared at him, but said nothing. Nevertheless, he placed a shot in front of me. I watched the yellow liquid quiver in the glass.

"You need to lighten up," he went on. "*Sanctum's Savior* deserves to get wasted, at least tonight."

I laughed. "Sanctum has no saviors."

Since I'd been called a vagina, I held the shot glass up to the rest of our table in salutation. Then, all four of us threw back our heads and let the pungent, disgusting poison slide down our throats.

"You know," Garan said, looking between Ara and I, "you two could be twins."

Ara and I looked very similar, save for our eye color. He was also shorter than me, and his hair was a little wavier than mine. That said, we could have been twins if you'd had as much to drink as Garan. His pupils were dilated and he was swaying in his seat.

Ara scoffed. "No we don't. I'm *way* better looking than Qaira."

Yet all the women I'd ever brought home were ten times better looking than his girlfriend. I didn't say that, though. Those were fighting words.

"So this raid," Uless began, slurring, "are we taking civilians into custody, or interrogating them on the spot?"

I looked around, unsure if we should have this conversation or not. In about an hour, Uless would probably pass out in the men's restroom like he'd done every other time, and wake up without a single memory of tonight. It all seemed like a giant waste of breath.

But now I was fiercely buzzed, so I'd entertain him. No one was within ear's reach so I didn't have to worry about an eavesdropper. "I don't plan on taking anyone back with me."

Uless shrugged. His tan complexion and hazel eyes were muted by the spotlight on the stage. He looked translucent. "Fine with me. I just wanted to know how long we were going to stay there. I can't stand that heat."

"Yeah," I muttered, gulping down the rest of my drink, "I hear you."

"Fucking angels," my brother growled, shaking his head.

"Save your anger for the field, Ara."

He gave me a serrated grin, but it melted as he looked over my face. "Your ink is fading again."

"Yeah, I know." I didn't really care, either.

Nehelians painted their skin with semi-permanent ink. It was tradition for Sanctum upper-echelon to use ink as a form of identity. I was required to wear my family symbol underneath my eye, but I often let it fade to near-invisibility. I didn't like walking around with the equivalent of a name tag on my face. Especially given my status.

25

Besides, I could think of a thousand better ways to spend two hours than having someone draw all over me.

There was a war to wage, but Ara wouldn't understand. He was still young. I was five hundred years older than him. He paraded the Eltruan symbol like it was a crown. Technically it was, but it was a crown of thorns.

As we finished our drinks, Garan left the table.

"Where are you going?" asked Uless.

"To take a leak. Do you want to come and hold my dick for me?"

We laughed.

Uless grimaced. "Get lost, you fucking queer."

Garan grinned, backing away. "Aw, that hurts. Especially coming from y—"

He bumped into a group of women, and their drinks crashed to the floor. I hid my face in my hand, unable to watch the scene that would unfold.

"What's your problem?!" one of the girls cried.

Garan was red-faced and stuttering. "I-I'm sorry, I didn't see you there!" He tried to help them pick up their spilt drinks, but was too intoxicated and tumbled to the floor as he bent down. Ara and Uless were laughing so hard that they had to rest their heads on the table, and the girls were shouting at Garan as he tried to get up. Some of the other customers were starting to stare.

I slid from my seat and gave the squawking women a smile. No sooner had they seen me (and my ink), they dismissed Garan. My brother used this time to pull him to his feet and shove him toward the restrooms.

"I'm sorry," I said. "My friend is loaded. Let me buy you another round of drinks to make up for it."

There were only four of them, so I figured it couldn't be that expensive. My request was met with nervous giggles.

While I noted their orders, I couldn't help but notice one girl in particular. She had long, brown hair and green eyes; a tiny waist and broad hips. Her full, pink lips curled into a coy smile as my eyes lingered on her.

"I'd never guess the Regent's son would come to a place like this."

"I don't usually," I said. "My friends are celebrating. Do you live in Sanctum?"

"I'm a college student from *Celca*. My name is Talia," she extended a hand. "You're Qaira, right?"

Ah, Celca. It was a smaller city outside of Sanctum. For the first time ever, my ink had given me an advantage. Talia would love nothing better than to cling to the arm of an Eltruan, and I was determined to fuck her. Hooray, mutualism.

"Would you like to come with me while I order the drinks?" I asked, taking her hand in my own.

"Sure."

My prey led me through the crowd, toward the bar.

* * *

Two hours later, I ditched my group to drive Talia to her apartment in Lower Sanctum. I parked my aero-craft in the lot outside, and we spent another half an hour doing malay.

"Be gentle," she cooed, splaying her arm across my lap.

As I filled a syringe, I stared at her arm. The light from the street lamps cast an eerie glow across her skin, making it look pale and necrotic. Track marks covered the underside of her elbow; little black puncture wounds across yellowed flesh, like a worn pin cushion.

I slipped the needle into a fresh spot, glancing at her face as she leaned her head against the seat. The lights in Sapyr had muted the dark circles under eyes and hid the shadows of her hollow cheeks. Talia was a junkie, and had been one for a while. She was still beautiful, but she looked sick. For a second I wondered what I was doing here.

After her euphoria faded, she grabbed her purse. "You want to come up?"

No, I just spent three hundred usos worth of malay on you for nothing. "Sure."

I followed Talia to her third-story apartment. She lived in a space that was the equivalent of a studio. Sections of her house were partitioned with beaded curtains to make up for the lack of rooms. The place smelled like flowers, probably from the incense that was burning on her coffee table.

Lower Sanctum was a ghetto. I didn't like being here; it was a reality check to how my people were forced to live. I paused in the doorway, taking all of this in. I was being delivered a personal message of how bad it had grown through war. Through malay.

Talia slid out of her dress, waiting for me on her bed. I closed the door and approached her, loosening my tie. She straddled me for half an hour, but after only fifteen minutes I knew I wasn't going to come. Malay made it difficult to orgasm, and she was ruining the mood with her whiny female sex-talk. Every time she mentioned how much she loved my *'huge cock'* I was jarred from the act.

Again, I wondered what I was doing here.

After we were done, I dressed in silence. This should have made me feel something, but that hollow nothingness was still there. I didn't know why I even bothered anymore.

"Where are you going?" she asked.

"Uh, home? It's three in the morning."

She was lying naked on her side behind me. I felt her finger tracing circles on my bicep. "Well, can you at least give me one more hit before you leave?"

Fucking junkie.

"No, you've had enough."

Users didn't make a habit of sharing their malay; it was too expensive. The fact that she had the nerve to ask for another hit when I'd already wasted an entire syringe on her was appalling. But the only one to blame was me, considering I'd given her some at all.

She tugged on my arm. "Come on, please?"

I shook her off. "I said *no*."

I made a quick escape to her door, murmuring a goodbye. As I turned the handle, something shattered over the back of my head.

The impact staggered me, and I whirled around in shock. Fragments of her broken bedside lamp lay at my feet. My hair felt wet; I was bleeding.

"What the *fuck?!*" I screamed. "*You crazy, junkie whore!*"

"You think you can just fuck me and walk out of here without giving me anything in return?!" she shouted back.

"I already *gave* you a hit! I didn't realize you were a fucking prostitute!"

Her eyes were wild. The distant gaze in them made me realize that she wasn't all there. "I want your stash. *All* of it."

"Yeah, like that's happening."

"I'll scream from the rooftops that the Regent's son is an addict," she said, smiling.

I closed her door, *locking it.*

Talia saw the look on my face, and then her smile faded. Somewhere in her malay-deluded mind she had realized that I wasn't a person to fuck with. But it was too late now.

As I advanced on her she tried to run, but her apartment was too small and there was nowhere to flee. I backhanded her and she fell, smacking her head against the wall. Blood trickled down the corners of her mouth, and she looked up at me in terrified confusion. Before she could scream, I wrapped my hands around her neck and squeezed.

She thrashed, trying to claw at my face. I didn't let up.

"I'm more than just the Regent's son, you stupid bitch. Guess you're going to find that out the hard way."

As if my statement was ataractic, Talia stopped fighting. She stared up at me with a glazed look in her eyes as I ripped the last threads of life from her. The glazed look became a distant stare, and then I let go. She fell sideways on the floor.

I sank to the edge of her bed and put my face in my hands. This wasn't supposed to happen. I was supposed to fuck Talia, and make it home before three o'clock. Now what?

I was seen leaving Sapyr with her. They would believe me if I told them all I did was drive her home, but I didn't want the hassle. With a sigh, I left her apartment and opened the door to my craft, grabbing my stash. Making sure no one was around to see me, I ran back inside.

It looked like Talia was going to get what she'd asked for.

I pumped her with more than the lethal dose, propping her body up against the wall. I left the needle in her arm. Although forensics could have found evidence of murder, there wasn't going to be an investigation. She was a junkie, and Sanctum authorities had better things to do with their time than carry out an in depth investigation of an overdose. They probably saw twenty of these a day.

I knelt in front of her and wiped a strand of hair away from her cold, bluing face. "Was it worth it?" I whispered.

After I cleaned up the shattered lamp, I made sure to take the spare key I'd found stashed above one of her kitchen cabinets and locked the door.

I got in my craft and started the ignition, but then everything sank in. Anger and despair coalesced and I punched the steering wheel three times, denting it. My knuckles bled, and the outer pain numbed the inner. I left Talia's apartment and flew home.

Soon, the spires of Eroqam crept over Upper Sanctum's horizon. The curtains rose again, concluding this brief intermission to the evident façade of *Sanctum's Savior.*

IV
THE SCHOLAR

THE NEXT MORNING BEGAN LIKE EVERY OTHER.

My alarm clock blared and I knocked it to the floor trying to press the snooze button.

The obnoxious sound continued, now just out of reach. I'd barely gotten more than three hours of sleep. I could have used the extra fifteen minutes, but I was forced to get out of bed and grab the fucking thing. The moment I set it back on my nightstand, my glassy, red eyes rose to the door.

Waking up was probably the worst part of my day. Perhaps I would feel differently if I ever got any sleep, but I was stupid and often reluctant to go to bed on time. I didn't like the idea of another day's end; I didn't like knowing I'd have to go to work in the morning.

My eye was twitching, and there was an icy tremor shuddering up and down my arm. I reached for my case, opening it up. I filled another syringe, trying to stave off the memories of what had happened several hours ago. The image of Talia's body circled through my thoughts, her empty, green eyes staring at nothing as she lay on the floor of her apartment. Through my bedroom window, newborn light left an eerie glow that I felt across my back. For some reason, I knew that today would be different.

I slipped the needle into my arm and closed my eyes.

After my shower, I dressed into a suit and headed for the dining room. Epa, our maid, would have already laid out our breakfast. My sister found me along the way.

"No one has told you yet, but…" she began.

The last time she began a sentence like that, my father had snuck out of his room in the middle of the night and built a castle out of condiments from our refrigerator. I braced myself.

"The scholar has moved in with us."

I froze, looking at her. "What?"

Tae's gaze wandered to the end of the hall, settling on the dining room. I followed her stare. "Dad said the Eye of Akul hired a scholar to be your new advisor."

An *advisor?* Since when did I have an advisor? "And who is he?"

Tae smiled, like what I said was funny. "Go and see for yourself. In the dining room."

Pastries, juice and tea lay across the table, while Epa stacked dishes on a tray beside it. This was all very ordinary scenery, except there was a woman sitting at the head of the table, *in* my seat.

I lingered in the doorway, staring at her. My surprise gave way to confusion, which then gave way to anger when I thought about the Eye of Akul going behind my back and hiring an advisor. A *woman* advisor.

I had nothing against women, but there weren't very many in the Sanctum forces. My job wasn't for the faint of heart. Was this some kind of sick joke?

"Who are you?" I asked.

She looked at me, and my confusion returned. Her eyes were pale violet, shimmering in the overhead light. There were no red rings around them. She wasn't Nehel.

But she wasn't an angel, either.

Tae stood beside me, smiling at the woman. I tilted my head toward her. "Tae, go and get our father."

"But he's sleeping," she whispered.

"Then wake him up!" I hissed. Did I really have to point out that *this* was more important than my father's beauty rest?

Tae frowned and slipped away. The woman and I were left studying each other. I noticed other discrepancies in her appearance; tiny details of her face that were different than ours.

Her ears were round while ours were triangular. She had a little nose and huge eyes, with straight black hair that hung to the small of her back. She looked unnatural, like a doll.

More than a minute passed. She said nothing, her expression a mask of stoicism.

"Who are you?" I asked again, needing to break the silence.

Instead of answering my question, she gestured to the empty chair beside her. "Are you going to sit? Or are you going to just stand there and stare at me like an idiot all morning?"

I bristled, about to give her a piece of my mind, but my father and sister returned.

"Good morning, son!" Qalam almost shouted. "I told Epa to order the cala muffins you—"

"Who is *that?*" I interrupted, pointing at the woman.

My father looked at her, blinking. Then his face filled with revelation. "Oh, yes. That's the scholar."

Was I the only one who found this situation *completely* weird? "What's a scholar? What is she?"

"Qaira," the woman said, and I stiffened at the sound of my name on her tongue. She was gesturing to the empty seat again. "Please."

My lip curled. "I'm not doing anything until I know what's going on."

"Well that's a shame, because I'm not telling you anything until you sit."

She was treating me like a dog. I'd been in her presence for less than ten minutes and I already couldn't stand her. No, this wouldn't do.

But for now I wanted answers, specifically what she was and where she came from. Since the angels' arrival I'd known we weren't the only ones in the cosmos, yet....

I sat, glaring at her.

She looked at the pastries. "Are you going to eat?"

"No."

"Breakfast is the most important meal of the day."

"Who are you?!" I shouted.

Her smile faded. "My name is Leid Koseling. I've been assigned by your council to advise you in your war against the Archaeans."

"That didn't tell me a fucking thing."

"Language!" my father cried.

"Leave us!" I shouted.

My sister dragged our father off.

Leid poured herself a cup of tea and grabbed a pastry, placing it on her plate. I watched her with a measure of indignation. She had already made herself right at home.

"What are you?" I said.

"I'm a scholar."

"And what's a scholar?"

"You wouldn't know. We haven't been here for a long time."

"Then how does the council know about you?"

She looked at the breakfast tray. "Eat something and then I'll tell you."

"I'm not hungry."

Leid smiled. "Eat anyway."

Cursing under my breath, I grabbed a muffin and threw it on my plate. She stared at me until I was forced to take a bite. It slid down my throat like tree bark. I felt humiliated, but I needed answers.

"Scholars are only employed by those fortunate enough to know about us," Leid continued. "With that said, the members of your council haven't told you everything."

"So when are you going to tell me something I don't know?" I glanced at my watch. "I'm late for work."

Leid stood, grabbing her long white coat. "We can talk more on the way, then."

I blanched. "Excuse me?"

"I've been hired as your advisor, Qaira. I go everywhere you do until our contract expires."

What. The. Fuck. "No, I refuse."

She sighed. "Please don't make this any harder than it already is."

"And what exactly is that supposed to mean?"

"It means you're an obnoxious prick, but a job is a job. Trust me, I don't want to be here either."

My eyes widened, but all I did was laugh. Without another word I left the dining room, storming toward the port. I could hear Leid's heels clicking close behind.

The Eye of Akul would answer for this.

* * *

It was going to rain.

Sanctum's clouds were a deep gray, and fog blanketed the ground like a sheet would a corpse. Only the tallest buildings were visible. The weather made my drive even more complicated.

Leid said nothing on the way to Parliament, staring out the passenger seat window. I kept glancing at her, wondering if this was all a dream. I was expecting to wake up at any moment, but it never happened. The most appalling thing about this was that everyone seemed absolutely fine with some strange alien female just showing up and surgically attaching herself to my hip.

"Sanctum looks different than how I remember," Leid mentioned.

I didn't respond.

"Your market place is in ruins," she continued, despite my blatant reluctance to speak to her. "Was that a recent Archaean attack? I haven't been officially briefed yet because I arrived late last n—"

"I'm not talking to you until I find out what's going on," I interjected. "So you might as well just shut your mouth and sit there."

"Your hostility is impressive."

"Says the woman who called me an obnoxious prick."

"That wasn't hostility," Leid said, smiling. "That was honesty."

I wondered how much trouble I'd get into if I opened the passenger-side door and kicked her out of my craft in mid-air. "How do you know our language?"

She was looking out the window again. "I know all languages."

I raised a brow. "*All* languages?"

"Yes."

"Do you know Archaean?"

"Do I need to tell you the definition of *all*?"

Bitch. "So what exactly is a scholar?"

"We're multiversal mentors. When our services are requested and the job seems interesting enough, we aid other beings in whatever task requires our knowledge."

"I thought you said you didn't want to be here."

Leid hesitated, looking out the window again. "This job wasn't my choice. I was assigned here by someone else."

"One second," I said, raising a hand. I needed to concentrate on landing my craft. The Parliament's flight dock was almost too narrow, and my formal complaint about it had been ignored. Maybe my nerves were shot this morning because I crashed the tail end of the craft into a cargo dock, knocking over a pile of packages. Leid and I jolted forward on impact.

"Fuck me," I sighed, massaging my head. This was *exactly* what I needed.

Leid grinned. "Doesn't seem like it's your day, Commandant."

I shot her a look and got out of the craft, ignoring the muttering laborers hovering around the scattered packages. One of the Parliament liaisons was approaching me with a questioning gaze.

I threw my keys at him. "Park this thing. I don't have time for it."

Leid joined me as I walked through the glass hall of the Parliament Bridge. "So, the Eye of Akul hired you to follow me around to make snide remarks?" I asked, shoving my hands into my pockets. "Somehow, that seems typical of them."

"On the contrary," she replied. "My charm is simply a bonus."

I laughed. She was a real piece of work. The thought of her constant presence made me want to leap off the bridge.

As I stormed by the secretary guarding the council room, he stood to protest. "Commandant, the Council is busy—"

"Sitting there doing nothing, I know," I muttered, exploding through the door.

The Eye of Akul were expecting me. It was a little unsettling to realize I was *that* predictable.

"Qaira, just in time," greeted Isa, seated behind the center podium. There was a collection of papers in front of her. "I hope you've brought a pen."

I pointed at Leid. "What's the meaning of this?"

"The scholar has introduced herself, hasn't she?" Isa asked, evading my question.

"She says you've hired her to advise me."

Kanar nodded. He was seated third from the center. "Yes, we have."

"Advise me on *what?*"

"The Archaean conflict. What else?"

It was getting pretty hard to keep my cool. "I don't need an advisor. I'm handling the situation just fine."

"He doesn't seem to like me very much," Leid said, amused. "Perhaps you might explain to Qaira why you chose me to advise him?"

"The scholar has extensive information on the Archaeans," Isa said. "She knows about their technology and their combat strategy. She's an invaluable asset, and you are going to welcome her to Sanctum whether you like it or not."

I looked down at her. She was five foot nothing and barely made it to my shoulder. "How do you know about the Archaeans?"

"We've been contracted to the Archaeans numerous times on Felor," she said.

I was shocked. "Are you saying that you've worked *for* our enemy?"

"I haven't, but others have and we share notes."

I looked back at the council. "We can't trust her. She's too neutral."

"Neutral?" Kanar repeated.

"We need someone with passion; not a brains-for-hire who might harbor empathy for her past clients."

Leid's amusement vanished. She gave me an irritated frown. "We have no interest in affairs outside of our contracts. I'm here to do exactly as I'm instructed. I don't care whether this planet goes up in my flames or the Archaeans get blown out of the sky. I hold no biases. I just do my job. And believe me," her eyes narrowed, cutting through my soul like a piece of broken glass, "I have empathy for no one."

I was speechless. All I could do was look away, running a hand through my hair.

"I'll be useful to you," Leid pressed. "If you'll let me."

"All you've done so far is distracted me."

"I'm sorry, Qaira, but it isn't your decision," Isa said.

"Isn't it? You get to decide what I do? I'm technically the Regent!"

"Are you putting your pride before the prospect of Sanctum's victory?" asked Shev, giving me a disappointed look.

My jaw clenched. I was cornered.

"I want a construction team assembled to make that landing dock wider."

Isa blinked. "What?"

"The Parliament dock is too narrow. If I'm going to sign my life away to a little girl, then you need to at least give me that."

Beside me, Leid smiled.

"Agreed. I'd like you to get the scholar acquainted with Parliament and Sanctum. She'll be by your side during all working hours until the contract expires."

"About that contract," I said, crossing my arms. "I'd like to see the terms."

"Ah yes, I almost forgot." Isa handed me the papers from her desk. I took them.

DECLARATION OF AID FROM THE COURT OF ENIGMUS

It is hereby announced that Scholar Leid Koseling of the Court of Enigmus shall be sent to The Atrium to serve as council to the Regent and the Eye of Akul in their escalating conflict with the Archaeans. The parties involved must read the terms of agreement and sign their names should they find the following terms suitable:

1) The Scholar will serve as aid to Sanctum for exactly ten years, or until the conflict has been resolved. The means of payment requested by the Scholar should be delivered no later than ten days after the contract expires.

2) The Scholar is not permitted to aid Sanctum in any form of physical combat. If this should happen, the contract will be voided and both the Scholar and those that paid for their services will be punished accordingly.

3) The Scholar is not permitted to help design or construct objects that might sway the fate of the conflict. The Scholar is allowed to educate the Regent and the Council so that they will acquire the knowledge necessary to design or construct said objects on their own.

4) The Scholar should act as a companion to the Regent and the Council, but it is not their duty to protect them from harm. The Scholar is solely responsible for offering aid in verbal form.

5) The Scholar must be protected from harm by Sanctum. The Regent and the Council will make it a priority to keep the Scholar safe from any danger. The death of a Scholar is seen as negligence by the Court of Enigmus, and punishment will be severe.

6) The identities of the Scholar and the Court of Enigmus will not be disclosed to anyone outside of the parties involved.

There were numerous signatures at the bottom of the page, as well as an empty line. I looked at the tiny print under the line. It was my name.

After reading this, it was like Leid was nothing more than a piece of rental property. What was the Court of Enigmus?

"Ten years," I recited, letting that sink in.

"I don't think it'll be long enough," Leid said.

"Oh really?"

She nodded. "Sanctum has many obstacles to overcome."

"We've been handling it fine so far," I said, icily. "We've managed to stave them back for half a century."

"Commander Raith is not looking to kill you," said Leid. "If he was, you would have been dead a long time ago." She looked at the council. "How much do you know about angel technology?"

"That's where we need your services the most, Leid," Kanar said. "Several days ago, Qaira managed to secure one of their combat crafts after an assault on Eroqam, but it's left our research scientists baffled."

Leid tapped her chin. "Well, I suppose that's a good start. When can I see it?"

"Your eagerness is appreciated," Isa began, "but for the rest of the day I think you and Qaira should get a little more acquainted with one another. Perhaps you could find a way to quell his doubts about you."

The scholar glanced at the papers in my hand. "I can't do anything until he signs that."

I signed the contract, smirking to myself. Leid didn't realize how much blood there was going to be. The violence we faced on a day to day basis was too much for most of us to handle, let alone a little alien girl. I'd give it less than a year before she'd break.

I handed the contract back to Isa and she said, "Sanctum welcomes you, Leid Koseling."

"I hope I bring your city and its people victory," said Leid.

I was already walking out. It wasn't long before Leid caught up to me. We climbed the stairs and traversed the hallway to my office. As I opened the door, I paused. "What's your repayment?"

"Pardon?"

"What are we giving you in return for your services?"

"My payment isn't of any concern to you."

My stare hardened. "Isn't it?"

"No. I assure you, Qaira, that what I am getting isn't anything remotely valuable to Sanctum."

"Okay then." I opened the door and stood aside. "After you, *scholar*."

"Thank you," Leid said. As she stepped inside, I stared daggers at the back of her head. Sure, I'd agreed to work with her—;

But nowhere in the contract did it state that I had to *like* her.

V

POLARITY

MY EYES FLUTTERED OPEN, GAZING ahead in a confused fog. At first I had no idea where I was but then my gaze settled on the alarm clock that I'd forgotten to set the night before. The fog cleared and I realized I only had fifteen minutes to get ready for work.

Shit.

I jumped out of bed and near-sprinted to the shower. Somehow I managed to bathe, dress and shoot up in only ten minutes. I was planning to skip breakfast but my stomach was already growling. If I didn't eat now, I'd have a stomach ache all day. Leaving it empty for hours on end tended to do that to me.

Ara and Tae were at the dining table. My father never woke up this early, so Epa always saved him a plate to take to his room later on.

Leid was reading a news periodical, sitting in my seat again. She didn't even glance up when I exploded in, fumbling with my tie. I shot her a look when I noticed where she'd chosen to sit, but was too preoccupied with my tie to get angry. I wasn't going to use the chair anyway.

I threw a pastry on my plate and reached for the kettle on the tray. Then I froze, holding the kettle, glaring at Leid. Still, she didn't look at me.

"How many cups did you have?" I asked, shaking the empty kettle for emphasis.

She turned a page of her periodical. "Three."

"You drank it all," I said. "You *know* I have a cup every morning."

"Perhaps if you hadn't slept so late you might have gotten here in time to have some."

Tae and Ara exchanged looks of dread. They knew what was about to happen; the same thing that had happened countless times since Leid moved in two weeks ago.

"I can make you some more," offered my sister.

I didn't answer her, still glaring at Leid. "I'm not late. And it's none of your business what I do outside of work. If I sleep in a little later than normal, that's my right."

"Well, it's also my right to drink as many cups of tea as I want."

"Okay, *you* listen to *me* you fu—" I caught myself, counting to four in my head.

"The world doesn't wait for you, Qaira. You should stop expecting it to." Leid threw on her coat, flashing me a smile. "You didn't go to bed until two o'clock this morning. Sleeping less than four hours a night affects your work performance."

"… Are you implying that you don't think I'm doing my job well enough?"

Ara scoffed, covering his mouth.

Leid moved by me, heading into the hall. "*Now* you're late."

I watched her disappear toward the port, fuming. My siblings could practically see the steam coming from my ears. Tae acted uncomfortable, while Ara was beaming. He seemed to enjoy watching Leid's treatment of me. Karmic justice, he'd said.

"Remember to show up for the briefing this afternoon," I muttered, heading for the hall as well.

"Roger," my brother said to my back. "Wouldn't miss it for the world."

* * *

Traffic was horrible.

You'd think the Regent's son and the Commandant of the Enforcers would get some bonuses, like having a special lane in which he could bypass all the normal people on their way to their less important jobs. But my only bonuses were chauffeuring Leid around and putting up with the council's bullshit.

I was still pissed about breakfast and didn't say anything to Leid on the way to Parliament. My only saving grace was that she was nice to look at. It was kind of annoying that I found her so attractive, given the fact that she wasn't even a part of my *species* and I couldn't help but feel like I was partaking in some kind of bestiality fetish whenever I thought about her.

She wasn't really my type, either. Leid was thin and her breasts weren't nearly as large as I'd have liked them to be, but there was a certain allure to her that I couldn't put my finger on. Too bad it was ruined whenever she opened her mouth.

We had been sitting in a traffic jam for fifteen minutes, and when we finally reached Parliament I'd forgotten that the landing port construction started today. Now I had to go all the way to the front and try to find parking there.

"Fucking beautiful," I muttered, glaring at the NO PARKING SIGN.

Leid grinned. "How ironic."

I turned the craft, jerking the wheel hard enough to throw her against the passenger seat window. She stared angrily at me, and now *I* was grinning.

Twenty minutes later we were in Parliament, and I ducked by Isa and Shev while they were speaking to my receptionist. Maybe the council wouldn't notice I was late.

Things were pretty quiet since the attack on Eroqam. I spent most of the day handling matters my father was no longer capable of, like budgeting, law-mediating and delegating with the higher-ups who worked for the city. A Regent's day only lasted from seven to three, but I was also the Commandant and would go directly to Eroqam's military wing after my desk job. Needless to say, work days sometimes lasted well into the early morning.

And they only seemed longer with Leid as my shadow.

I tried to stay afloat amid the sea of paperwork that had been waiting on my desk when I'd arrived. Leid paced behind my desk, analyzing my weekly schedule.

"You double-booked a meeting with Upper Sanctum's Chancellor and the Sanctum Education Director," she noted.

I didn't respond, signing a budget report.

"Would you like me to change it?"

"Yeah, whatever."

I heard her flipping through my schedule. "The only other opening you have is at three-thirty."

"Guess that'll have to do."

"You leave at three."

"Guess I won't today."

"Would you like me to postpone the meeting until the next day?"

"Leid," I sighed, massaging my head, "just schedule whatever you think is best and let me know. You're going to do that anyway."

I didn't need to turn around to know that she was smiling. "As you wish, Commandant."

Several hours later I had completed most of the work that had deadlines for tomorrow. I took a moment to stretch and noticed Leid was sitting on the leather armchair across from my desk, staring at me.

"What is it?" I asked.

"I want to see the Archaean aero-craft."

I blinked. "Right now?"

"No, after the briefing tonight."

"That's fine. I was waiting until our research scientists could give us anything conclusive, but they're still at a loss."

Leid reclined across the arm, smiling. "I'm sure I could fill in some blanks."

"You're quit sure of yourself, aren't you?"

"Says the flesh and blood epitome of arrogance."

I sighed and returned to my work. Despite her cue to shut up, Leid kept talking.

"Do you have the outline for your briefing?"

My eyes rose from the report, settling on her. "Why?"

"I'd like to see it."

"Why?"

"To make sure it's a good plan?"

I smirked, looking back at my report. "Thanks, but I don't need your advice on military tactics."

"Because I'm a woman?"

"Among other things."

"It's very unfortunate that the soon-to-be Regent of Sanctum is an ignorant, chauvinistic pig."

I put my pen down and stared at her. She met my irritated frown with an icy smile.

"Is there somewhere you can go for a while?" I asked through my teeth. "There isn't anything productive about you hovering over me all morning."

She looked at the door. "Is there somewhere that I can get food?"

"The cafeteria is on the first floor; take a left down the stairs. What, *all* of my tea and three pastries weren't enough for you?"

Leid ignored my jab. "What do you usually get when you're there?"

"Why would that matter?"

"I don't know much about Nehelian food, and most of it gives me indigestion."

Charming. "Their leriza sandwiches are pretty good."

"Thank you," she murmured, slipping out of my office.

I sighed in relief, reclining in my seat. Relishing this moment of peace, I closed my eyes. My exhaustion gave me a floaty, dizzy feeling, and since Leid ruined breakfast my empty stomach was churning bile up my throat.

I glanced at the clock; two more hours until I could go to lunch. I had another dozen budget reports to sift through. It was going to be the most painful two hours of my life. But at least I was alone now.

Ten minutes later, Leid came back into my office, holding a lunch tray.

I scowled at the sight of her. "Why didn't you eat in the cafeteria? I don't want you getting crumbs on my—"

She placed the tray in front of me. My annoyance switched to confusion.

"I could hear your stomach growling," she said. "And I thought maybe if you ate something you wouldn't be so grouchy."

I stared at the food. "Thank you."

Leid returned to the chair. "So, can I have your outline now?"

Clever. "It's in the front compartment of my briefcase," I said, wolfing my sandwich. "Help yourself."

As she read it over, I saw her face darken. "Qaira, this is inhumane."

"And attacking my city and killing hundreds of people isn't?"

"Those were soldiers. The angels in the refugee camp aren't soldiers."

"I'm willing to bet that some of them are." When she only looked at me, I sighed. "I shouldn't have given that to you."

"Are you planning to hurt them?"

"If it comes to that."

"If you cut off communications with their base ship, it'll only provoke them."

"Well maybe Commander Raith will actually grow a pair and face us."

Leid hesitated, tucking my notes back into my briefcase. "You don't want them to attack you. Not yet."

"I suppose you're entitled to your own opinion. End of discussion."

"But Qaira—"

"End of discussion!" I shouted, making her jump. I was perfectly capable of military strategy. She knew nothing of me, or this war.

Leid stared at me, crestfallen. "As you wish, Commandant."

I returned to my work.

* * *

At three-thirty, I watched as the eleven Enforcers I had handpicked filtered into the briefing room. I stood on the stage, in front of a large projection screen, going over my notes. Leid sat front and center, *staring* at me. It was annoying, and I was sure she knew that.

Although the rest of the council opted to trust me, Kanar entered as the Enforcers took their seats. He stood at the very back, giving me a nod of encouragement. When everyone was ready, I hit a button on the remote control lying on the podium. The projection monitor flickered behind me.

"Lieutenant Eltruan, hit the lights," I said.

Ara stood, doing as I'd ordered.

"Thank you all for coming," I began. "You are here because I have personally selected you to be part of our interrogation team for the raid on Crylle, happening three days from now. Our mission objective is to find out who among the angels are relaying intel to the Archaean base ship. We will be departing from Eroqam at nine in the evening—just a little after the camp's curfew. That way, everyone is where they're supposed to be when we arrive."

I pressed another button on the remote. A map of Crylle flashed onto the screen.

"Lieutenants Eltruan and Geiss will take the left-side sweep of the camp, while Narish and Tem will take the right," I continued, pointing out their paths with my finger. "Lieutenants Fedaz and Cama, I want you to go to their medical facility and evacuate their staff. I'll be stationed at the southeast communications building. Make sure you all are taking headcounts as you move. I'll be comparing them to the manifest to verify every white is accounted for. Everyone else will be on stand-by with me." I paused. "Questions?"

Ara raised his hand.

"Lieutenant Eltruan."

"Are we cutting the communications before or after we arrive?"

"Eroqam will jam their transmission signals when we arrive in Crylle. We don't want to do it too soon or it could serve as a warning to the perpetrators in the camp."

Uless raised his hand.

"Lieutenant Fedaz."

"How are we treating hostiles?"

"Kill anyone who resists us."

I glanced at Leid. She looked back at me, devoid of expression.

Garan raised his hand.

"Lieutenant Geiss."

"What exactly are we looking for? How are we supposed to identify the mole?"

"We're looking for weapons and incendiaries. If you find any questionable documentation, take that as well. The whites who tried to destroy our grain supply facility a few weeks ago were not soldiers. They were camp rebels, or so I'm suspecting. The rebels are *in* that camp, and we're going to find them."

"How are we to know if the documentation is questionable? We can't read Archaean."

A job requirement of an Enforcer was to be able to *speak* Archaean. Very few of us could read it. It looked like Leid was going to come in handy for once. "My advisor is fluent in Archaean, so you don't have to worry about that. Lastly, we are not taking any angels back for questioning, and will be doing all of our interrogations in the Crylle communications building. It's going to be a long, hot night, gentlemen."

The crowd groaned. I ignored them. "Any more questions?"

Leid raised her hand.

I glared at her. "*Yes*, Advisor Koseling?"

"Commandant Eltruan, I've had a chance to look over the Crylle manifest. There are over five thousand children living there. What will be done about them while your fear-mongering is going on?"

A few of the Enforcers turned to look at her. She kept her eyes on me.

I was still trying to register her question. "Uh, what?"

"Are you telling me that you're planning on storming the refugee camp, killing anyone that gets in your way, in front of *children?*"

Anger began to rise from my chest, moving over my head. It made my ears hot and left pinpricks along the nape of my neck. "Advisor Koseling, an angel is an angel."

Leid seemed to anticipate my response, because she reclined in her seat with a knowing smile. "Commandant, that is exactly how you create these alleged rebels in the first place."

The anger had now returned to my chest, quickening my pulse. That bitch never knew when to shut up.

"You go in there, kill their parents, and then they end up hating you enough to volunteer to blow your city to smithereens. To my understanding, most of the attacks on Sanctum were caused by adolescents, correct?"

"Most of them, yes."

"So why don't you instruct a team to round up the children and keep them out of harm's way? It will be good publicity for you; showing your people and theirs that you at least have a heart."

I looked at Kanar. His expression said it all. Once again, I was cornered. "Advisor Koseling, would you like to come up here and take over?"

"Of course not. You're a *wonderful* tactician, Commandant."

I clenched my jaw, realizing that she was getting back at me for this morning. "Very well. Lieutenant Samay, you'll be in charge of rounding up all the children in the camp. Does that suit you, Advisor Koseling?"

Leid smiled. "It suits me fine."

"Are you sure? Is there anything else we could do to make the angels more comfortable while we raid their camp for weapons of mass destruction?"

"Commandant Eltruan," Kanar warned.

I swallowed my pride and moved on. For the rest of the briefing, Leid stared at me with that pretentious smile of hers, and I fantasized about peeling off her face and hanging it from Eroqam like a flag.

VI
FROM WITHIN

LIGHT REFLECTED OFF THE WINDSHIELD, creating blinding beams that made me squint. The sun was insufferable up here.

I sat quietly in the back of our Enforcer craft, trying to assemble my assault rifle through the sun's glare. We were fifteen minutes from Crylle, and my soldiers were preparing for landing. Although I was leading the raid, I was nervous and everyone knew it. It made *them* nervous, but there was a good reason to worry. Even with the awaiting militia that would aid our charge, we were outnumbered twenty-five to one. We had firearms, but I had a hunch that at least some of the whites did as well.

I latched the rifle to the strap around my shoulder, settling my gaze on Leid as she stared out of the cabin window. By some act of a miracle, she hadn't said a thing since we'd left Eroqam.

"You're violating your contract, you know," I said.

She looked at me. The light made her hair and eyes shimmer. "How so?"

"Your contract said you shouldn't be placed into harm's way. Actively participating in a raid is as close to *harm's way* as you can get."

Leid smiled. "I'll be just fine, Qaira, but thank you for your concern."

In reality I hoped she got blown to pieces in crossfire, but all I did was nod and head to the empty co-pilot seat.

"How much longer?" I asked Lakash.

"Ten minutes, sir."

I grabbed my radio. "Eroqam, come in. This is Commandant Qaira Eltruan."

"This is Eroqam; go ahead, Commandant."

"Jam all signals across Crylle airwaves. Let me know when that's complete."

"Yes, sir."

I switched channels. "Crylle communications tower, this is Commandant Qaira Eltruan of the Sanctum Enforcer Division. Come in, please."

After a few moments, I heard, *"Good evening, Commandant. This is General Akrah Kalesh. Are you ready for our troops?"*

"Just about. We land in ten."

"I'll have them assemble near the northwestern gate."

"Good. We'll see you soon."

I let the radio fall to my lap. Lakash glanced at me. "I don't like that look," he said.

"Sorry," I muttered.

Lakash reached into his coat pocket and handed me a flask. I shot him a look that relayed my disapproval of drinking and flying, but accepted it nonetheless. "It helps with my nerves," he explained. "I keep thinking about Tela."

I watched the scenery, recalling the ambush on Eroqam. A migraine was slowly settling in, one of the many side-effects of long-term malay use. The light was making it worse. "It was my fault."

"No it wasn't. You couldn't have known it was an ambush." I handed him his flask and he took another gulp before putting it back into his coat. "I'm just glad I showed up late."

"That isn't funny."

"I wasn't trying to be funny."

The clouds parted and the ramshackle rooftops of Crylle came into view; shacks and tents with only a few stone edifices, enclosed in a dome of chain mesh. The sky was guarded as well, since angels had wings. Like us.

The similarities in our appearance were a little overwhelming. Archaeans and Nehel hailed from different planets yet we looked identical, save for our eyes, hair and wing structure. The angels were pale skinned, with ice blonde hair and white wings. We were tanner-skinned, with dark hair and black wings. The Nehel had various shades of eye color, but I'd only ever seen blue eyes on angels. It was hard to tell them apart; they all looked the same to us.

Leid looked like us, too. She just didn't have wings. It made me wonder how many other creatures there were across the galaxy, living similar lives on similar worlds. But then I remembered I was about to raid Crylle, so I returned my attention to the matter at hand.

As Lakash drew the craft into a slow descent, I caught a glimpse of soldiers aligned at the northwestern gate. Then I looked at my radio, frowning. Eroqam should have jammed Crylle's signal by now. Soon the angels would see us, and without a jam they could alert their base ship.

"Eroqam, come in."

"Interference is complete, sir."

"About time."

We landed two minutes later. As my Enforces exited to greet the Sanctum squadron, I moved to block Leid from leaving the craft.

"I want you to stay beside me at all times," I said, while she peered up at me with an amused grin.

"Such is the terms of my contract."

"I mean it. You could get killed."

"I have faith that you'll protect me, Qaira."

"I can't afford to protect you when I have fifty thousand hostile whites to worry about. When we get to the southwestern communications building, you will *stay* there. Even if I leave."

Leid crossed her arms, the grin fading. "Fine. Can you get out of my way now?"

I moved aside and she exited the craft without another word. Her agreement had seemed disingenuous. Surprise, surprise.

I'd thought my only obligation to Leid's contract was to take her advice, but it seemed like I was going to have to keep her from catching a bullet, too.

Only nine years and eleven months more to go.

* * *

The heat was killing me.

I'd been outside for thirty seconds and I was already about to die. Crylle was located on the highest layer of The Atrium, and it was *scorching*. The sun never set, not even at night, so it was like living in a furnace all day, every day. General Kalesh must have really pissed someone off to be stationed here. I couldn't imagine anyone volunteering to guard Crylle.

My men stood in a line, facing the Sanctum militia. I walked to the front and shook Kalesh's hand. "Thank you for your help," I said.

"The pleasure is all mine, Commandant," he respond. His gaze shifted to Leid and stayed there. It was unusual for a woman to be in a place like this, and she didn't look like a soldier. "Who is that?"

"This is Leid Koseling," I said, gesturing to her. "She's my appointed advisor from the Eye of Akul."

General Kalesh smiled, holding out his hand. "Crylle is no place for such a beautiful lady, Advisor Koseling."

I rolled my eyes as Leid took his hand. She looked at the camp behind us, wearing a conflicted frown. "Crylle is no place for anyone, General."

"I need a lock-down of the perimeter," I said, trying to break them up. If Kalesh's attention stayed on her, he might notice her eyes. Nehelians had thin, red rings around their irises, and Leid did not. She was usually able to hide them in the shadows of her hair, but we weren't in Sanctum anymore.

Three Enforcers and thirty guards followed us as we made our way toward the communications building. Most of the whites ran the moment they saw us, although some stayed to watch us pass.

They were frail with hunger, dirty and poverty-stricken. Piles of trash lined the streets, as if they'd used them to mark out a system of roads. Despite my feelings about the angels, Crylle was a little hard to swallow.

There was nothing we could do for them; we had our own societal ills to treat. I was just baffled that Commander Raith would let his people live like this. Even if they couldn't find another sustainable planet, death seemed like a better option than Crylle.

"Qaira," Leid called. I looked down at her. "Could you please radio Lieutenant Samay and tell him to bring the children to the communications building?"

"Why?"

"I'll explain in due time; but not here, Commandant."

I didn't feel like arguing with her. "Alright."

A couple of hours later, Lt. Samay herded in as many angel children as the Sanctum militia could find. Leid ordered my men to line them up and she walked through the rows, inspecting every filthy, tear-stained face. After looking over them, she shook her head, appearing disappointed.

I might have been sour about the time and resources that she was wasting, but the Enforcers hadn't found anything in Crylle yet. I could faintly hear gunfire and screams from the window. The militia was heading our way with whites under suspicion. Something, *finally*.

Leid tugged on my arm. "Lt. Samay didn't bring all of them."

"What?"

"There are children that he missed. We need them all."

I stared at her. "*Who* are you looking for, Advisor Koseling?"

Instead of answering me, she looked away and tapped her chin. She always did that whenever she was thinking. "Can I have the map of Crylle?"

I'd had about enough of this. "I'm not giving you anything until you tell me what you're doing."

"Qaira, I can't say it here."

"Why not?"

"Can you please just give me that map so I can get us *something* out of your pointless raid?"

I felt my lip curl. "If you don't shut up and back off, I'll have you detained with the whites."

At first Leid looked surprised, but then she smiled. "As you wish, Commandant."

She slipped into the crowd, while my attention turned toward a group of guards marching the first wave of suspected insurgents through the door. I directed them to the vacated offices down the hall.

When I returned, I spotted Leid outside of the communications building, talking to several guards in front of a land craft.

My eyes narrowed, and I approached them.

"What's going on?" I demanded, glancing at the map in Leid's hand. How she'd gotten that, I didn't know. Probably from one of the other Enforcers.

"They're taking me to the Crylle Medical Facility," she said.

"No, they're *not,*" I said through my teeth, waving the guards away.

When we were alone I took a step toward her, eyes fierce. "I thought we agreed that you wouldn't leave the communications building?"

"I wouldn't have to if you'd listen to me."

"Maybe I would listen if you told me your plan."

Leid surveyed our surroundings, making sure we were alone. "I'm looking for a boy."

"… A boy."

"Yes, an angel boy. He's extremely valuable."

"What's so valuable about him?"

She opened her mouth to respond, but another group of guards moved through the doors. "Sir," one of them addressed me, "should we begin the interrogations now?"

"Yes," I said. "Make sure someone is recording them, too."

When I looked back at Leid, I realized that I didn't care to hear her story. I needed to be here, exacting *my* operation; not running around Crylle in search of a little white. "Come on, we're going inside."

"I'm going to the Medical Facility with or without you, Commandant," Leid said, giving me a defiant frown.

"Leid," I said, dropping all formalities, "if you take another step, I'll have my men detain you for—"

"I will kill your men."

My voice caught in my throat. As surprising as that had been, I laughed. Yeah, that was real threatening coming from a five-foot-nothing girl in a fancy dress. But before I could tell her that, she marched off to the land mech.

I didn't budge, watching her departure. A part of me wanted her to wander off and get killed, but then another part of me thought about the backlash I'd receive from the Eye of Akul.

'The death of a Scholar is seen as negligence by the Court of Enigmus, and punishment will be severe.'

Ugh, fuck.

"You two," I said, pointing at a pair of idle guards by the door. "Come with me."

* * *

The medical facility was located on the northwestern side of camp, one of the few concrete buildings in Crylle. It looked out of place with the rest of the scenery. Our land mech was the only one around, so my team hadn't made it here yet. That was a little annoying, considering I'd clearly said their objective was to *secure* the medical facility. I was about to radio them and ask where the fuck they were, but Leid hopped off the mech and sauntered to the door. I jumped off after her and grabbed her arm, wrenching her back with a snarl.

"I can't protect you if you keep running off. I told you to stay by my side, Advisor Koseling, and I *meant* it."

She ripped from my grasp, smoothing her shirt. "I'm sorry. I keep forgetting."

"Keep forgetting what?"

"Sir, what do you want us to do?" called one of the guards.

"Stay there and protect our ride." We could have flown and made it here faster, but Leid didn't have wings and I refused to carry her. That was way too intimate.

Leid waited for me by the door; I entered first, keeping a steady hand on my rifle.

The cool air came as a relief. Sweat matted my hair to my head and my clothes clung to my body. It didn't help that I was wearing armor.

We traversed a dim, shadowy hall that was covered in grime. We weaved around blood-stained gurneys and bewildered patients in wheelchairs, peering into every room along the way. The stench of feces and malady almost made me gag.

Again, guilt crept through my insides. This all was becoming a little too much to bear.

"What's the meaning of this?" said a youthful voice ahead.

Leid and I looked toward the sound. At the end of a hall stood a child; not even an adolescent. Despite that, he wore a white physician coat and an irritated frown, hugging a clipboard to his chest. It didn't take a genius to know that he was who Leid was looking for.

But I was stunned by the sight of him, and froze.

Leid stepped in front of me, smiling. "There he is."

"This is a hospital, Nehelians," the kid continued, not at all afraid of us. "There are only sick people here. Could you please raid somewhere else?"

His voice was that of a kid, but he spoke like an adult. Was he *really* the doctor here?

"We're not here to raid anything," Leid said, speaking Archaean. Unlike us, she was completely fluent. No accent.

That surprised the kid as well. "Then what are you doing here?"

Her smile grew. "We're here for *you*."

The kid stared at her, widening his eyes.

"Qaira, point your weapon at him before he runs," she whispered.

I did, with a measure of disgust. Pointing guns at children, white or not, wasn't really my style. "What are we doing?" I whispered back.

The kid raised his hands. "No, put it down. Don't scare anyone, *please*. I'll come along quietly so long as none of my patients or staff are harmed." He moved toward us, but froze when he stepped into the light and got a good look at Leid's face. His expression twisted with confusion. "Oh."

I looked between Leid and the kid. "What's going on?"

"Nothing," Leid said, smile unfaltering. "Everything is fine, isn't it?"

"Yes," the kid murmured, continuing his approach.

When he was close enough, I grabbed the back of his neck and shoved him in front of us. As we vacated the medical facility, I leaned into Leid. "Who is he?"

"His name is Yahweh Telei."

"That isn't what I meant."

"I'll tell you once we get back to the communications building." She glanced over the crowd of patients and medical staff. "There's too much of an audience right now."

Right as we exited the facility, my radio beeped.

"Commandant Eltruan, come in. This is Lt. Uless Fedaz."

"Hi, Lt. Fedaz. Can you tell me why you and your team aren't at the medical facility?"

"Sir, we've got a situation."

My frown melted. "What's your status?"

"There's a rebel angel; she has Ara."

There were screams behind his transmission. Gunfire.

"Where are you?" I asked, trying to hide the panic in my voice.

"Southwestern Crylle. Qaira, she's strapped to a bunch of fucking explosives! I don't know what to do! We keep telling her to stand down but she's not complying!"

"Keep talking her down. I'll be there in a minute."

I severed the call, and my wings released from my back with a thunderous clap. I looked at the guards. "Take the boy and my advisor back to the communications building."

Leid grabbed my arm in protest. "I'm to be at your side at *all* times, remember?"

I wrenched free of her grasp. "Not this time. Because of *you*, I'm all the way on the other side of the city!"

The look in my eyes warned her to back away. She did, frowning sullenly.

And then I was off, soaring over the dilapidated shacks, praying my brother was still alive when I got there.

*   *   *

That had been the longest two minutes of my life.

I landed in the middle of a crowd that had gathered in the street, the gust of air accompanying my descent blew trash in every direction. Before me, an angel girl had her arm wrapped around my brother's neck, forcing him on his knees. In her hand was a remote control—a trigger—to the incendiaries wired around her waist.

My brother stared at me with wide, fearful eyes. His mask lay several feet away. The angel girl was crying, and her face looked all messed up. Bruises and a bloody nose. I looked at Lieutenants Fedaz and Geiss, questioningly.

They were still shouting to release my brother, shaking their rifles at her. It was only making her more frightened. The crowd was screaming at them, about ready to storm us.

"Stop!" I shouted, pushing them back. *"Stand down!"*

They conceded, and the crowd grew silent. There were armed guards encircling us, but none dared to move.

I looked at the girl, holding out my hand. "You don't want to do this. I know you don't; I can see it on your face."

"Don't come near me!" she screamed, strangling my brother even harder. *"I know who you are!"*

"Let my soldier go, and we can—"

"They shot my parents!" she sobbed. "They didn't even do anything and they *shot* them! Your men barged into my house and forced me to undress, and my parents tried to stop them! *They're not men, they're monsters!*"

I looked at Uless and Garan. Now I knew why they weren't at the medical facility. They had decided to ignore my orders and have some fun of their own. This was the final straw.

"What's your name?" I asked the girl.

She didn't respond.

"Tell me your name," I pressed.

"Ariel," she sobbed. "Ariel Triev."

"Ariel, if you let my soldier go then I won't kill you. You have my word. Release him and we can talk."

"You expect me to believe that?" she cried. "The only reason I'm alive right now is *because* I have him."

"Ariel, my patience is thinning. I'm willing to work with you but first you have to let my soldier go."

The environment changed in my peripherals. I looked over my shoulder, spotting Leid among the crowd. She was unaccompanied, and I couldn't hide my shock. How did she get here so quickly?

She caught my gaze, smiling. I frowned and looked ahead. Apparently *no one* listened to me anymore. "You have ten seconds to release him, Ariel. After that, my offer expires."

I couldn't blame her for doubting me. Even I didn't think that had sounded very convincing. She knew she was dead either way.

"No," she almost whispered, thumbing her trigger.

Alright, I'd tried the civil route.

I raised my hand, sweeping it behind me. That was a cue for the guards to start pushing the crowd back. My men had seen this gesture before, and knew what it meant. Get out of the way, and *fast.*

The girl watched the crowd recede with waning courage. She looked back at me, unsure of what was happening.

"Last chance, Ariel; let my soldier go."

"No!" Ara was screaming. "No, Qaira, *don't!"*

I ignored him. My brother had made his bed.

Ariel was noncompliant, and I squinted.

She brought her hands to her head, screaming. Blood began to trickle from her nose, ears and eyes. She dropped the trigger and sank to her knees. Even though she'd released my brother, he didn't move. He couldn't. He was screaming and bleeding, too.

To the rest of Sanctum, I was a deity. A man born with the ability of murder by thought. They looked to me for salvation, because my people believed that I was born for that very reason. *Sanctum's Savior.*

But my gift had come with consequences. Severe ones. Such was the balance of the cosmos.

I released my psychokinetic grip and nodded to my men. Uless and Garan swooped in and dragged my brother off. Ara was still clawing at his head and screaming, but he'd live—albeit with a migraine for a couple of days.

In an act of desperation Ariel tried to crawl to her remote, her bloodied face twisted in a frozen sob. I walked after her, raising my rifle.

Right before Ariel could reach it, I shot her in the back of the head. She collapsed face-down on the road, hand still outstretched, a growing pool of blood beneath her.

I watched her bleed out at my feet, feeling something twisting and snapping inside of me. Lt. Fedaz was approaching from behind.

"Commandant, I'm sorry," he said. "We didn't know that she had weapons—"

I spun and punched him in the face, feeling his nose crunch under my knuckles. I would make Uless Fedaz an example of what happened when my soldiers ignored my charge.

He stumbled and fell, holding his broken, bleeding face. I grabbed him up by the collar with another fist wound.

"I *SPECIFICALLY* SAID—"

I punched him again.

"NOT TO—"

And again.

"FUCK AROUND WHILE YOU'RE—"

And again.

"ON THE JOB!"

I threw him down and he curled into a fetal position.

"What part of that was unclear, you fucking twats?!" I looked at Garan, who backed away with his hands up. I walked toward him. *"If I have to say it again then you're going to end up like that angel bitch!"*

Very seldom did I lose control like this, but when I did, everyone took heed.

Most of the crowd had already scattered. Leid stood amid the stragglers, watching the ordeal. She was placid.

"Sir, I'm sorry!" Garan screamed, still backing away. "Never again, I swear!"

I turned to the remaining crowd and shot my gun at the sky. *"Get out of here before you join your friend!"*

Within seconds, my team and I were alone. Leid was helping Ara to his feet. He was clearly in pain, but relieved to be alive.

"Do you need medical assistance?" I asked. I was angry at him, but he was still my brother.

"I'm good. My head is killing me, though."

"Consider yourself lucky." I turned the nearest guards, nodding at the dead angel in the middle of the street. "Search her house and find out who her associates are. I want to know where she got those incendiaries."

As Ara was carried off into a land craft, Leid wandered to my side. There was a hint of reverence behind her stare, but she said nothing.

"How did you get here?" I asked.

"I ran." When I only glared at her, she smirked. "I can run very quickly. But it seems like we *both* have unique talents."

I glanced away, shrugging. I hadn't wanted her to see that. I didn't parade my ability around.

"So, do I have to run back or can you carry me this time?"

I eyed her. "Fine, but watch my jacket."

* * *

My enforcers rounded up over twenty rebels. Most of them had weapons stashed in their houses, given to them by Archaean soldiers or stolen from our guards.

Two hours of interrogations later, we discovered that the Archaean soldiers were bartering acts of terror for food rations. The same problems were occurring on their base ship. Even though the Archaean Forces were giving the refugees food rations, it was barely enough. Rebel leaders, kept anonymous onboard the ship, stole rations and gave them to refugees willing and desperate enough to attack us.

As helpful as this information was, none of the rebels said anything about a Nehelian insurgent. The goal of our raid was left unfulfilled.

My soldiers lined the rebel men and women along the outer side of the communications building, blindfolded with their backs turned. The enforcers assembled into a line as well, pointing their rifles at them. I stood in the window, watching.

They waited for my signal.

I looked over the trembling whites, a flicker of conflict in my gaze. Then, I nodded.

My soldiers opened fire. Within moments, all of them were dead and sprawled across the ground. Blood splatter decorated the wall.

Leid stood beside me, watching the soldiers pile the bodies into the back of a cargo craft. I had sorely underestimated her. She was just as desensitized toward death and violence as me.

"You've done this before," I said.

"I am a specialist of my field," Leid replied, her eyes on the window.

"And what field is that?"

"War philosopher and tactician."

"How many wars have you aided?"

"I've lost count, Commandant."

"How many have you won?"

"As many as I've aided." Before I could pry any more, she turned. "We're taking the angel boy back to Sanctum."

"That's not your decision to make, Advisor Koseling."

"That boy is an asset that Commander Raith can't afford to lose. Yahweh Telei is his son."

My eyes widened. "Why would his son be working at a medical facility in Crylle?"

"He's a physician, among other things. A prodigy."

"How do you know that?" I asked, incredulous.

"As I said, scholars share notes. One of them has aided the Archaeans more than once. If you want to find out whether or not there's an insurgent, this is the way to do it. With Crylle's radio transmissions jammed, the only way Lucifer Raith could find out that his son is being taken hostage is by an outside source. One of yours. If there is an insurgent, Commandant, you'll hear from Commander Raith, and *soon*."

All I could do was stare. "Why didn't you tell me about this sooner? I would have made it a priority to find that boy."

Leid smiled. "You're worried about an insurgent, Qaira. Have you ever considered the possibility that the insurgent is one of your men? I wasn't going to take that chance."

Without another word, she vacated the hall. I watched her disappear around the corner.

I'd been wrong. Advisor Koseling had served me well today. She was smarter than I'd given her credit for, and I felt like an asshole.

I grabbed my radio. "Lakash, come in."

"There you are, sir. I think I fell asleep for a while." He'd been waiting in our craft for nearly eight hours. Poor him.

"Get the craft ready; we're moving out."

VII
TENUITY

"ARE YOU GOING TO KILL ME?"

I looked over my shoulder, responding with an irritated frown. My obvious want of silence went ignored.

"I deserve to know if you're going to kill me."

"Could you shut up? I'm trying to concentrate here."

I was checking the digital lock on Yahweh's door, installed by our analysts an hour ago. We had arranged a room for him in the Commons, as Leid had insisted that no harm come to the boy and we treated him with a bit of decency. Since I couldn't chain him to a wall, a computerized lock would have to do.

Yahweh sat on the edge of the bed, staring daggers at my head. As smart as Leid claimed he was, he couldn't be *that* ingenious if he thought I'd go to all this trouble just to kill him.

"You know, that really isn't necessary," he said.

"Oh?"

"It's not like I'd try to escape. Where would I go?"

"If you won't try to escape, why do you care if there's a lock on your door?"

The kid frowned. "It almost seems like you're afraid of me."

"Yeah, you're absolutely terrifying." The lock was activated and I stood up, brushing off my pants. "A guard will be by in a couple of hours to bring you something to eat."

I lingered in the door, staring at him. His eyes glittered like blue diamonds, and his unevenly cut ice blond hair spilled across the bridge of his nose. I hated angels. So nauseatingly perfect-looking.

I slammed the door behind me.

It was almost five o'clock in the morning, and there was little point in sleeping since I had to be at Parliament in three hours. The enforcers who had accompanied me were given the day off, but there was no one to replace the Regent.

I headed for the dining room to down four cups of coffee, but I froze in the hall when I heard music. A cello.

I stopped, listening. The sound of it made my heart race.

Then, my eyes narrowed.

The sound was coming from the music room, which had been unused since my mother's death. That was once her place to escape the world, and my father had built it for her when she was forced to quit the Sanctum orchestra after having me.

I moved to the door, freezing on the threshold.

Leid sat on a stool, my mother's cello between her legs. Her face was hidden by her hair, and her arm danced to and fro with the bow clutched in a tiny fist.

My anger faded. For some reason I found this sight… *beautiful.* I couldn't tell if it was the music or the cadence. Either way, I leaned against the frame, crossing my arms.

Leid eventually sensed my presence, and her eyes rose to mine. She stopped playing, letting the bow fall to her side.

"What are you doing in here?" I asked.

"Playing the cello."

"Why?"

"Why *not?*"

I nodded at the instrument. "That belongs to my mother."

"And your mother is dead."

My stare hardened. "Who have you been talking to you?"

"No one."

"How did you know that?"

"Because you just told me. With your eyes."

I looked away, uncomfortable. "You shouldn't be in here. Put the cello away and return to your quarters."

Instead, she reached over and ran a hand across a dusty violin case lying on the stool beside her. She opened it up, glancing at me. "Is this yours?"

"Yeah, sort of." When she only stared, I explained, "My mother gave it to me. She was going to teach me how to play when I was old enough."

Leid looked back at the violin, sadness etched across her face. "Oh."

Without another word we left the music room, pausing at the fork.

"Are you going to sleep?" she asked.

"I don't see any point in that," I said.

Leid gave me a smile. I was beginning to find it pretty. "Neither do I. We've had a long day, Commandant. Would you like to have a drink with me?"

I glanced at my watch. "Alcohol now? It's five in the morning."

"You've never shown up to work drunk?"

"... Is that a joke?"

Instead of replying, she headed for the dining room.

I followed her, frowning.

* * *

Thirty minutes later, the room was spinning.

I really shouldn't have taken that last shot, but Leid was goading me. In fact she'd drunk twice as much and seemed completely fine. I wasn't about to let a little girl drink me under the table, alien or not.

Nausea crept up my throat, but I swallowed it and closed my eyes. I opened them to find her pouring us *another* round. "No," I conceded, pushing away the glass. "I can't."

She laughed. "Done already?"

"How are you still conscious? I'm probably twice the size of you."

"I'm cheating," she said, fingering the cork. "My kind can tolerate an impossible amount of liquor."

"I knew it had to be something."

"Is Yahweh secure?"

I nodded, reaching for the pitcher of water. We didn't say anything for a while.

"Your name means bliss," Leid stated, downing another shot. *"Qaira fortunega."* She'd just recited a welcoming phrase from the ancient priests of Moritoria. *Bliss and fortune.*

"I didn't choose it."

"I find it kind of ironic, given who you are; *how* you are."

I glared at her. "And *how* am I, Leid?"

"You're the unhappiest person I've ever met."

I glanced away, not particularly liking her analysis. "You don't know anything about me."

"But I do. I practically knew the moment I laid eyes on you."

I didn't respond. What was she trying to prove?

"I'm telling you this because I want you to succeed, Qaira."

"By giving me a characterization beat-down?" I asked, shooting her a sidelong glance. Before she could respond, I added, "What the fuck do you care, anyway? Why are you so invested in me? You get what you want regardless, and then you're off to serve some other unlucky idiot."

Leid said nothing, her face marked with hurt.

I took a sip of water, unable to meet her gaze. After a moment she left her chair.

"I'm sorry," she said. "This was a mistake."

As she passed, I grabbed her arm. My grip wasn't rough, but firm enough to make her stop. "You don't know me," I repeated, quietly. "You don't know of the things I've done, and I don't appreciate your insight when it's based on ignorance."

I released her, and Leid looked down at me. I hadn't realized how close we were to each other until now. There was a moment between us, a tiny fraction of a second where things could have taken a very drastic turn. However, that window was lost when she stepped back.

"Take comfort in the fact that whatever you've done, Qaira Eltruan," she paused, moving to the door, "I've done far worse. Oh, by the way; you have the day off. I've arranged for the council to take care of your duties. You honestly think I'd load you up and send you off to work? I'm insulted."

She smiled, and then was gone.

I looked back at the table, trying to stop my vision from spinning. I was far beyond loaded, and the only thing that could cure it was sleep. Which I could do now.

"What are you doing up so early?" my sister demanded, breaking the silence and making me jump in my seat. Before I could respond she looked at the bottle of Cardinal. "Have you been *drinking?*"

"It's fine," I slurred. "I have the day off."

"Wow, I don't think I've seen you this drunk in… ever."

"I was peer-pressured."

My sister sighed and placed the bottle back into our liquor cabinet. I watched her set a kettle on the stove, smoothing her disheveled, wavy brown hair. She was still in her robe.

"How's Ara?" I asked.

"He was okay, but didn't say much. I don't suppose you'll tell me what happened?"

My dear sister; there was so much about the world that I had to hide from her. "Trust me, you don't want to know."

I got out of my seat and began for the exit. My sister looked at me. "Where are you going?"

"To bed."

"You don't want any tea?"

"Tae, I'm about to puke all over the fucking floor!"

She cringed. "Okay, go to bed."

I didn't need her permission. I was already staggering down the hall before Tae had even finished her sentence.

VIII
ONUS

I COULDN'T BREATHE.

I couldn't breathe!

My chest heaved and I shot up in bed, coated in sweat. I couldn't get any air in me.

And then I knew why. I'd forgotten to take my dose of malay before I went to sleep. I hadn't taken *any* malay for more than twenty hours. I'd gone to bed so drunk that I had forgotten.

I collapsed to the floor, tangled in sheets, knocking everything off my nightstand. I crawled to the dresser, extending a trembling hand to the top drawer. It was too far. I couldn't stand up.

The room was getting foggy. My vision was tunneling. I was going to die.

I lay on my side, wheezing, eyes glazing with defeat.

The door opened. "Qaira, I'm sorry."

Leid.

"I know I said you didn't have to go to work today, but—"

She froze at the sight of me. All I did was look at her, helpless.

She closed the door. "Where is it?"

How did she know? How *could* she know?

I pointed at the top drawer, battling consciousness.

Leid bolted to the dresser and threw open the drawer, tearing through it. A second later she found my syringes and case and knelt beside me.

"Don't move," she said, rolling up my sleeve. She paused, stricken by all the track marks on my arm. Then she found a clean spot and ripped open the container cap with her teeth, filling the syringe with malay.

75

Leid injected the syringe into my arm and I cringed, looking away.

Cold air filled my lungs and I gasped, doubling over in a fit of coughs. I fell sideways, staring vacantly ahead, riding the most intense high ever.

Leid stayed by my side, watching. She seemed concerned, and surprised.

I didn't like the way she was looking at me. *That disappointment.* Shame marked my face and I tried to hide it, but as everything sank in the shame turned into anger, then into *fury.*

This was all her fault. If Leid hadn't gotten me drunk I would have remembered to take my dose. I wouldn't be here feeling like a piece of shit. Now she knew. Now she'd always look at me with that air of sad disappointment.

"As I was saying," she almost whispered, "I know I said that you didn't have to go to work today, but our—"

Leid was cut off when my fingers curled around her neck and I rammed her into the wall, teeth clenched. For a second I fantasized about killing her as red inked across my vision. But she didn't even scream. She just stared up at me, expressionless. My anger waned, switching to confusion at the idea that that hadn't frightened her.

And then the malay-fog cleared and I realized what I was doing. I recoiled, hands encasing my face.

Leid said nothing, standing and smoothing her skirt-suit. I stayed down, trying to get a hold of myself.

"Get dressed," she said. "Commander Raith just contacted Eroqam. He wants to speak to you." She moved toward the door.

"Wait," I rasped.

She turned. There was nothing in her eyes when she looked at me.

"D-Don't tell any—"

"I won't." She closed the door.

I was left in the darkness of my room.

Beside me, my alarm went off. I threw it at the wall.

* * *

The Eroqam Communications room was located in the northern wing, just a little ways past the Commons. Linguists and information systems analysts kept our servers and databases running smoothly, surveyed our radio channels, and also listened in on the whites' transmissions between Crylle and their base ship.

Leid was already waiting for me when I arrived, standing off to the side so she wouldn't be in view of the giant projection screen that covered the wall. Isa, Shev and Kanar sat in the third row, between the analysts preparing to connect to our live video feed.

Another analyst handed me a portable microphone that hooked around my ear. "We're ready when you are, sir."

I was hardly ready, especially with this hangover shredding my brain like razorblades, but that was life. "Connect to telecom line five."

The screen flickered, and then Commander Lucifer Raith appeared on-screen.

The room he sat in mirrored ours, with Archaean analysts stationed in rows behind him. But their computers looked nothing like Eroqam's, their panels clear and emanating strange, blue light. I also noticed that Raith didn't have an earpiece. I couldn't see a mic anywhere on him. He wore a white and black military uniform with a gold pendant pinned across his breast.

Raith said nothing at first, letting the tension rise. His long, ice-blond hair fell over one eye; the other gleamed with contempt. "Qaira Eltruan, it's been too long."

"I can't say the feeling's mutual."

"I heard you and your savages raided my camp yesterday."

I didn't reply, crossing my arms.

Raith tilted his head. "Did you have fun slaughtering my people?"

"Just returning the favor, white. We might as well stop dancing around the real reason for your call."

Hesitation.

Raith sighed. "Did you kill him?"

I smirked. "Of course I didn't. What good would that do me? But I'd love to know how you found out so quickly considering Crylle lines are still jammed, last I checked."

"I'm not at liberty to discuss that."

"Well how about you tell me or I'll put a bullet in your son's head?"

Commander Raith stared vacantly at me, his thoughts on my threat imperceptible. "If Yahweh Telei dies, then so does Sanctum."

I laughed quietly. "That's quite a threat, Commander Raith, especially coming from someone who has yet to even talk to me face to face."

He leaned in, eyes fierce. "You have absolutely *no* idea what we're capable of, Nehelian. And even though you're poking the beast with a stick, I'm still willing to negotiate terms for Yahweh's safety."

"Given that Yahweh's *in* Sanctum, it'd be counterintuitive to destroy it, right?"

"... What do you want?"

"No more attacks on Sanctum, or your son dies."

"That last attack wasn't my doing. I can't account for all the Archaeans on my ship who hate you, Commandant."

"Maybe you should try a little harder."

"How did you know?"

I paused. "Sorry?"

"How did you know about my son?"

I resisted the urge to glance at Leid. "Your rebels sing a pretty song after they're stuck with enough sharp objects."

Raith smiled. "I don't believe that. No one would have ever given Yahweh up."

"Truth hurts. Maybe you should walk it off."

"Let me see him."

"That sounded like an order. Let me remind you that you're in no position to make demands."

"I don't believe Yahweh is unharmed; and even if he is, I don't believe he will stay that way in *your* care."

"That stings. I'll have you know that I *love* kids."

"Let me see him!" Raith screamed, slamming his fist against his desk. The feed broke for a second and the screen flickered to static. *"If you don't let me see my son right now, I'll launch everything we have on Sanctum!"*

I was glad the feed broke, since I hadn't wanted him to see me flinch. I looked at Leid. "Go and get the kid."

Lucifer's image returned as Leid stepped out of the room. All we did was glare at each other.

There was an insurgent in Sanctum, and now I had proof. It was a bittersweet discovery, because even though I'd just provided the evidence to back my hunch, I had no idea who the insurgent was. I also had no idea *where* to start looking.

On second thought, I did. The only people who knew about Yahweh's capture worked for Eroqam. Leid had been right, again.

She returned with the angel boy moments later, placing a gentle hand on his shoulder to nudge him forward. Yahweh looked at the screen and fell beside me. At the sight of him, the hardened frown on Lucifer's face softened.

"Are you hurt?" he asked.

The boy shook his head. "Don't waste your resources trying to free me, father. I'm only one of many."

I stared at the kid, caught off guard by his sense of selflessness.

"You are more valuable than you know," Raith said. "Don't you dare try to play a martyr, do you hear me?"

Yahweh nodded, glancing away. Their conversation was very awkward.

"Sorry to interrupt this moment between you," I interjected, "but my time, like your son, is invaluable and I'd really like it if you could agree to my terms so I can get back to work."

"So long as you keep to your word, Commandant."

I gave him a serrated grin. "What, you don't trust me?"

Raith smiled, bleakly. "When will Yahweh be returned to us?"

"I haven't really decided yet. Let's see if you can stop the attacks, and then we'll talk."

"You'll be hearing from me *very* soon."

The screen went black.

Kanar stood, applauding. "Excellent job, Commandant. It looks like we're finally making some progress."

"Don't count on it," I sighed, handing the earpiece back to the analyst. "Are all the supplies at the Aeroway?"

"We're working on transferring the last shipments now," Isa said. "We'll discuss the specifics tomorrow morning."

I looked at Yahweh, who stood there with his eyes cast to the floor, hands shoved into his pockets. "I'll take the kid back to his room."

* * *

Nothing was said until we reached his holding room. As I punched in the code to the digital lock, he looked up at me.

"That was foolish, you know."

"Oh yeah?" I said, barely listening.

"You should have demanded that Lucifer leave The Atrium."

I laughed, opening the door.

Yahweh wrinkled his nose. "Why is that funny?"

"Because I don't want Raith gone, kid. I want him *dead*. You're biding me some time to figure out how to get on his ship." I shoved the boy inside, and he stared defiantly at me.

"Your malice will be the death of you, Qaira Eltruan."

"Everyone keeps saying that, but here I am." I shut the door, locking it.

Raith and his filthy whites had poisoned our world for too long. They'd taken a proud city, a proud world, and disassembled it piece by piece. Sanctum was in a state of decay because of the seventy-year we'd been forced to endure. No, Raith wasn't getting off scot-free. I wouldn't let him rock up on another planet and do the same thing to *them*. They were parasites, and parasites deserved to die.

I turned and found Leid standing in the hall, flashing me a grin. I watched her with trepidation; she was acting like this morning had never happened. How could she?

"I commend you on a performance well done," she praised. "So, what are you going to do with the rest of your evening off?"

IX
A LESSON OF DOMINANCE

LEID LOOKED OVER THE MENU, HER WARY frown falling to a grimace. "Nothing on here looks good."

"*You* chose the place."

"I know."

"You've been mulling that over for twenty minutes. You better pick something soon or we're going to look like idiots."

Her grimace faded and she gave me a smile, but it didn't reach her eyes. "Must you always be so unpleasant?"

"Only when I'm being terribly inconvenienced. It's not my fault that that happens all the time."

We were sitting at a fancy restaurant in Upper Sanctum. *Kesa* was well known for their wine and rice dishes, not to mention their staggering prices for near-microscopic portions. Leid had seen a review column in our news journal and wanted to come. Even though I was the richest man in Sanctum, I seldom ventured to these kinds of places. But I understood Leid was getting cabin fever, and I still felt guilty about almost breaking her neck this morning.

It was late in the evening so the dinner crowd was already gone. That was a good thing, considering I didn't need any more media attention. The press would have loved to report rumors of *Commandant Qaira Eltruan's flourishing romance with his Advisor*, which would then force the spotlight on Leid. I couldn't have that. In passing she may have looked ordinary, but anyone interested enough to look twice would be able to tell she wasn't Nehelian.

The only thing I could hope for was that logical reasoning would force curious spectators into questioning their sanity should they think she was some kind of alien. But with the whites around, who knew.

"Is this any good?" She held the menu out, pointing to an entrée. I leaned in to read it. Another leriza dish. I was about to complain about her eating the same thing all the time, but thought better of it. I just wanted her to choose something so I could have dinner.

"Yeah, it's good."

Leid wore a black-laced dress with white knee-high boots. The height of her heels almost made *me* stagger. Her hair was tied in a bun and she wore heavy-lidded liner, trying to make her eyes appear smaller. I hated to admit it but she was the prettiest woman in the restaurant. I didn't *want* her to be the prettiest woman in the restaurant because people kept staring and I was afraid they'd notice who she was with.

She put the menu down and pointed at the wine bottle. "Want any more?"

"Not until we eat." I was still hung-over.

Leid shrugged and poured the rest of it into her glass, filling it to the rim.

The waiter came by for the thousandth time. "Are you and your date ready to eat, Commandant?"

"She is not my date," I said curtly, handing him the menu. "She is my advisor and we are having a business meeting."

"Can I have another bottle of wine?" asked Leid.

I shot her a look. "I'll have the artegna with legumes. She'll have the grilled leriza with tevra sauce, and *another* bottle of wine."

"What would the lady like with her side?" asked the waiter, glancing at Leid.

Leid blinked. "What?"

I sighed, massaging my forehead.

"Your choice of setsa, canai or the sautéed poi."

She looked at me; her expression read *'save me'*.

I did. "She'll have the canai."

After the waiter left with our menus, she asked, "What's canai?"

I smirked. "Pickled gizzards."

"You're horrible."

"I know."

We fell silent, waiting for our dinner. I stared at Leid as she unfolded and refolded her cloth napkin. Only three weeks ago I was plotting her demise, and now we were at a restaurant together. The irony didn't elude me.

In my defense I didn't have anything else to do. This was the first day off I'd ever had. Tae, Ara and my father were already finished with dinner by now. I was never able to participate in my family life because I left early each morning and didn't get home until late at night. I probably saw them for about an hour per day, if that.

Leid was the first person who I'd spent this much time with since... forever. The isolation my job forced on me left me uncomfortable in most social situations. But then again, Leid was weird, too. Her lack of empathy was appalling. She'd say just about anything on her mind without any regard as to how it came across. Sometimes it was funny, other times it was annoying.

"Your ink is fading, Qaira."

I rolled my eyes. "Yes, I know. I haven't had a chance to call my artist."

"I could fill it for you."

I stared at her, saying nothing. She smiled.

"For free, even."

"Nothing comes free with you," I said. "Since when do you ink?"

"Since always. Inking is a long-practiced tradition of the Nehel."

"Oh, yeah? I didn't know that."

She frowned at my sarcasm. "Will you let me?"

"As long as you don't fuck my face up."

"Well then you better be nicer to me."

"I'm nicer to you than I am anyone else."

"That's scary."

We shared a grin.

Our food arrived and I dug in. I hadn't realized how hungry I was until I took my first bite. Several minutes later my plate was half clean. My eyes rose to Leid as she sat there picking at hers.

"Are you going to eat?" I asked.

Reluctantly she took a bite. Her face lit up. "Hey, this is pretty good."

"Fantastic."

When we were done I poured myself a glass of wine, refilling Leid's as well. This had to be her sixth. She nodded her thanks, taking a sip.

"I want to see that Archaean craft tomorrow."

With all of the commotion over the past week, I hadn't taken her to our research laboratory yet. "I planned on it."

"Good."

"What do you hope to achieve by seeing it?"

"Wrong question."

I lifted a brow.

"What do *you* hope to achieve by *me* seeing it?"

Ah, technicalities. "The craft came from their base ship, which means it can return there. I want to know how it works, and whether we can replicate it."

"So you want to upgrade your crafts."

I nodded.

"I'm beginning to suspect that you don't simply want the angels to *leave* The Atrium."

"I plan to kill Lucifer Raith," I said plainly, watching her expression. "I want to destroy their base ship."

Leid glanced at her lap. "Your plan will take a while, Qaira."

"That's fine. We have Yahweh to keep the whites at bay."

Her eyes widened with revelation. "That's *right!* We have Yahweh!"

I tilted my head at her sudden display of enthusiasm. "Hooray?"

"The fact that we have him could speed up your plan exponentially!"

"What do you mean?"

"Yahweh Telei has developed over twenty percent of the Archaean's technological advances over the course of three centuries."

"… Shut up."

"I told you he wasn't just a kid, Qaira. The contract forbids me to from building the crafts myself, but—"

"Yahweh could," I finished. "Well at least he'll be somewhat useful."

"Now all we have to do is convince him to work for us. That won't be easy."

I smirked. "I'm sure I can think of something."

"You can't hurt him."

My smirk fell. "Okay, what is it with you and that white? What do you care if I smack him around a bit?"

Leid looked away, conflict in her gaze. "He won't comply with violence. You need to get him to respect you. To *like* you."

"It sounds like you know him personally."

"I don't. Another scholar does, though."

"Who?"

"I can't disclose that. It's against my contract to talk about Enigmus affairs."

"Yahweh is an angel under *my* supervision. It's important that I know these things."

"No, it isn't. Unless Lucifer learned of my involvement there would be no reason for him to contact the Court of Enigmus. If we keep it that way, everything will be fine. But you *mustn't* hurt Yahweh."

We fell silent as the waiter returned with our check. I muttered thanks and opened the book to inspect the bill.

Seriously? Two hundred usos?

"Promise me, Qaira. This is important."

"So have you taken my place as Regent? Last time I checked, you serve me. I don't have to promise you anything."

Leid's face darkened. "Without me you wouldn't last another year, *Regent*. I suggest you reflect on that before you try to undermine me."

Anger began to resettle in my chest, rising to my face. My pulse beat like a war drum. Instead of replying, I jammed the money into the checkbook and slammed it on the table.

"Get up, we're leaving."

* * *

The ride back to Eroqam was quiet, obviously.

It was nearly midnight and Upper Sanctum was closing down. Lower Sanctum was just opening for business. The working class crowds filtered into bars and shops as we flew overhead, like little ant drones marching in and out of their hives. Lights below flickered in the dark like stars reflected off water.

"Are you going to give me the silent treatment for the rest of the night?" asked Leid.

I frowned, keeping my eyes ahead. "That was the plan, yeah."

"Your methods of resolution are comparable to a child's."

"Totally not helping your case right now."

"Qaira, stop it."

"You first. If my memory serves correct, you were the one who started this."

"I didn't start anything. You approach every problem with violence."

"I do not."

"You do so."

"Let's take a survey," I said, gesturing between her and I. "We have a problem, right?"

Leid said nothing, crossing her arms.

"And I haven't resorted to violence."

"Yes, I suppose laying your hands on me twice in a day would be overkill."

"Cheap shot. You know I didn't mean to do that."

"Do you have any malay in your craft?" she asked.

"Yes."

"May I see it?"

I gave her a sidelong glance. "What for?"

"I'd like to try some."

"… Are you fucking serious?"

"Don't worry; I can't get addicted to substances like your lot. I just want to see what all the fuss is about."

Our conversation revived memories of Talia, and I didn't want to think about that. I was fairly certain my scholar wouldn't go insane and throw a lamp at my head if I refused to give her another dose, but then again anything was possible when it came to Leid.

I nodded at my dashboard. "It's in there."

Leid opened it up and removed my case. It contained fifteen canisters and forty-six syringes. "Goodness," she gasped, examining the size of my stash. "How many do you take per day?"

"Three," I said. "I buy it in bulk."

She filled a syringe and injected it into her arm. Even though I did that numerous times a day, I still couldn't watch. Then she sat there, looking around. Suddenly, her eyes widened.

"Oh *my*."

I grinned at her reaction. It was funny.

"I can see the appeal," Leid said, reclining in her seat and closing her eyes. Her dress slid up her legs, and my eyes trailed to her exposed thigh. Something in my stomach twisted. I found myself wondering what she looked like underneath that dress, and an image of her straddling me flashed through my mind. I'd never fucked a strong-willed woman before. I was curious to know if she'd keep up that act while I was buried in her. She was so tiny that I'd probably break her in half.

Whoa, Qaira. Whoa.

I forced my attention ahead, trying to get a hold of myself. I hadn't had my needs filled since Leid showed up a month ago. Since she was more or less attached to me, I was practically celibate. Ten years of celibacy. Someone kill me.

89

"Is this all you have?" she asked.

"No, I have more in my room. You saw it this morning."

"How much is in there?"

"A little less than this."

"Is your brother an addict, too?"

"No."

"Does he know about you?"

"He hasn't ever asked, but he might. I don't know."

I also didn't know why she was asking me these questions. By the time my suspicion was fully instated, I'd turned my head just in time to watch her open the passenger window and dump my *entire* case. It plummeted two thousand feet into the darkness of Sanctum.

It felt like my eyes were about to pop out of my head. As I stared at her in utter disbelief, she leaned back in her seat, seeming quite satisfied with herself. My hands cramped up and I realized I was clutching the wheel so hard that my knuckles were white.

"LEID, WHAT THE *FUCK?!*"

"Now, now; this is for your own good."

I floored the pedal and we shot into Eroqam's landing port. I turned off the ignition and whirled to her, snarling. "Do you know how expensive those are?! You just dumped five thousand usos out the fucking window!"

"Doesn't matter," she said, unflinching. "You aren't buying any more."

I glared at her.

Leid opened the door, moving to get out, but I reached over her and shut it again. We weren't finished. "What do you think you're doing? You can't *force* me to quit. Don't you remember what happened this morning?"

"You still have some in your room. I'm not cutting you off completely, but from now on I'm going to hold onto your malay for you. I'll administer your doses in smaller amounts over time. We're going to wean you off."

"You... you *can't*," I stammered. "You have no right to dictate my life!"

"Then try to stop me," she dared, flicking my nose.

I shot back into my seat, enraged. She darted from the craft before I could say anything else. How could that bitch run so fast in those *shoes?!*

I chased her, knowing exactly where she was headed. The events that followed were surreal.

Leid burst into my room right as I caught up to her. As she lunged for the dresser, I tackled her to the floor. We rolled around my bedroom, entangled in a vicious struggle. She was holding her own a little *too* well, and my surprise made me clumsy. She managed to kick me off and I was sent into the wall.

By the time I got back up, she had my case.

"You can't do this!" I shouted. *"I'll be worthless if you cut my doses!"*

"For a while I imagine you will be," she agreed. "But that will change. You can't keep this up, Qaira. Malay kills people. You're *killing* yourself. Not to mention you're impulsive, violent and angry. Those aren't suitable traits for a world leader."

"You're not my mother! You can't treat me like a fucking child!"

"It seems like someone needs to."

And that was it; I snapped. I lunged at her again, swinging.

My fist caught air. Leid had disappeared.

Something wrenched my arm behind my back and shoved me forward. My face hit the wall and I spun, swinging again. She caught my hand and bent my wrist back, nearly snapping it. I fell to my knees, crying out in shock.

She held me there, eyes gleaming with malice. "Don't play with me, Qaira. You might get hurt."

"What... *what are you?!*"

"I am a scholar," she said evenly. "And I'm doing what's best for you. You want to win this war? Start acting like it."

Leid let go of me and I recoiled, holding my near-broken wrist. She rummaged through my case and took out a syringe, filling it with malay.

"Here is your night's dose," she said, slapping it on my nightstand. "I'll give you another before you go to work."

I stared at it, still trying to process what just happened. Getting spanked by a girl half my size was an impossible fact to swallow.

Leid moved to the door, stopping over the threshold. "Thanks for dinner, Qaira. I'll see you tomorrow morning."

A smile, and then she was gone.

I sank to my bed, putting my face in my hands. Leid's contract returned to me, specifically the clause about how she couldn't aid us in physical combat. Back then I'd laughed about that, but now everything was crystal clear. She'd snapped a collar on me. Leid had never intended to serve me. I was serving *her*.

"Qairaaaaaaa," Ara called from my door.

I didn't even look at him.

"We're going to Sapyr! You wanna come?" he was already drunk; I could barely understand what he was saying.

"Get out," I muttered.

Ara's face scrunched up with confusion. "What's wrong?"

"I said *get out!*"

He flinched. "What the fuck is your problem lately?"

The question was rhetorical, because the door slammed a second later. Ara hadn't noticed the needle on my nightstand. He was probably too loaded to see straight.

I glanced at the syringe, daydreaming of stabbing it through Leid's pretty little eyes. I felt like destroying everything around me, but I was too tired to move. All I did was sit there, staring at the wall.

Only nine years and ten months more to go.

X

CHAINS

"THE AERO-CRAFTS THAT THE ANGELS use are made from a thin, metal alloy found only on their planet," Leid began, seated at the head of the conference table. Her eyes were lowered to the folder in her hands. "Your scientists were nice enough to test the colligative properties for me, and there are several metals in The Atrium that are capable of producing the same effect."

The Eye of Akul were on the edges of their seats. The director of Sanctum Science Research, Kada Ysam, and his team of aerophysicists were also present for the briefing.

As Leid explained the mechanics of our enemy's crafts, I stared ahead in a fog. I should have been listening to her, especially since I'd been pushing for the results all week, but I couldn't hold a single cohesive thought long enough to even speak a sentence, let alone listen to one.

For the last several weeks, I'd been a zombie. Perspiration coated my skin; droplets of sweat threatened to trickle from my trembling upper lip. My hands were a shaking mess. My brain felt like it was being shocked. I wanted to die.

Every three days or so Leid would decrease my malay dose just enough for me to suffer. And, no sooner had I gotten used to the adjusted amount, I was forced to suffer again.

Life moved by in a blur, a hazy form of incoherence. Work days came and went as I floated aimlessly through a chemical dream. I was surprised no one had noticed my evident decline.

"What do you think, Commandant?" asked Kanar, and I snapped back to reality. Everyone was staring at me, awaiting an answer to a question I hadn't heard.

"Uh," I stalled, looking to Leid with a desperate wince, "I..."

"We discussed it yesterday evening," she said, swooping in to my rescue. She handed Kanar a sheet of paper. "Here is the list of materials I will need in order to begin building the necessary components of the craft. Dr. Ysam, I want to get you acquainted with our angel detainee, Yahweh Telei, who I'm hoping can come up with a prototype."

"The Archaean has agreed to help us?" asked Isa.

"Agreed," I recited, laughing dryly. "As if he has an option."

They looked at me.

"Please excuse the Commandant," Leid said, clearing her throat. "He hasn't been getting much sleep lately, as we've been working around the clock to get our project in order."

More like I hadn't gotten much sleep lately because I woke up three times a night choking and shaking. When everyone went to bed, Leid slipped into my room and slept in my armchair. She kept me under heavy supervision in case my lungs failed in the middle of the night. That had happened three times.

While she did everything in her power to keep me alive, I thought about murdering her a dozen times a day. In fact, I was doing it right now.

Shev glanced over the materials list. "The angel detainee will tell us how his people built their crafts, and based on what we have here, we'll replicate them. Is that what you're saying?"

Leid nodded. "Expect some deviations because we aren't using the same protocols."

"Understood."

"I can't tell you how delighted I am to see how far we've come. Saying it's a pleasure to have you with us is an understatement, Advisor Koseling," praised Isa.

Ugh, that bitch was stealing my life.

Leid patted my arm. "Please, I can't take all of the credit. I'm only doing what the Commandant instructed me to."

"Your father would be very proud," said Kanar.

I shot him a look. "You make it sound like he's dead."

Leid squeezed my arm, hard enough to hurt. "Thank you all for coming. We'll be sure to keep the Eye of Akul updated as we proceed."

When everyone filtered out of the council room, she gave me a venomous look. "Could you please be professional?"

I said nothing, shoving my stuff into my briefcase. She held the door for me as I left.

"You're almost to half your regular dose, Qaira. It won't be long until you're completely rid of malay."

I paused in the doorway, leaning down until our noses almost touched. "And how long until I'm rid of *you?*"

Leid tried to shake that off, but I could see the hurt in her eyes. "Hate me if you must. Meet me before dinner so I can give you another dose."

She walked away, not looking back.

I headed in the opposite direction, off to enforcer training.

* * *

The only upside to quitting malay so far was that my appetite came back. That evening my family watched me plow through seconds, and then *thirds* of dinner.

But I paid for that a little while later, when I spent the better part of an hour puking all the dinner I'd eaten into the toilet. Leid had injected a dose before I'd sat down at the table, but it was less than that of this morning's. Her decrease was premature; I hadn't been given enough time to adjust. It was probably her way of getting back at me for my remark this afternoon. Fucking bitch.

I staggered to my bedroom and collapsed in bed, curling onto my side. I must have passed out then, because when I opened my eyes again there was someone shaking my arm, and the light from my window was gone. The room was pitch-black.

A whisper. "Qaira."

Leid.

I shook her off, not turning around. "Get out."

"No."

"What do you want?"

She didn't say anything.

"Come to enjoy the show?" I asked, laughing. The laugh turned into a cough a second later. I shivered.

The bed shifted as she sat on the edge of it. Her silhouette crept into my peripherals. "I don't enjoy seeing you like this. I know you think I'm doing this for some sick form of entertainment, and that really upsets me."

"Get out!" I shouted. *"You've practically turned me into a cripple, reduced me to nothing, and now you're trying to invade the only hour away from you that I have?"*

"I won't get out until you stop moping around and feeling sorry for yourself."

"I'm not moping! I was *sleeping* because I spent the evening puking up my insides!"

"Get up."

"I can't move."

"Get up!"

Leid ripped me out of bed and I fell to the floor. Before I could even respond she grabbed my shirt and pulled me up, slamming my back into the wall. My tired, blood-shot eyes were wild with disbelief.

"The pity party is getting old, Commandant. If you're such a strong man, why don't you fight this? You're going to let some drug get the better of *you?* You're Qaira Eltruan, the Savior of Sanctum, son of the Regent and the man who can—"

"I know what you're trying to do, and it isn't working."

Even in the darkness, her eyes gleamed violet. "We're almost there, Qaira. You're *so* close to being free of this drug. You think I've put a leash on you but you've been in chains for decades. You are a slave to malay, and it's time to take the shackles off."

"I don't think I can take it. It feels like I'm dying. You don't understand."

"You're right, I don't. But if you give up, then you're going to die. And... I don't want you to die."

Slowly, I looked down at her. Leid looked up at me. There was a moment.

"So, how hard was that to say?" I asked, smirking.

She only smiled and looked away, heading for the door. "Come, I want to show you something."

"What?"

"See for yourself."

* * *

Leid had spent several days cleaning up the music room. The layers of dust were gone, the instruments shined on display, and my mother's cello and violin were waiting for us beside two chairs in the center of the room.

Seeing this stirred up a few emotions in me, not all of them good ones. In part I felt like Leid had desecrated the only sacred memories I'd had left of my mother, but at the same time she'd brought life back into a decaying place that everyone else had forgotten.

"What's the meaning of this?" I asked.

"I'm going to honor your mother and teach you how to play that violin. Every time you feel like life's about to crush you, I want you to come in here and play."

Leid took a seat beside the cello and looked at me, but I hadn't moved. She could sense the wariness in my gaze. As I debated whether or not to follow her in, she tucked the cello between her legs and began to play. The song she played this time was sad.

I watched her, entranced. The world fell away, and I floated in stasis. She was right; it was helping. Her music was ataractic, and for a second I forgot how sick I felt.

After a minute or two she stopped playing. I moved inside and took a seat beside her. Leid's eyes lowered to the floor; raven threads of hair slid across her shoulders, hiding her face.

"How did you learn to play so well?"

"There are almost identical versions of the cello on numerous planets throughout the multiverse," she whispered. "I learned to play the strings several centuries ago, when something terrible happened to me. Music is a language that needs no words to express how I feel. And like this, my agony is beautiful."

I looked away, silent. When the silence became too much to bear, I said, "I don't hate you, you know."

She turned to me.

"I wanted to. *Tried* to. But I can't."

I picked up the violin, looking over the polished white wood. My eyes lingered on the engraving my mother had designed for it: *Q*.

When I looked back at Leid, she was smiling. The smile wasn't one I'd ever seen on her before.

"I'm very happy to hear that, Qaira."

XI
COMPOSURE

I WAS RELIEVED TO FIND THAT I WAS still on time for our detainee's morning meal schedule; even after I'd spent half an hour in Eroqam's private restrooms puking my guts out. That was becoming ritual for me. I didn't know why I kept trying to eat breakfast.

Tae and Ara had begun making remarks about how sick I looked, telling me they were worried. I'd told them it was because I wasn't getting much sleep from all the work I had, but I'm pretty sure they didn't believe me.

Despite all that, I was in a good mood today. Leid gave me an injection this morning and it was the first time that I didn't think of killing her. Instead we spoke about the weather.

And since I was in such a good mood, it was time to try to persuade the white kid into working for us. Because Leid had (repeatedly) emphasized the fact of not laying a finger on him, I didn't want to go into his holding room without some level of patience.

I caught one of my guards in the hall. He was carrying Yahweh's breakfast tray to his room.

"I'll take over," I said, snatching the tray. I punched in the code and opened the door, finding the boy sprawled over the bed on his stomach, reading a book. He didn't even look at me as I walked in.

"This must be a special occasion," he said as I placed the tray on the desk beside the bed. "Commandant Qaira Eltruan has come to grace me with his presence."

I smirked at his indignation, taking a seat across his bed. I'd spoken to Yahweh three times before now, but he still made me uncomfortable. A kid his age shouldn't have been able to anticipate an out-of-routine event just from my appearance, let alone critically analyze it using an impressive vocabulary. I glanced at the book he was reading.

"How are you finding the *History and Political Inflections of Sanctum in the Adoria Era?*"

Yahweh shrugged. "Not sure. I can't read it."

"Just enjoying the pictures?"

"I'm trying to learn Nehelian in written form."

"And how's that going for you?"

"Not so well."

"I'm sorry."

"If you're really sorry, you'll get me some paper and writing utensils so I can take notes while I'm trying to learn."

"Writing utensils are sharp."

Yahweh looked at me, annoyed. "Must I really promise not to kill myself?"

I laughed quietly.

"So what do you want, Qaira Eltruan?"

"You don't have to say my last name every time you address me."

"Being on a first name basis represents a level of intimacy that I don't care to have with you."

I made a face. "Intimacy."

"Again, why are you here?"

I decided to cut the small talk, since the kid wasn't biting. "We need you to help our science research team replicate your angel crafts."

Yahweh smiled. "No."

"That isn't really an option; sorry if I made it sound like one."

He leaned into my face, looking me over. "Are you sick? You look terrible."

"We've gathered the materials that we need," I said, ignoring him, "and would like you to draw us up protocols for a design—"

"I'm not doing it."

I stared at him.

"You don't really need me anyway," he said, pouting at his book. "I'm sure your scholar could do all that for you."

"You know about Leid?"

"Of course I do. I've seen a dozen scholars in my lifetime, not to mention she looks nothing like you. But tell me; do you know what they *really* are?"

I was sure the kid could tell that I didn't.

"Eroqam is playing with fire, Commandant. You have no idea of the lines you're crossing right now."

I sighed. "So, this can go one of two ways. Either you help us willingly or I'm going to have to make you help us."

"You can't hurt me. Your scholar said that, didn't she?"

I leaned in, narrowing my eyes. "Leid said that I couldn't lay a finger on you. She never said I couldn't hurt you, and I am a resourceful man. There are plenty of ways that I could hurt you without touching you, Yahweh *Telei*. Would you like to see them?"

The defiance melted from the kid's face. He looked away, at the bed. "No."

"*No* as in you still won't help us, or *no* as in you don't want to find out how I can hurt you?"

"What do you want me to do?"

I reclined in my seat, smiling victoriously. "Smart boy."

"I really wish that wasn't the case right now."

Getting out of the chair, I slid his breakfast tray to him. "Eat something. Leid and I will return for you later on with all of the details."

"Can I *please* have something that will stimulate me?" he begged. "I'm going insane with boredom in here. And I won't be much help to you if I have a psychotic breakdown."

I grinned, heading for the door. "If I were you I'd relish the boredom, because pretty soon you're going to be very, *very* busy."

* * *

Leid waited for me in the flight port hallway, holding my briefcase.

She always had my briefcase, though I had no idea why. At first I was late three days in a row because I turned our house upside down trying to find it, only to discover Leid had taken it to the port. She'd said it was one less thing I had to worry about. I never looked for it anymore.

I nodded at Leid and she held my briefcase out to me. I took it, and we walked to my craft.

Nothing was said for the first half of our trip. Leid couldn't seem to handle the anticipation anymore and looked at me. *"So?"*

"So what?" I asked, smirking.

She frowned at my playfulness. "Did Yahweh agree?"

"Yes."

"Did he agree *without* you hitting him?"

"Yes."

With a satisfied smile, she leaned back in her seat. "Good."

And then we hit traffic. I cursed under my breath, looking at the clock on my dash. At least we still had another twenty minutes.

"You didn't eat very much this morning," Leid noted.

"Technically I didn't eat anything, since it all went into the toilet."

"You need to try to keep some food down. You're losing a lot of weight."

"Well why don't you try convincing my stomach of that with your stunning logic. I'm sure it will listen."

"I bet clear liquids would go down easier than pastries and tea. Why don't you try water and broth?"

"That sounds fucking delicious, Leid." She opened her mouth to protest, but I said, "Stop mothering me. I'm fine."

She shrugged and glanced out the window. "Suit yourself."

It'd been five minutes and we'd only moved ten feet. We were going to be late. I glanced at Leid as she stared out of the passenger side window, recalling what Yahweh said earlier this morning. Curiosity was settling in.

"Tell me about the Court of Enigmus," I said.

She looked at me, surprised. "What do you want to know?"

"Where are they?"

"Far away; another universe."

"Another *universe?* There's more than one?"

"There are thirteen that we know of."

"What's your definition of a universe? I was always taught to understand that a universe was infinite."

"A universe is not infinite, though to lesser beings it would seem that way. Universes are actually spherical; it's like a giant planet, so you'd never reach an end per se."

"How do you get to another one?"

"A being from one universe cannot enter another universe. The multiverse is a web of universes connected only by their situation. They sit side by side in almost a flower arrangement."

"You said the Court of Enigmus was from another universe."

"We're different. To my knowledge we're the only beings able to cross universes without succumbing to the effects of their alternate physical laws."

"Alternate effects?"

She smiled. "In my world, Qaira, I would not be nearly as strong as you. The laws are different in your universe. It changes my strength and speed."

The traffic cleared and we were able to move again. "How do you travel to different universes?"

Leid arched a brow. "Why are you so curious?"

"I don't know. Why wouldn't I be?"

"We travel through tears."

"Tears?"

"Portals, sort of; ripples in the space-time continuum. There are over a hundred across your galaxy alone, and they bridge us to another universe."

I stared at her, baffled.

Leid sensed my confusion and paused, tapping her chin. "Okay, think of it like this: each universe is connected in a sort of flower/web type order, like a wall connecting two offices together.

All matter vibrates, even if you can't see it. In certain areas, resonance is strong enough that the matter moves aside and we can travel through it."

"So you can travel throguh the wall."

"Yes, precisely."

"Does your body's matter get displaced when you go through?"

Leid blinked. "How do you know about that?"

"I almost got a degree in aerophysics."

She seemed surprised. "Really?"

"Yeah," I muttered. "I know you thought I was stupid. Sorry to burst your bubble."

"I never thought you were stupid," she said, frowning. "What degree did you get instead?"

"Two. Linguistics and Military Philosophy."

"I suppose that makes sense. Is education a requirement for military personnel?"

"No, but it is for people in office."

"Ah."

"So, you're pretty much saying that the only way to get to other universes is by taking one of those tears?"

"Pretty much, yes."

"Are you immortal?"

Leid smiled, amused. "No one is immortal, Qaira. It defies the laws of the multiverse."

"How do you find these tears?"

"We can see them."

"Can *I* see them?"

"No. Lesser beings aren't able to detect resonance shifts like we can."

"Lesser beings."

"I don't mean that in a quality way. That's just what we call everyone who isn't one of us."

"Where's the tear in Sanctum?"

"A few blocks from Eroqam."

I flew into the parking lot of Sanctum Parliament. Pulling my keys from the ignition and snatching my briefcase, I opened the door but Leid grabbed my arm.

"What's wrong?" she asked, sensing the sudden change in my mood.

"It's nothing," I sighed. "I just…"

She tilted her head, waiting.

"This whole time I've been amazed by how alike we are. But now I know that we aren't alike at all."

Leid reached over, cupping the side of my face.

"That isn't true," she whispered. "We're very much alike, you and I."

I froze, having not expected her to do that, and my eyes stayed on her lips as she spoke. Despite what she just said, there was something about Leid that was unlike that of any other Nehelian woman I'd ever known. She made me weak.

She made me weak, and I *liked* it.

Leid's eyes moved to the clock. "Shoot, you're late."

Without another word she slipped out of the craft. After a second of confused silence, I followed her.

* * *

Meetings, meetings and more meetings.

Just when I promised I'd kill myself if I had to stare at another politician's face, it was lunch time. But I wasn't hungry, I was craving.

It happened every so often, usually when I thought about malay. I made myself as busy as I could, but sometimes the thought still managed to sneak in.

My hands were shaking as I pushed aside the files on my desk. I told my secretary I'd be out of the office for an hour, and then I glanced at Leid. Half her face was hidden behind the ugly plant I was forced to keep because my sister had bought it for my birthday. She was writing something in my schedule, having taken it upon herself to become my personal assistant. Which was fine by me, since I didn't have to pay her.

Then again the amount of wine Leid drank in a week could have covered someone's salary. I didn't know if I could call her an alcoholic, though, since she never actually got drunk.

As I moved to the door, she looked up. "Lunch already?"

"Yeah, are you coming?"

"I'm not really hungry today."

"Oh," I said, trying to hide my disappointment. I'd gotten used to her joining me for lunch. "Want to come anyway?"

She smiled. "Will you miss my company?"

I glanced away, uncomfortable. "No, I just don't want you alone in my office for an hour. Who knows what you'll get into?"

Leid laughed. "Where are we going?"

* * *

Ciala was Upper Sanctum's favorite lunch hour restaurant.

Usually we ate in Parliament's cafeteria, but I was feeling pretty cagey and wanted to get out for a while.

The customer line wasn't massive since we missed rush hour. Leid and I stood amid other Nehelians decorated with fancy suits, briefcases and portable computers, and I watched the scenery shift from full-scale windows that surrounded the restaurant. Another attractive feature of this place was that it rotated atop a twenty story high-rise. People ate to a pretty view.

During the day Sanctum didn't seem so ugly, but I knew that façade better than anyone. Upper Sanctum was a corporate district; only twenty-five percent of the population could actually afford to live here. Lower Sanctum housed seventy-five percent of our residents— prostitutes, junkies, and all the other naturally-unfortunates, packed into a ghetto like old shoes into a moldy storage box.

We could paint a pretty picture all we like; reality was cold and cruel. Sanctum was falling, and there was nothing I could do about it. Not yet. First, I had to get rid of the angels.

Leid and I sat across from one another in a booth. I ate my lunch while Leid stared jadedly out at Fadja Memorial Park. I watched her, chewing.

"Are you sure you're not hungry?"

"No, but thank you."

Leid removed her white coat, laying it on the cushion beside her. She rested her arms on the table, idly running her fingers across her black mesh, elbow-length gloves. Her fashion sense was eccentric, but somehow it worked.

"Would you like to practice your violin later?"

"If I have time. I'm running the enforcer drill tonight."

"It seems like you need it, though."

"What do you mean?"

"You're shaking."

Shame on me for thinking she wouldn't notice. "I'm fine, and I said we'll see."

"So, what did you think about this morning's education tax-cut conundrum?"

"Yeah, because I totally want to talk about work while I'm on lunch."

"Do you have anything else to talk about?"

"Eroqam barely taxes education as is. Even the early academia teachers make a decent living. I'm not cutting taxes."

Leid arched a brow. "You think thirty-two thousand usos a year is a decent living?"

"It's better than what the other half of Sanctum lives on."

"The other half of Sanctum is below the poverty line."

I put my sandwich down, glaring at her. "Why are you trying to take a stab at me? What have I done now?"

"I'm just asking you a question. I'm not trying to start an argument. I want you to explain your opinion."

"My opinion on tax-cuts is irrelevant. You're taking little jabs at me because you don't agree with the way I run this city."

"You're right, I don't."

"Well that's too bad. You're here to advise me on the war; not tax-cuts."

"Could *you* live on a thirty-two thousand uso salary?"

Good-fucking-grief.

"Eroqam brings in more than four million usos a year," she went on.

"Half of which goes to our army and technology," I said.

"And the other two million?"

"Employee salaries, insurance… look at me, Leid. I drive to work every day in a standard craft, I wait in line with commoners at lunch. I don't live a grandeur life. I might be the richest man in Sanctum, but in reality I'm not that richer than my subjects. *You're* the one buying hundred uso bottles of wine in bulk."

Leid smiled, shifting her attention to the window. The smile was a taunt, like she was saying I was full of shit. I was starting to wish I'd left her at my office.

Then I looked out at the city as well, losing myself in the scenery. I thought about absolutely nothing, and it was such a relief. The food had calmed my nerves, and my craving was gone. I was relieved for that, too.

"Qaira," I heard Leid call, but at first I couldn't refocus my gaze. *"Qaira."*

I looked at her, but she wasn't looking at me. Her stare was directed behind me, at the televised screen above the serving table. I turned, following her eyes. A news report was being broadcasted, one with a headline that read:

COMMANDANT QAIRA ELTRUAN: SAVIOR OR TYRANT?

I reread the headline several times, my heart sinking into my stomach.

A news anchor was speaking to the head chairman of Sanctum's Department of Social Affairs, Lev Gia. He'd been in office as long as my father, and I could still recall all the parties he'd ever attended in the Regent's name.

"The level of authority that our Regent has is obsolete," he was saying. "His son is running the show behind the scenes, twisting Sanctum in order to carry out his own machinations."

"Machinations?" asked the news anchor.

"Everything that the Commandant is doing refutes his father's method of ruling. The Sanctum Enforcers and our guards are ignoring the very laws that they created. Qalam Eltruan is infirm, that we all know, but ever since his leave we've had a twenty percent spike in poverty and violent crime. Qaira Eltruan has cut programs for malay addicts and aid for low income citizens. He's placed almost the entirety of Sanctum's money into its militia, which he uses to slaughter angel refugees and silence peaceful protests for their freedom. His father spent years striving for peace, and in less than a decade we are right back to where we started. Qaira Eltruan's war on the Archaeans isn't a Sanctum-supported war. It almost seems like it's personal. We've practically deified him *because* of his tendency for violence."

I looked around the restaurant. Everyone was staring at me.

"Leid," I whispered, "get up. We're leaving."

She was out of her seat before I finished my sentence. We escaped Ciala as a recording of the Crylle raid blared on the screen. Ariel Triev's screams filtered into the reception area, and I heard myself:

"If I have to say it again then you're going to end up like that angel bitch!"

The raid had been a confidential matter. Someone had secretly recorded it and handed the recording to the press. The insurgent was in Eroqam, indubitably.

The backlash of that report was going to be severe, but all I could think about was how Tae and my father were going to take this. That video was going to destroy me.

The elevator ride was silent. Leid stared at me with concern, but she didn't dare speak. She knew me well enough by now to know when I had a certain look in my eyes, it was best to stay quiet.

By the time we reached the main floor, I'd come up with a plan. Hopefully the report hadn't been aired all morning, but I doubted it or else someone would have told me at Parliament. It was lunch time, but not every Nehelian was eating lunch right now, and not everyone had access to a television.

The media wanted to call me a tyrant? Fine, I'd *give* them a tyrant.

I reached for my radio as we climbed into my craft. "Ara, come in."

"Qaira, have you seen the fucking news?!"

"Yes. I have a job for you and the others. Head down to Sanctum Public Broadcast and confiscate that recording. Arrest the people involved in that news report. Do it quietly. Make sure you take any copies they may have made."

"...Can we do that?"

"They just publicized confidential government property. That's technically treason, Lt. Eltruan."

"Good enough reason for me. We're on our way."

When I severed the link, Leid was glaring at me.

I glared back. "Please, say something. I'd love to hear your fucking insight right now."

She only looked away, shaking her head.

Our trip to Parliament was silent.

When we got back, Leid vacated the craft without a word. I lingered in the driver seat, watching her disappear into the lobby. As the door shut, I grabbed my radio again.

"Lt. Geiss, come in."

"Commandant," said Garan. We hadn't spoken since I nearly beat Uless to death. *"What can I do for you?"*

"I'm about to give you and Lt. Fedaz an opportunity to redeem yourselves."

"Go ahead, Commandant."

I'd had to face dozens of hard decisions within the short time since I'd risen to office, and this wouldn't be the worst thing I had ever done. I knew that. But eventually these kinds of things weighed you down; took little bites out of your soul.

And they were getting harder and harder each time.

* * *

Late that evening, I returned home with blood all over my hands.

It was long past dinner, and I hoped I could sneak to my room and take a shower before anyone saw me. Unfortunately nothing ever seemed to go as I hoped. As soon as I darted past the dining room, I heard:

"Qaira, is that you?" *Tae.*

I covered my hands with my briefcase as she peeked into the hall. She seemed normal enough, which meant she hadn't seen the broadcast.

"Hi," I said.

"Why are you so late?"

"Drill."

"Oh, right."

That wasn't entirely true. I'd cancelled drill, but no one knew that. Including Leid.

My sister disappeared into the kitchen. "I left a plate in the oven."

"I'll be there in a second. I really need a shower."

"Long day?"

"Like you wouldn't believe."

The shower felt good, and I closed my eyes as near-scalding water beat against my back. I lowered my head and watched the blood run from my knuckles and down my forearms in thin, pink streams. My hands stung from the water, but the pain felt kind of good.

I dressed casually and headed back to the dining room, where my plate awaited me at the table next to a glass of wine. I watched my sister scrub a pot through the open doorway, and a smile spread across my lips. In many ways, she reminded me of our mother. At least what I could remember of her.

"I forgot to tell you," she said as I ate. "Leid went to check on the military craft progress, whatever that means, and she said she would meet you for practice at nine."

"Okay."

"What are you two practicing?"

I hesitated, wiping my mouth. I didn't want to tell her because she'd make a big deal of it, but I had done enough lying for one day. "She's teaching me how to play the violin."

Tae froze, looking at me in disbelief. *"Really?"*

"Really."

"Qaira, that's wonderful!"

"… Is it?"

"I'm sorry; I'm just so happy to hear you found a hobby. Music runs in the family, after all."

So did murder. "Leid thinks it'll take the edge off my job."

Tae sat beside me, placing a cup of steaming tea next to my wine. Apparently she was trying to make me piss all night. "Is it working?"

"I don't know. We just started."

"I'm glad you're growing fond of her."

"Uh, what?"

"Aren't you?"

"Well if you mean we aren't at each other's throats any more, then yes."

My sister rolled her eyes. "You don't have to be so defensive about it. I only meant the two of you seem to be getting along better."

I finished eating and Tae stood to grab my plate. I stood as well.

"Here," she said, reaching for it. "Let me take—"

I held it away from her. "No, you've done enough. Sit down."

She sat, reluctantly. "Where's Ara? Isn't drill finished?"

I rinsed off the plate and placed it into a cabinet over the sink. "He stayed back with Garan and Uless." To clean up all the blood. "He'll be here shortly."

There was a noise from the living room. Then we heard:

"Arcia! *Arcia!* Why didn't you wake me? I'm going to be late for work!"

My father had fallen asleep on the couch again.

"I need to take him to bed," Tae murmured, rolling her eyes.

I didn't say anything, only nodded. *Arcia.*

Wrapping the woolen frock around her shoulders, Tae slipped into the living room and I was left staring after her with a hollow feeling in my gut. I drained the wine but left the tea and reached for my briefcase, but then paused when I realized I wasn't going to work. Instead I slipped through the door and down the hall, toward the music room.

I was late; Leid had started without me.

I watched her play from the doorway. Head down, eyes closed, lips pursed seductively. Her fingers danced along the board and the bow glided across the strings.

And then I realized that I didn't deserve to be here, in her presence, surrounded by all of this beauty. I didn't deserve the happiness I felt. And if only Leid knew who—no, *what*—I really was, I was sure that she'd feel the same.

"Qaira."

I looked at her, and she smiled.

"Yeah, I'm here."

XII
WORTHY OPPONENTS

LEID SLID THE NEEDLE INTO MY ARM with as much precision as a blind knife thrower. I jerked, and she blew a vein.

"Fuck!"

"It would be a lot easier to do this if you'd stop moving."

"I'm moving because you're gouging out my arm!"

"You're so dramatic."

"I'm going to have a bruise the size of a continent!"

She got it right on the third try. "There. Sorry."

I closed my eyes as euphoria took over. It only lasted a minute. When I was fully-functional again, I headed to my closet and started pulling out some clothes for this morning. Leid watched me in my full-length mirror.

"Yes?" I asked.

"Your ink is fading again."

"Uh huh."

"I'm going to fill it for you tonight."

"Sure thing."

I headed to the shower room, leaving her on my bed.

An hour later we were headed to Parliament. I switched the radio frequency to Sanctum's Public Broadcast, waiting for the inevitable. When Leid tried to switch it to music, I swatted her hand away. Several minutes later, the report came:

"Yesterday night, at approximately eleven o'clock, the body of Chairman Lev Gia was found in his aero-craft at an abandoned storage facility in Lower Sanctum."

I feigned surprise, turning up the volume.

"Reports show that he was severely beaten and shot multiple times. The Sanctum authorities have deemed this a drug-related homicide, as two cartridges of malay, along with malay paraphernalia were found on the body."

I shut off the report, switching it to Leid's music.

She was glaring at me, and I kept my eyes ahead.

Eventually she looked away, staring out the passenger side window. I'd thought she was going to say something about that, but she didn't. That had been my way of confessing what I'd done, and it seemed like she didn't even care.

We hit traffic. I sighed.

"About that *deserving a special pass through traffic for being the Regent's son* law," she began, leaning into a palm. "You've got my vote."

"What's the hurry? My entire day is booked with meetings."

"Yes, I know. I planned your schedule, remember?"

"Well, you're fired."

* * *

Leid and I crunched numbers with our Parliament's accountants, lowering taxes on some things while raising them on others.

I'd decided to raise the alcohol tax by two usos, since it might lower the frequency of alcohol related violence in Lower Sanctum. I also signed off on a budget approval for law enforcement to crack down on malay distribution, as commemoration to Lev Gia's death. Irony.

Due to the messy recent events, I wanted my father to address the public, but he was in a steady decline as of this week and I would have to do it myself. I was now the face of Eroqam from here on out. The only upside to the press meeting was that I might be able to change the public's opinion of me in light of Gia's drug-related homicide.

Later that evening, Leid and I oversaw an Archaean craft protocol discussion between Yahweh Telei and Ysam Kada in the science research laboratory. The first half of it was spent with

Yahweh going over momentum and torque lectures while Dr. Kada kept staring at me with a 'what the fuck' look on his face. I didn't blame him, considering he was getting schooled by a child.

Our science team had already gathered most of the items on Leid's material list. It was enough to start construction of the prototype shell, and while Yahweh and Dr. Kada went over appropriate dimensions, I was reading the diagnostic report for the electrical configurations of the prototype controls. Leid stood over the team, making sure our hostage didn't *accidentally* miscalculate anything.

As I skimmed over the report, my brow rose higher and higher. "Leid, come here for a second."

She hovered over me, and I pointed to the passage that explained how to program the *voice automated system*. "Does that mean we're going to have to talk to our crafts?"

Leid hesitated, reading it over. "No. Yahweh is only suggesting a way to strengthen security by making the ignition voice-key automated."

"So the craft won't start unless it recognizes the voice of the pilot who owns it."

"Correct."

"Wow, that's genius."

"When are we working on the controls?"

"Tomorrow evening. We're waiting on our system engineers to get all the wiring in order."

Leid smiled, surveying the crowded lab. "This is really coming along."

"Yeah."

She went back to standing watch, and my gaze fell on Yahweh. He stood amid a group of analysts, nodding as they spoke to him. I knew it was all an act, but he looked like he really wanted to be here.

Yahweh Telei had become more than just a white to me. There was something enigmatic about him, and it made me question whether we had the Archaeans' deadliest weapon in the palm of our hands. Intelligence as a deadly weapon; what an interesting thought.

As the crowd around the kid cleared, he glanced at me.

I looked away, returning to his report.

* * *

At midnight, I escorted Yahweh back to his room.

He never fought me, and I didn't even have to lead him by the arm. We quietly walked side by side like comrades at the end of a long day at work.

Yahweh stepped back as I punched in the code. I opened the door, motioning for him to enter first. When he stepped inside, the kid turned and looked up at me with those gigantic, sparkly eyes. "I've heard you're able to make people's heads explode. Is that true?"

I blinked, wondering who he had been talking to. "Yes."

His eyes grew even wider. If that was possible. "So you could make my head explode right now if you wanted to."

"If I wanted to."

"How does it work?" he asked, tilting his head.

"You're guess is as good as mine.

"I'm sure my guess would be much better."

I smirked. "I'm sure."

Yahweh sat cross-legged on the end of his bed as I grabbed his empty dinner tray. "Are you the only one among your people able to do it?"

"Do what? Remove dirty plates from your room?"

He frowned.

"Yeah, I'm the only one."

My tone had been a lot drier than I intended, and unfortunately the kid picked up on that.

"You see it as a burden."

"How I see it is really none of your business; but no, I don't think of it as a gift."

He smiled. "You should. Lucifer knows about you. You're the reason why he's so reluctant to step in."

"You call your father by his first name?"

"He's not my father."

I stared at him. "But he called you—"

"I'm his adopted son."

"Oh."

"What makes your ability such a burden?"

"Why do you care?"

"It's the most interesting thing I've heard all week."

I had no idea why I was humoring him. "It doesn't work like how you think it does. It's not selective."

"You mean you can't control whose head you explode?"

"Sort of," I said, sitting in the chair across from him. "Let's say I want to make your head explode, but you're standing in a crowd of people—"

"Area of effect."

"Right."

Yahweh looked away, deep in thought. "I assumed you had the ability to telepathically link to the minds of other people, but now I think you might be releasing some form of high-energy radiation."

Eyebrow. "Like microwaves?"

"Maybe something a little stronger. Of course there's no way for me to know for certain. Not without a lab and proper equip—"

"Okay, what the fuck is your problem?"

Yahweh looked startled. "I beg your pardon?"

"I beg your pardon?" I mocked in his childlike voice.

"I don't sound like that," he huffed.

"You're not even old enough to work and you're sitting here talking to me about area of effect radiation, not to mention you're constructing state of the art military crafts. I could barely make sense of your electrical configurations because they were far too complex for my tiny Nehelian brain."

119

Yahweh said nothing.

"What happened to your childhood?"

"I didn't have one."

"No kidding. Why not?"

"I'd rather not talk about that."

Judging by the look on his face, he hadn't had too great of a life before Lucifer snatched him up. I had several theories, but I wouldn't share them. Besides, I'd wasted enough time. I just had a heart-to-heart with a white. Kill me, please.

Without another word I left the seat, tray in hand. As I opened the door, Yahweh said, "Do you hate me, Qaira Eltruan?"

I paused. "I hate angels."

"If I write down a list of things that I want, will you get them for me?"

"As long as it isn't sharp."

When I looked over my shoulder, he was smiling.

"Goodnight, Qaira Eltruan."

I left the room in silence, closing the door behind me.

XIII
THE INSPECTION

I WOKE TO FIND A MALAY SYRINGE ON my bedside table. Leid wasn't around. There was a note beside the syringe, kept in place by the weight of my alarm clock.

'*I went to the research lab to check on the progress of the craft shell. I figured I would give your arms a rest for one day. Also, you might want to try sleeping on your side because you snore. If my room was right next to yours, you'd keep me up all night. I'll meet you on the flight deck at seven.*

Leid ☺'

Funny.

I tossed the note into the wastebasket and shot up, then took a shower and got dressed. I was twenty minutes ahead of schedule because Leid wasn't around to distract me. The dining room was dark; Tae wasn't awake yet, and Epa wouldn't start setting breakfast out for another fifteen minutes. I was about to hit the light switch but I heard something in the kitchen. *Clinking* glass.

"Tae?"

No answer.

"Ara?"

No answer.

I crept into the kitchen to investigate. And there was my father, setting up all the condiments along the counter. He'd even gone into our pantry and brought out all the jars of preserved fruits.

He sat on the floor scribbling on their labels with a permanent marker. There was a psychotic look in his eyes.

"What are you doing?" I asked.

"Labeling them," he said. "Then I'm going to put them back in alphabetical order. This house is chaotic; there's no order. You just place everything everywhere. How is anyone supposed to find anything?"

I hit the lights. My father shielded his eyes, while I gaped at all the writing on the walls. I held my head, unable to believe what I was seeing. "Dad, what have you done!?"

"Your mother used to label everything by hand, you know," he said, ignoring me. The psychotic look was getting more intense. "But now she's gone and no one makes anything from scratch anymore."

I snatched the marker out of his hands. "Get out of the kitchen!"

"I'm not done!"

"Tae!" I shouted into the hall. *"Tae, will you get in here, please?!"*

"You can't leave it unfinished!" my father snarled. Once upon a time he had a temper like mine. "I'm just trying to clean up the place! Arcia would have never left it like this!"

"You wrote all over the walls with permanent marker!"

"How else was I supposed to remember where everything goes?!"

My sister appeared, eyes bulging when she saw us. "Dad, oh goodness; come on, let's get you something to eat."

My father's expression softened at the sight of her, and he let her guide him out of the kitchen. Tae and I shared a look.

But then Qalam wrenched from her grasp and turned on me. "It's *your* fault that she's gone!"

I stood there, stunned.

"Dad!" Tae shouted, trying to recapture his attention, but he wouldn't look at her.

"I wouldn't have to do this if you hadn't killed her! You're a *murderer!*"

My pulse beat in my ears. Even though I knew I should have walked away, I didn't. I couldn't move. My father kept chanting *murderer* at the top of his lungs, and each time my heart pounded just a little faster until I couldn't stand to hear it anymore. Red inked across my vision.

It had to stop. *Now.*

I punched him in the face as hard as I could, and my father stumbled into the dining table, taking a breakfast tray and two chairs with him on his way down. Everything hit the floor with a *crash.*

My sister screamed, and my father started to cry. He curled atop pastries and spilled tea, sobbing for his dead wife.

"What is the matter with you?!" Tae shouted at me, collapsing on her knees at my father's side. *"He doesn't know what he's saying! He's* sick*!"*

All I did was stand there, numb.

And then I couldn't take the sight anymore. I grabbed my briefcase and fled for the door.

"Qaira?" my sister called over my father's wails. *"Qaira, wait!"*

I slammed the door and hurried to the flight deck. Leid was already waiting for me in our craft. I got in and jammed the key into the ignition, nearly crashing into one of the pillars when I backed out.

"What happened?" asked Leid when we'd left Eroqam's port.

I didn't say anything and turned the radio up. She turned it down.

"Qaira, *what happened?*"

And then it all came flooding out.

"Will you shut the fuck up?!" I screamed, and she flinched. *"Why don't you ever shut the fuck up?! I just want to drive to work without hearing the sound of your fucking voice for once! Can I have that? Can I?"*

End of conversation.

* * *

"How's everything in Sanctum lately, Commandant? I heard word this morning that things are getting a little tumultuous down there."

I didn't say anything, rolling my pen along the desk.

Commander Raith reclined in his seat, tilting his head. "You don't seem like your insulting self today. Are you alright?"

"I have to spend my lunch break staring at your face. What do you think?"

"Yes, but we're ten minutes in and you have yet to call me a vulgar synonym for female genitalia."

Commander Raith and I met once a week over the televised screen to discuss Yahweh's status. He often used these meetings to try to get under my skin. Today it was working.

"You're wasting my time, white. If you have nothing else to say then I have a thousand more important things to do."

"Just one more thing, Commandant, and then you can be on your way."

I waited.

"I'm sending an inspector to see Yahweh for himself, not that I would ever distrust your word, but—"

I blanched. "Forget it."

Lucifer frowned; his pale, blue eyes shined with indignation. Angels were very androgynous. He almost looked like a woman, deep voice and no tits aside. "He'll come unarmed and you can supervise him personally, if that'll make you feel any better. I want assurance that my son is still in good health."

"Then I'll bring him in here and you can talk to him."

"I want to know if you've been feeding him properly and keeping up with his hygienic needs. That kind of information can't be gathered from seeing him through a screen, and I'm sure you've intimidated him into silence by now."

"Apparently you don't know your own son. I can't get him to shut up. Care to share your secret?"

Raith smiled, showing me a row of perfect teeth. "Commandant, I've kept up my part of the bargain—with great duress, mind you—and I want you to do the same. A single angel

124

at your military headquarters couldn't possibly pose a threat, could he?"

I was beginning to lose my patience. "That isn't the point, you stupid cunt."

"Ah, there it is. I spoke too soon."

"Eroqam isn't a five star hotel. Your son isn't on vacation. We agreed that I would keep Yahweh alive so long as you keep your whites from attacking my city. Nowhere in our agreement was there a clause about making sure the kid had his full servings of vegetables each day."

"The inspector will bring some medications and maybe a few of Yahweh's things to keep him occupied. He gets bored easily, and if he gets sick you have no way of treating him."

I was about to protest again, but realized he had a point.

"Fine. When?

"I'll send the inspector in an hour."

"No, we'll meet him at our airspace borders, and the angel can come in our craft the rest of the way."

"Very well. I'll speak to you soon, Commandant."

Lucifer disconnected the call.

I reached for my radio with a sigh. "Lt. Eltruan, assemble a team for an enforcer pick-up at our airspace borders."

"For what?"

I said nothing, waiting for him to remember the talk we'd had about his lack of professionalism over the radio.

"... For what, Commandant?"

"I've just permitted an angel to cross into Sanctum territory. We're giving him a ride to Eroqam."

"Roger. I'll let you know when we're ready."

* * *

Leid stayed at Parliament while my brother, Uless, Garan, Samay and I flew to Sanctum's airspace border. We had another enforcer craft following us as back up. I didn't really think this was a trick, but it was better to be safe than sorry.

As we ascended, an angel vessel descended. We met, hovering twenty feet apart. Our doors slid open simultaneously, presenting a mirror image of soldiers pointing firearms.

An unarmed angel in a long white coat pushed through the line, hugging a brown satchel to his chest. Unfolding his wings, he leapt from the Archaean craft and flew to ours. I stepped back, allowing him entry. When he landed inside, Ara and Garan shut the door and both crafts parted ways.

The angel inspector sat on a bench while we rifled through his satchel, making sure there wasn't anything suspicious in it. A bunch of clothes and books. Garan tossed it back to him and nothing was said for the rest of the flight.

I led the angel through the Commons, ignoring the sharp stares of soldiers as they passed. Our visitor had an air of arrogance to him, a sort of pompous demeanor that made me think he didn't want to be here as much as *I* didn't want him here. He was young, perhaps my age, with white-blond hair cut unevenly to his shoulders. He wore a serious look, eyes darting across the hall that we traversed.

When I opened the door to Yahweh's room, the kid shot from his bed wearing a look of shock.

"Namah?"

"Good afternoon, Dr. Telei," the angel greeted. His voice was deeper than I'd expected.

"What are you doing here? Are they releasing me?"

"Unfortunately, no. Commander Raith has sent you some personal items, and this Nehelian has agreed to let you have them." Namah shot me a disdainful look.

Yahweh took the satchel and placed the contents on his desk. Several articles of clothing, about five books, and a wooden box that, when opened, revealed a board covered in black and white squares, along with a plastic bag of white and black figurines.

"My chessboard!" Yahweh cried, hugging it.

I arched a brow.

Namah smiled. "Commander Raith wants you to practice. Maybe you'll be able to beat him when you return."

Yahweh pouted. "I've never beaten him."

"Sorry to interrupt your family reunion," I interjected. "But can we get to the inspection? I'm supposed to be at work."

Namah pulled a stethoscope and auriscope from his pockets. He checked Yahweh's breathing and looked inside his ears. After that he looked inside of his mouth, and for some reason he flashed a light in the kid's eyes.

"My father sent you to give me a check-up?" asked Yahweh, slightly amused.

"Silly, I know. Has the Commandant fed you regularly?"

"Yes."

"How is the quality of food that you are given?"

"Spicy, but fair."

"Does he let you bathe?"

"Three times a week. Not quite as much as I'd like."

Namah wrote his answers down on a type-set document. It looked like a survey. From his seemingly bottomless pockets, he pulled out two bottles of medication. "I'll leave these with you. I'm sure you know how to take them."

"No," I said. "Those are coming with me."

"Qaira thinks I'm suicidal," said Yahweh.

Namah handed me the bottles, frowning. "It was good seeing you again, Dr. Telei. I'll let the Commander know that you're in good health."

"Tell him I said thank you for the chessboard."

As we left, Yahweh sat on his bed and started placing figurines across the board.

"What now?" I asked the white when we stepped into the hall.

"Now I head to Crylle and let Commander Raith know that his son is healthy."

"Crylle?"

"If you haven't noticed, I'm a physician. Since you kidnapped Crylle's *only* doctor, I've been assigned there in his place."

I glared at him. "Am I taking you to Crylle?"

"You're the one who wanted to pick me up at the rendezvous."

"Your Commander failed to mention that I'd have to be your chauffeur."

"Intentionally, I'm sure."

That devious fuck. "Lt. Eltruan and Fedaz, meet me at the port. I need you to escort our angel visitor to Crylle."

"Commandant," Ara responded, *"can't one of the Sanctum guards do that?"*

"… I'm sorry, Lt. Eltruan, but did you just question my order?"

There was a moment of silence.

"No, sir."

* * *

The rest of the day flew by.

After an hour-long press conference and several meetings with Sanctum chairmen, it was already time to leave. On a normal day I would have flung myself from my office and cartwheeled all the way to the port.

But it wasn't a normal day. Today was the day that I'd punched my infirm father in the face, and then bailed on my sister. I didn't want to face the music.

I ignored my growling stomach and found other things to do around the office. An hour later, Leid was staring at me.

"Are we ever leaving? It's getting late."

"In a minute," I said. "I have a few deadlines I didn't make today."

"What happened this morning?" she asked, clearly suspicious. She knew the end of the day was *fuck-this-o'clock* for me, no matter how many deadlines I'd missed.

"I don't want to talk about it."

"Well are you planning on staying here all night? Because *I* don't want to stay here all night. And I'm hungry."

Sigh. Listening to her whine almost made facing Tae sound like fun. But I was hungry, too. "Want to go out for dinner?"

Leid stood by the door, crossing her arms. "Are you avoiding your family?"

"No," I lied. "I just feel like I need to step outside of my life for a little while. Can you stop interrogating me?"

Her frown melted and she grabbed my briefcase from the chair. "Alright, fine. Where are we going?"

XIV
DIVULGENCE

I TOOK LEID TO A SMALLER RESTAURANT AT the western edge of Upper Sanctum, one with very few customers on weeknights.

The Red Curtain was near Sanctum's Aeroway port and not particularly close to any neighborhoods. No one traveled much during the week, so it came as no surprise when there were only a handful of customers scattered amid a gymnasium-sized dining hall.

Our server seated us at the very back of the hall, out of direct view of other customers. Spectacular service was one of the only perks of being an Eltruan in public.

We were given menus and wine. Long after I'd decided on what I wanted, Leid sat there with a disgruntled frown, like she was having trouble again.

"What is it with you and menus?"

"This place doesn't serve leriza."

I rolled my eyes. "The world isn't going to end if you try another form of meat. In fact *everything* is better than leriza."

"What are you getting?"

"Secca. It's on the second page."

"Pain-fried bluta with sautéed greens on a bed of white rice," she read aloud, wrinkling her nose. "What's bluta?"

"Fish."

"Is it good?"

"No, it's terrible. Totally disgusting. That's why I'm ordering it."

"Order me the same," she said, pouring some wine.

The waiter took our menus away a few minutes later. We didn't talk for a while. Leid kept shooting me looks, like she was waiting for me to tell her why we were here instead of at home. I pretended not to notice them.

"The craft shell should be finished this evening," she mentioned. "Tomorrow we'll start working on the engine. That'll be the most challenging part. Judging by the way things are going, we should be finished the prototype in a week; maybe two if we run into any snags."

"Sounds good."

"How did the inspection go today?"

I smirked, having forgotten all about it until now. "We ended up flying that white all the way to Crylle. He was in transit to replace Yahweh as their practicing physician."

"A doctor?" Leid asked, arching her brows.

"Yeah, his name was Namah or something."

There was a change in her expression, but only momentary. Before I could ask about it, she said, "Tae wants to take me shopping."

"Have fun with that."

"I don't really want to go, but it would have been rude to decline. I want your family to like me."

"Join the club."

Leid tilted her head. "What?"

"Nothing."

The waiter returned with our wine. I downed the first glass in two gulps. Leid watched me with a brow raised.

By the time dinner showed up, I was *loaded.*

Leid kept going on and on about tax cuts and other crap I didn't care about, and then I realized there was food in front of me. It took two tries to grab a fork.

"Alcohol is an addictive drug, Qaira. By raising the price of it, you're only condemning the drunks to further poverty. They'll pay *any* amount to drink."

I was extremely thankful to be shitfaced right now, otherwise I would have shoved my fork into her head. "Can we please talk about something other than work?"

"Fine, but seriously, you're going to lose money by cutting fuel taxes. You should have just given in and cut the taxes on education so that—"

"Leid."

She slumped in her seat, sulking.

We ate the rest of our dinner in silence. I finished first and pushed the plate aside, pouring myself another glass of wine. The bottle was nearly empty, so I refilled Leid's glass with the rest of it. The food had sobered me up a bit.

"Are you getting desert?" she asked.

"No. Do you want any?"

"Not really."

"Okay. I might order some more wine, though." Anything to stall for time.

She eyed me, but didn't comment. I wasn't a heavy drinker, and Leid knew that.

"Qaira, are you there?"

It was Ara. I'd forgotten to unclip the radio from my belt.

"Yeah," I muttered.

"Why haven't you come home yet? Tae is worried sick about you."

"Leid and I are eating out."

"Are you planning to come home tonight? I heard about what happened and—"

And there he went, blowing my cover. "I'm not alone, you retarded fuck!"

Ara was quiet for a second. Leid was staring at me.

"Fine, just come home soon. Tae isn't going to bed until you speak to her, so don't make her stay up all night."

I hung up on him and turned my radio off. Leid kept staring at me. That was it; now I had to talk about it.

"I hit my father this morning."

Leid didn't even bat an eye. "Why?"

"He was having one of his... *episodes*, and said something that I..." I hesitated, trying to figure out how to explain it to her. I couldn't, so I just got to the point. "I lost it."

"What did he say to you?"

"It isn't important. He didn't mean it, but at the time..."

I glanced away, saying nothing else.

Leid didn't press, and resumed picking at her plate. "It isn't a secret how his illness affects you. Do you miss him?"

"What?"

"Do you miss the man he was before?"

"I don't know. He used to be my counsel. Whenever things got really, *really* bad, he was there to fix them. Now things get really bad and I don't have anyone to talk to."

"You don't need anyone to talk to. Time has forced your right of passage. Your father prepared you for everything you'll have to face, and now you hold the torch. Instead of being bitter about the fact that he can't provide you with any more advice, remember what he taught you."

I looked at my empty plate, unable to come up with a response.

"People get old and become useless, Qaira. That's just how life is."

That actually made me laugh. "I never took my father's advice. Our worldviews are very different."

"Yes, I've noticed. That isn't necessarily a bad thing."

"Oh?"

"Your father's benevolence for the angels anchored their belief that they have a chance at a permanent life on The Atrium. He didn't persuade them to move on like he should have."

That was pretty surprising to hear, considering how often she criticized my tactics.

"Sanctum needs a Regent with a stern hand. In this way, I think you're more suitable for the position."

"Tell that to the Eye of Akul."

"They're upset because you aren't as easy to manipulate as your father was. But although I think your sternness is suitable for war, I think you need to be less stern with your own people."

I hesitated, sharpening my stare. "What do you mean?"

Her eyes gleamed with condescension. "Must I give you a recent example?"

She was talking about Gia. I looked away, confirming that we were on the same wavelength.

"I doubt you'd be surprised if I told you that you have an issue with rage."

I wasn't.

"And though I don't know the specific events of your life that led you down this path—and I don't mean to judge you at all—but the future Regent of Sanctum should show a little empathy."

"Are you done?" I asked, icing over. "I don't need you pointing out my flaws. I'm already aware of them."

Leid took a sip of wine. "What do you plan on doing about them?"

"I don't know. Why don't we revisit that topic when I'm actually the Regent?"

"I fear by then it will be too late. You'll be too far gone."

I'd had enough of this. "Come on, we're leaving."

It was raining, and after paying our waiter I found Leid lingering in the lobby, sulking at the storm from the window. She hadn't brought a jacket, and although I would have *loved* to watch her get rained on, I decided to be the better man and removed my coat. When I draped it over her shoulders, she looked up at me in surprise.

"There," I said, opening the door, "is that empathetic enough for you?"

* * *

Tae was waiting for me in the dining room when we arrived home. Leid left to her room before I'd made it there, knowing my sister and I would want a word alone. We planned to meet later on that evening at the research lab, but for now, I was stranded.

My sister and I stared at each other in silence, until I plopped on to a chair across from her, looking like a child about to be scolded.

Tae sniffed the air, wrinkling her nose. "Have you been drinking?"

"Yeah, but I'm not drunk. Anymore."

"What could possibly be going on in your head to make you want to *hit* our father?" she demanded, diving right in.

While I couldn't even *count* all the shit going on in my head, I said, "Nothing."

"He didn't mean what he said."

"I know."

"The doctors told us that there were going to be times when Dad would say rotten things, and we mustn't—"

"I know, Tae. I was there."

"Then why did you..." She paused, her face filling with revelation. "You don't actually *believe* what he said, do you?"

I looked away, guilty as charged.

She paid me a sad frown. I didn't like the pity behind her gaze. "It wasn't your fault, Qaira."

"Yes it was."

"You were just a child. You had no idea what you were doing."

"Doesn't mean it wasn't my fault."

Tae sat there, staring at me. My gaze fell.

"It's alright," I said. "I just don't like hearing about it, that's all."

"Qaira, look at me."

I did, reluctantly.

"Dad doesn't blame you. He loves you. He's done nothing but love you, even after Mom died."

"Yeah," I said, placidly.

"You don't seem like yourself. I feel like I don't even know you right now."

She'd never known me; not the *real* me. "I'm sorry."

"Don't say that to me. You need to say that to Dad."

"Does he even remember what happened?"

"No, he doesn't remember that you hit him. He's asked several times about the bruise on his jaw and I..." She looked away, ashamed. "I told him that he fell."

I massaged my forehead, sighing.

"Even if he doesn't remember what happened—or your apology for that matter, I'm certain you'll feel better if you talk to him."

"I'll do it in the morning," I said, conceding. "I don't want to wake him up."

"I'm going to bed," Tae announced, getting out of her seat. That was my cue.

"I'll see you tomorrow," I said, heading for the hall.

"Where are you going?"

"Leid and I need to work on the prototype."

"My dear brother; do you ever sleep?"

"I'll sleep when I'm dead."

My sister murmured a goodnight while I left our residence, heading for the Commons.

XV
WHAT COMES WITH LOSS

MY EYES OPENED AND I STARED AT my closet mirror. There was a heavy feeling in my chest, making it hard to breathe. If I'd been dreaming, I couldn't remember it. But my room felt ominous and unfamiliar. Maybe I was still asleep.

I glanced at the clock, finding I had woken up three minutes before my alarm. I sat up and yawned, a tear of exhaustion trickling down the side of my left cheek. I felt like shit, and couldn't remember the last time I'd had more than four hours of sleep.

I threw off my blankets and forced myself to my feet, heading to the closet to fetch a suit. I pulled off the shirt I'd slept in and then Leid barged in without knocking.

She froze several steps in, staring at me. Or more specifically, at my chest.

"I didn't realize you were inked anywhere but your face," she remarked, filling a syringe with malay. Leid had never seen me without a shirt before.

Nehelian scripture covered me from collarbone to ribs, spreading and wrapping around my biceps. She'd filled my ink before, but I hadn't told her about all of it. As a consequence most of it had faded, yet was still prominent enough to read. For some reason ink stayed longer on your body than your face.

Along with a form of identification, the Nehel believed that ink gave you power depending on what you wrote. My father believed I was the reincarnation of King Malkhet from the epic *Kelkrah* (Nehelian for retribution), and to honor his belief I wore its passages. Kelkrah was the story of a warrior whose wife is killed in battle. His sorrow and lust for revenge immortalizes him, and he kills his way through the rival army, leaving a blood-soaked trail all the way to their king. Even though I wasn't very superstitious, I actually liked that epic and thought the story was worth wearing.

"Most Nehelian men ink their bodies," I said, throwing on a shirt. I sat beside her on the bed and rolled up my sleeve, watching her tiny fingers curl around my forearm. Everything about Leid was little, except for her attitude.

Surprisingly, she administered the malay on the first try.

"I'll see you at breakfast," she said, heading for the hall.

I had decided against a shower, as I'd taken one last night. But I was groggy and a shower was the only thing that could wake me up, so I headed out. Halfway there I remembered my discussion with Tae, and I made a detour to my father's bedroom. I didn't really want to wake him, but who knew when I was coming home tonight?

I knocked on his door. There was no answer, but I wasn't surprised. My father could sleep through a nuke.

When I cracked his door, an interesting odor of stale liquor and cologne wafted into the hall. I stepped inside, fumbling for the lamp on his dresser.

"Dad?" I whispered.

No answer.

Shadows played across the room; I could see him on the bed, the contours of his body lumping out beneath the sheets. I found the lamp, and the room was cast into a haze of soft yellow.

"Dad?"

Still nothing. I really didn't want to shake him.

But as I drew closer I realized that something wasn't right. There was something wrong with his face. It was too pale, and his chest wasn't moving. He wasn't breathing.

I touched his cheek. It was ice cold.

The air left his room, and I collapsed on the seat at his desk. I gazed at him in a blank stupor, too shocked to even wear an expression. My father was dead, and I'd spent our last moment together punching him in the face.

And now I had no idea what to do. How the fuck was I supposed to tell Tae? A part of me wanted to just walk out of his room and pretend I was never here, but that was cowardly. Then, my eyes settled on the bruise at the bottom of his cheek, and something else occurred to me—;

What if *I* had killed him?

I closed my eyes and held my face, hoping that this was all just a dream and I would wake up any second. Someone touched my shoulder.

"Qaira, go and get your sister."

My hands slid from my face and I opened my eyes. Leid was beside me, gazing at my father with a forlorn look. I had no idea how long I'd been in here, but it must have been a while if she had come looking for me.

"I... I-I can't move."

"I'm sure your sister would rather hear the news from you."

I didn't respond and she helped me out of the chair, guiding me to the door. "I'll stay here until you get back, okay?"

I barely heard her as I wandered into the hall.

Tae was eating breakfast, reading a magazine. I lingered in the doorway, watching the happiness on my sister's face. In a few seconds that happiness was going to be gone, and it might never come back. I didn't want to be the one responsible for that, and stepped away from the dining room. But it was too late; she'd seen me.

"Good morning! Are you and Leid going into the office late today?"

I didn't say anything, looking at the floor.

"I made sure Epa saved you some tea," she tried again, wary. And then she noticed that my eyes were wet. "What happened?"

As my sister stood, I looked at her. My lips moved but my voice was gone.

Tae walked to me and took my hand, squeezing it. "Qaira, what happened?"

141

* * *

By noon, over a dozen people were in our house. The Health Division took our father's body away to determine the cause of death, while the Eye of Akul and a few other suits came to pay their respects.

I didn't really feel like talking to anyone so I just sat on our living room couch, staring jadedly into the untouched glass of wine in my hands. I kept replaying yesterday morning in my mind, and could have sworn that my father had hit his head on the dining table on his way to the floor. Cerebral contusion? Concussion? How would he have known? How would Tae have known? My father's brain could have been bleeding all day and they'd merely gone about their business. I'd walked out on them.

There was a tight feeling in my chest and I closed my eyes, trying not to cry. I couldn't cry in front of these people; it would ruin my image and I'd lose their respect. Nehelian men weren't supposed to cry. That was a behavior looked down upon once a boy stepped into manhood. Like any rule, there were a few exceptions, but this wasn't one of them. Of course they had no idea that I was putting myself on trial over here.

My sister was a fucking wreck. She floated around the room talking to our guests, her eyes puffy and swollen. Tae hadn't even gotten dressed, still in her sleep gown. No one blamed her. Every now and then she would burst into tears and everyone would comfort her with generic lines of assurance.

Leid wasn't here. She'd agreed to take over my office duties for the day so I could stay with my family. That was a good thing, too, since in my state I probably couldn't even drive.

Ara sat next to me, watching our guests. "We're burning Dad in two days," he said. "Shev and Kanar want to make speeches during the pyre."

I nodded.

"And I think you should say something as well?"

"I've got nothing to say."

"Then think of something."

I kept quiet. Ara glared at me.

"Will you snap out of it? This has nothing to do with yesterday morning."

"How do you know?"

"Because Eltruans don't die from getting punched in the face."

"He might have hit his head on the table when he fell."

"*Might* have? Do you know that happened for a fact?"

"I'm pretty sure it did."

Ara sighed. "Dad was old. He died of old age." When I didn't respond, he said, "I think you should make a speech, too. Our people will want to hear from the new Regent."

In all of the excitement, I'd completely forgotten that I was officially the Regent of Sanctum. I had been playing the part for years, but for some reason it never seemed so paramount.

"Fine, I'll think of something."

* * *

The coroner stopped by our estate late that evening to give us an official cause of our father's death. Heart failure.

Ara had been right, but the news didn't make me feel any better. In a way, it all was still my fault.

Nehel had a strong belief in the karmic system. I'd done a lot of bad shit lately, and my father had paid the price. Karma was the universe's way of keeping you in line; the only way you could really understand your mistakes. The prices of them.

Tae had gone to bed an hour ago. Ara was working on a bottle of Cardinal.

"You shouldn't be drinking. It's your shift to guard our supplies in two hours."

Ara looked at me like I'd just stomped on his nuts. "You're actually sending me to work? Our father *died* this morning."

"The world doesn't stop with his death. We should step up security for that reason."

"You didn't go to work today!"

"My work consists of budget reviews. Do you think the angels care that our father is dead? Are they sitting in their spaceship saying, *'Oh, let's give the Nehelians some time to mourn'?*"

Ara sneered. "Well then why don't you guard the post with me?"

"If I stay up with you all night, how am I supposed to go to work tomorrow?" I snatched the bottle from him, screwing on the cap. "You said it yourself; I'm the Regent now. When I give you an order, you'll do it."

"You're a heartless fuck, you know that?"

Before I could respond, Ara stormed off. I heard the door slam.

Sigh.

Now it was just me and Cardinal.

* * *

It was the early morning and I was shitfaced.

I'd taken about eleven shots, with one more left in the bottle. I had no idea how I was still conscious.

The dining room spun around as I sat there staring at that lost shot, gathering enough nerve to finish it. My ears pricked to the sound of our front door opening, and my eyes slid to the dining room doorway as Leid appeared in it. She had seen to the craft progress in my absence. She had done a lot for me today and I wanted to thank her, but I was too loaded to string a sentence together.

Leid could tell how far gone I was just by looking at me. Her face fell and she slipped into a chair across from mine, setting her bags on the table. "Is it working?"

"Sort of," I slurred.

"You should probably go to bed soon if you hope to ever wake up in the morning. I can't stand in for you tomorrow. You already have a backlog of meetings that I had to cancel today."

She'd been home for less than five minutes and I already wanted to scream. "You're not my mother. If I want to drink on the day my father died, I have every right. And if you're planning to sit there and make condescending remarks, you might as well go away."

"Your father died *yesterday*. It's two in the morning."

I glared at her, saying nothing.

"Fine," she said, getting up. "Ignore the good advice I'm trying to give you. And you're welcome for taking care of all your crap today. Good night."

Okay, that was *it*. "Do I not get a free pass just this once?"

She paused in the doorway, looking back.

"Am I forever being recorded in your log of disapproval?"

"You're drunk and angry," she said, coolly. "I understand, but you might want to curb your hostility before you regret it."

I laughed in spite of her. "Stop acting like you don't judge me at every turn. All you do is treat me like I'm an incompetent asshole."

"That's not true."

I shook my head, downing that last shot.

"Actually, it is true. Because you *are* an incompetent asshole."

My eyes slid to her.

"You have an entire world in the palm of your hand, yet you make the most appalling political and military decisions that I have *ever* seen. You clearly are not ready to take the throne, and me being here feels like a lost cause. You don't take any advice, and you treat everyone around you like an enemy. So no, I don't feel sorry for you, Qaira. I feel sorry for *me* and all the time I'm about to waste in this futile contract. Incompetent assholes don't deserve free passes."

"Go fuck yourself, you pretentious bitch."

"*You* fuck yourself, you cowardly prick."

I threw the shot glass at her. It missed her head by an inch, shattering against the doorframe.

She blurred from view, clearing the length of the dining room in a fraction of a second. Her fist cracked the side of my face and I was thrown *with* my chair into the kitchen. Before I could get up Leid was atop me with another fist wound.

145

"You piece of shit," she snarled, grabbing the collar of my shirt. "I could kill you in a heartbeat."

"Then do it."

Leid's fist trembled. I grinned, showing her my bloodstained teeth.

"Need more incentive?" I asked, goading. "I killed my mother when I was five hundred years old. She was scolding me for pulling out the flowers from her garden and I made her head explode. I stood there with her blood all over me and didn't shed a single tear."

The anger on Leid's face melted. Her fist stayed up.

"The night before you arrived, I strangled a college girl when she tried to steal my malay. I wrapped my hands around her neck," I explained, miming the action, "and crushed her throat. I looked right into her eyes as she died and I felt nothing. *Nothing.*"

Leid's fist fell. Her eyes trailed over my face, like I was an open window.

"Two days ago I beat chairman Lev Gia to death with my bare hands. When I was done, I shot him fourteen times and spat on his body."

"Qaira, stop—"

Leid was getting difficult to see. My vision was blurry and there was a tight feeling in my throat.

"You want to kill me? I think you should. It would do this world a favor." I winced, feeling hot tears roll down my cheeks. I hadn't realized my eyes were wet, and I looked away so she couldn't see me. "Get off."

Leid didn't move. I tried to shove her away.

"Get off! Stop looking at me!"

She pulled my hands from my face and pinned them to the floor beside my head.

I looked up at her, stunned.

"You're so beautiful when you cry," she whispered, heavy-lidded. "So very beautiful."

I opened my mouth to ask what she was doing but Leid silenced me, pressing her lips to mine. I jolted in shock as her tongue slid along my teeth. The tightness in my throat was kneaded away as a tingling sensation crept across my stomach and groin. She rocked her hips, dragging herself back and forth over my crotch.

And then we were rolling across the dining room floor, kissing savagely. I held her underneath me, burying my face into her neck; one hand clutched a fistful of her hair, the other disappeared up her dress, between her legs. Leid groaned, arching her back. She smelled like sex and flowers. My mind was spinning.

She threw me off and tried to straddle me again, but I wouldn't have it and picked her up, slamming her onto the dining table. The centerpiece and empty Cardinal crashed at my feet.

Leid unfastened my belt, looking up at me with those huge violet eyes. I watched her, my breathing heavy with anticipation.

When she freed me I leaned down, sliding up her dress. Her legs hooked my waist and her hands slid underneath my shirt, fingernails raking across my chest. Leid dragged her teeth along my neck, begging for it.

The rest was a blur of heat and ragged breaths. I gave Leid everything I had through clenched teeth and she bucked against me with equal fervor, until she tensed up and whimpered into my neck.

Leid was too warm; she felt *too* good. I couldn't take it anymore.

She sensed my nearness and kicked me off. I collapsed into the chair with a gasp. Before I could do anything she mounted me, burying me deep inside of her. Leid rode me through orgasm as I stared glassy-eyed at the ceiling, lips contorted in a silent scream.

We sat entwined on the chair long after our breathing had slowed. Neither of us said anything, letting it all sink in. I couldn't remember every clause in our contract, but I was pretty sure that I wasn't allowed to *fuck* the scholar.

We had been caught up in the moment, but something lingered even as we held each other. A sense of gravity and weightlessness; comfort and calamity.

"You're not a monster," Leid whispered in my ear. "Just a man; nothing more, nothing less."

XVI
THE PROMOTION

"ARE YOU EVER GOING TO MOVE?"

"No, this game sucks."

"Now, now; don't be such a sore loser."

My eyes lowered to our wooden battlefield, where my two pawns, rook and king were floundering. Yahweh still had his entire court, save for a couple of pawns and a bishop.

"Is this really what angels do for fun?"

"Our military uses chess as a way to practice strategy," he explained, twirling my queen in his fingers. "It builds patience and level-headedness."

"And boredom."

"Funny, I thought you liked this game."

"Yeah, until you beat me thirty-five consecutive times. Throw me a fucking bone over here."

The kid smirked. "Maybe you should work on your patience and level-headedness."

I left my stool, waving him off. "You win. I'm done."

Yahweh looked up, trying not to laugh. "Congratulations, by the way."

"For what?"

"I heard you're the Regent now."

"Oh."

"Your ceremony is tomorrow night, isn't it?"

"Where are you getting your information?"

He beamed. "Leid."

I rolled my eyes, heading for the door.

"And I'll have you know that I find your reason for her being in the lab very insulting. I don't make mistakes."

"Not even while you're working for your enemy?"

"I *never* make mistakes."

"Leid stays, kid."

Before Yahweh could protest, I shut the door. Punching in the code to the room's digital lock, I hurried through the Commons and toward the training block. Time for Drill. I was already five minutes late, thanks to that stupid game of chess.

The fifty Enforcers that I'd assigned tonight were assembling their gear and weapons in the armory. Ara was waiting for me at the arena entrance. I stopped at the foot of the stairs, looking him over.

He wore the Commandant coat, black with red embroidered seams, tails at his knees. A headset hugged his right ear, a microphone coiling all the way to his mouth. This was a big night for him. It would be the first time that he led Drill, and the last time I would watch it. As the official Regent, the Eye of Akul was forcing me out of the military domain. The Sanctum Enforcers were now entirely in my brother's hands.

My only task left was to train Ara to fly, as a prerequisite of being Commandant was to know every field in the Enforcer scope—piloting included. I'd decided to wait until Leid and Yahweh finished constructing our flight simulator.

The simulator, as Yahweh described using much bigger words, was a computerized game that perfectly mimicked flying our upgraded crafts. Using a simulator meant we wouldn't have any casualties during the training process.

The new crafts were one-manned, as opposed to the ten-man one pilot flight cruisers we were familiar with. That said, we needed *more* pilots. Ara and I had spent several days interviewing recruits from the Sanctum Militia. Everything was slowly coming together, but there were still a few hurdles to jump. That was okay; I was a patient man. Sort of.

"Keep a close eye on every team," I said as the soldiers took the field.

"Sir," Ara replied, opening the observation room door and letting me in first.

The Commandant stayed in the observation room during Drill. It was a room of glass above the field that gave you an excellent viewpoint of the arena. The field itself was a simulation of a city block in Sanctum and the scenery changed every several months to keep things fresh, otherwise soldiers would rely on memory instead of tactics.

Drill was held once a week, and its soldiers were rotated out. There were hundreds of Enforcers in Sanctum but only fifty were assigned to each Drill. Most of them looked forward to it, using it as a way to blow off steam. My men took the exercise very seriously; they knew I was watching each and every one of them, and I made a point to always play favorites. But in this case my idea of *favorite* coincided with skill. And you didn't want to make my shit-list, believe me.

"Teams *One* and *Two*, get into position," Ara ordered into the headset. "Teams *Three* and *Four,* wait behind the lines." While the soldiers did as he instructed, Ara said aside, "So now that I'm the Commandant, am I allowed to give our teams better titles?"

"Yes, Ara, because that matters."

"Teams One and Two? *Really?* How does it help our morale if you can't even bother to give them decent names?"

I sighed. "Do whatever you want. Just pay attention to Drill, please."

"The field is live, ladies!" my brother shouted, trying way too hard to sound like me. I couldn't help but smirk.

The battle began.

Each team had half an hour to take out their opposition. We used firearms with red ink bullets that made it impossible to argue a hit. As the soldiers decorated the arena with red splatter, Ara pushed the mic away from his mouth.

"I'm proposing to Ceram tomorrow," he said.

I tried to hide my shock. The idea of Ceram joining our family made me a little nauseous, but part of the discomfort was due to the fact that my younger brother would be betrothed before me. That wasn't tradition, and though I wasn't usually one for tradition, I knew the Eye of Akul (and my sister) would start pressuring me to marry. "Congratulations. Have you planned a date for her inking?"

Inking was a pre-marriage ceremony, where the bride was adorned in permanent ink with her husband's family name and her vows. It was kind of like a brand. Women didn't wear semi-permanent ink. The only time their bodies were decorated was when they were married, and those decorations lasted forever. You could imagine the complications of a divorce.

"Not yet. I haven't talked to her about it. Don't want to get ahead of myself; she might reject me."

"She won't."

"No?"

"You're an Eltruan."

"I'd like to think she won't reject me because I'm charming and intelligent."

"And an Eltruan."

Ara frowned. "Are you saying she's only with me because of my family name?"

I looked at the field. "No, I'm just saying she won't reject you. I wish you all the best." Before he could reply, I grabbed his mic and yanked him over to me so I could speak into it. "Lt. Samay, what the fuck are you doing? Stop standing in the middle of the street like a moron and take cover!"

As soon as I'd said that, Lt. Geiss nailed him in the head with an ink bullet. I sighed, while Ara laughed.

"Why is Lt. Samay acting like fresh meat?"

"He was up all night fighting with his girlfriend," explained Ara. "She kicked him out and now he's living in his craft until further notice."

"Wow, that sucks."

"Sure does. Not everyone has it like us."

No one had it like us.

"Lt. Assev, the enemy you're sniping is too far away!" my brother shouted into the mic. "Cover your team and let *them* get him!" He shot me a sidelong grin. "I could totally get used to this."

* * *

It was one in the morning when we wrapped it up at the research lab. We'd still had a lot to do, but called it quits when Yahweh fell asleep in mid-sentence.

Leid and I staggered back to my estate, our exhaustion mutual. All this work was starting to wear on us, and there was no rest in sight.

Tomorrow was going to suck even worse.

Work from seven to three, and then my induction ceremony from six to whenever. I couldn't leave until most of our guests did, and considering the ceremony was more like a party, I figured I'd be there at least until midnight. *Yay.*

That reminded me. "Did you buy a dress for tomorrow night?"

"No, I haven't had the time," Leid said, stifling a yawn.

"Why don't I take you to the Agora during lunch tomorrow?"

"Alright."

It'd been three weeks since my father died, and we never discussed the ordeal that had taken place that night. But things had changed between us. We held a strictly platonic relationship in public, but behind closed doors—;

Well, that was another matter.

When we got to my room, I changed into informal clothes while Leid groggily filled a syringe.

"This is your last week of injections," she said as I rolled up my sleeve. "How does that feel?"

I grimaced at the idea of her giving me a dose while half-asleep and reached for the syringe. "Here, let me do that. I don't want you severing an artery."

Leid handed it to me. After I injected it, I sat on my bed beside her. "Don't know," I murmured. "I don't even think about malay anymore."

"That's good to hear."

I held out the syringe and she reached for it. I grabbed her wrist with my other hand. "Why don't you stay in my room tonight?"

Leid shook me off. "No."

My grin fell. "Why not?"

"I'm fairly certain your idea of *staying* doesn't entail *sleeping*. If I don't get any rest before work, I'm going to croak."

She was right. I really needed some sleep, too. "I'll see you later this morning, then."

Leid took the syringe and headed for the door. "Goodnight, Qaira."

"Good morning, you mean."

"Yes, that too." And then she left.

I watched the door close, and then my gaze fell to the mirror on my closet. For a second, I didn't even recognize myself. The blight of worry and regret had all but vanished from my face, the dark circles under my eyes now only due to sleep-deprivation and not malay infirmity. Leid was my new drug of choice.

Everything was changing; little pieces at a time. If I thought about it for too long, it confused me. Scared me, even. For decades, the darkness was the only thing that had kept me going. It was the only thing that fed my ambition to see the angels dead. And now here I was, playing chess with one of them. What was happening to me?

Leid was making all the shadows recede, and I wasn't sure that I wanted them to. Happiness was a luxury I couldn't afford. Not yet.

First, Lucifer Raith had to die.

XVII
THE TROUBLE WITH COMMITTMENTS

"OW," I HISSED, FLINCHING. "Go easy!"

"Stop moving."

"You're gouging out my eye!"

"Because you're moving."

Leid squeezed my face and tilted my head; the ink pen pierced the tender flesh beneath my eye. It wasn't enough to draw blood, but it sure felt like it. My eyes watered up and I closed them. "Every time you fill for me I'm reminded why I used to pay for a professional."

"Quit your whining; I'm almost finished."

"You need to hurry. We're going to be late."

"Well it isn't *my* fault you didn't ask me to fill sooner."

"Yes, quite a mystery as to why."

"You can't have faded ink at your induction ceremony. It's disrespectful."

"And I giant handprint isn't?"

Leid laughed. "Stop distracting me." She finally let go and I jerked away, rubbing my face. "There, good as new."

I confirmed her statement in the mirror. She'd done a good job. After taking a minute to straighten my black suit and red tie, I stepped back and took a final look.

Leid stood beside me, applying some last minute make-up. I looked good, but she was the real stunner tonight. I'd bought her a white silk dress, form-fitting with a slit that ran up the side of her thigh. Her hair was tied in a halo braid, loose strands slithering over the small of her back. There was no doubt that Leid would get media attention tonight, and if rumor of a relationship happened, I'd let it.

"I feel naked," she murmured, wrapping her arms across her chest. All she did was emphasize her cleavage even more. I smirked.

"No you don't. I've seen you naked." Before she could respond I turned and pulled her against me, leaning my face into her neck and sniffing her perfume. I heard her sigh and my hand cupped her breast, thumbing her nipple. As it stood at attention, I whispered, "And I kind of want to see you naked right now."

"We can't," she objected, heavy-breathed. "Our driver is waiting for us at the port. You'll be late."

Leid was right. Damnit.

We headed for the flight deck, arm-in-arm.

* * *

When we landed at Yema Theater, the Eye of Akul were waiting for us at the end of a scarlet walkway, just in front of the rooftop entrance. Media personnel were allowed to stand at a distance, taking pictures and reporting live as Sanctum guards kept order. Four hundred Sanctum dignitaries and Parliament officials were here tonight, along with fifty of my favorite enforcers.

A server led us to our table, closest to the stage. It was round and draped in black tablecloth, candles housed in glass prisms atop it. Forty-five tables just like ours were scattered across the theater, immersing everything in hazy iridescence. A string quartet played on stage as guests took their seats, awaiting the show.

Leid and I sat with the council, along with Ara and Tae. And Ara's girlfriend, Ceram, who was whining at my brother about a new purse. I still had no idea why he wanted to marry her. She wasn't even pretty. Well, she wasn't ugly, but it wasn't like her looks made up for how superficial and annoying she was. Oh well; as long as he was happy.

The servers brought around our appetizers: fancy vegetable soup and bean salad with tulan cheese. I dug right in because I hadn't eaten since noon, but all Leid seemed interested in was the wine. Surprise, surprise.

After the servers took our empty plates away, I slipped a folded piece of paper from my pocket and read it over. I was pretty sure that I'd memorized my speech, but you could never be too careful.

"Your dress is beautiful!" squawked Ceram. "Where did you get it?"

"I can't remember," Leid said. "Qaira, where did we get my dress?"

"Opallas," I mumbled, not bothering to look up.

"Opallas! I love that place! You and I should go when their Kiorka season clothing line comes in!"

Leid smiled, wary. "Sure."

Looks like she made a new friend. Poor her.

Bzzt, bzzt, bzzt—

I glanced down at my radio, frowning.

Bzzt, bzzt, bzzt

The call was from Eroqam. I had to take it.

Ara's radio was going off as well. We shared a look. I nodded.

"Excuse me," I said, getting up and heading for the hall. The servers were still bringing around the main course, which meant I had some time.

Leaning against the wall, I brought the radio to my lips. "This is Qaira Eltruan, go ahead."

"Regent, this is Communications Analyst Tren. Commander Lucifer Raith is on hold at Eroqam, sir. He is asking to speak to you immediately."

"I can't. I'm at Yema Theater for the induction ceremony, which I'm sure he knows. Take a message."

"I've tried that already, sir. He refuses to speak to anyone but you."

Raith expected me to leave my *own* induction ceremony and drive all the way back to Eroqam? "If he won't leave a message with you, then it isn't that important. I'll call him in the morning."

"Yes, sir."

I disconnected the call and stared at the radio. What if Raith's message was important? No, whatever he wanted to tell me could wait until tomorrow. I wasn't going to cancel the ceremony because of him.

As I returned into the theater, the quartet was gone and spotlights flashed across the stage. The ceremony was beginning.

* * *

"I'd like to thank everyone for coming tonight, and a special thanks to the Eye of Akul for arranging all of this. I don't know what I'd do without them."

Applause.

"It was tough knowing that I was one day going to be the Regent. I admit there were times when I really had to stop and evaluate myself and my future—assess my actions in a way no one else ever had to. When I was six hundred, my father asked me what I thought the Regent did for Sanctum. He had come home from a long day at work and I hadn't seen him for almost a week. He would leave each morning before I'd wake for school, and arrive home after I'd gone to bed.

"After a long, hard thought, which coincidentally took the same amount of time as it did to chew my mouthful of cake—"

Laughter.

"—I said to him, 'The Regent controls all the men in Sanctum who carry big guns.' And at the time, that seemed like a good enough answer for him. But the Regent is much more than that, and I know that now.

"I was forced to take the mantle prematurely. As you all know, Qalam Eltruan was diagnosed with dementia ten years ago and since then I've strived to keep this city afloat. We have many, *many* troubles right now, and I want you to put your faith in me.

I'm not half the man my father was, but I promise to protect Sanctum with my life. Should the angels descend on us, I will be the first one on the field with our men, ready to taste the sting of their bullets. I promise to rid our society of malay once and for all; our Health Division is planning to open several new programs to treat addicts in a *safe* and steady climb to sobriety. Change is coming, Sanctum. We will see stability and prosperity equal to the Adoria Era. *Fhazia dia korti.*"

Fhazia dia korti. *Fire of eternity.*

"Fhazia dia korti!" chanted the audience. *"Di Sanctum!"*

"For Sanctum," I answered. "And without further ado, it is my pleasure to decorate my brother with the sigil of Enforcer Command. Please welcome Commandant Ara Eltruan."

I removed the badge from my breast as Ara took the stage to wild applause. After shaking hands, I pinned the sigil to his suit and together we gave the audience the Enforcer salute.

Isa and Kanar appeared at the other side of the stage as we descended, shaking our hands and pinning the Regent crest to my suit. Thousands of cameras flashed from the media-exclusive area, and I shook hands with all who rose to congratulate me on my way back to our table. The servers were clearing the tables and pulling them away in preparation for the after party. My sister hugged me and Leid watched us, smiling.

I had forgotten all about Raith's call.

* * *

Two hours later, everyone was drunk. The floor was packed and guests danced in pairs along the theater, moving in synch to the rhythm of the music. The dance was called *Jarahet*; men and women moved differently, forming lines and circles. It was a traditional dance and I knew it well, but I wasn't one for dancing unless it was a requirement for getting laid. That wasn't a problem in the foreseeable future.

Instead I watched my sister being courted by a young chairman of Sanctum's Commerce Division. Ara had proposed to

159

Ceram an hour ago and it seemed Tae felt pressured to start putting herself out there. Ara was the youngest among us, and the fact that he was getting married first put us both to shame. Well, only in a hypothetical sense. I didn't really care.

But I'd known this day would come. Soon my sister would get engaged to a well-to-do Upper Sanctum dignitary and leave our estate. I would miss her dearly.

Ara and Ceram twirled in the middle of the Jarahet. People were laughing and clapping. Leid stood next to me, sipping her drink.

"When is it considered not rude to leave?" she asked.

I glanced at my watch. It was nine. "Not for another few hours, sorry."

Leid surveyed the crowd. "Your council is gone."

"They're old. It's way past their bedtimes."

"Would you be terribly insulted if I went to check on the craft progress? We're running a week behind schedule already."

I frowned. "Yes, I would. I want you in that dress when I ravage you tonight."

She smiled. "Then dance with me."

I looked at her, hesitating with a response. The Jarahet had ended and the orchestra switched to a classical tune. Pairs of men and women danced closely together, arms locked, gliding across the floor.

"I didn't realize you liked to dance," I said.

"If I'm going to stand here for another three hours, then you better entertain me," she muttered, tossing her empty cup on a tray.

Sigh.

"Alright," I said, offering her my hand, "let's go."

Leid's smallness was never made more apparent than now. She was barely any taller than Yahweh, putting her at a height of *maybe* five foot nothing. Since I was over six feet, the mechanical issues of our dance made it kind of awkward.

But her frame added to her allure. I was the only one in the theater who knew that she could put me into a chokehold. Tiny but deadly.

"You dance well, Qaira."

"So do you. For someone who's never been to The Atrium, you know how to do practically everything."

She smiled. "I practiced."

"Practiced?"

"Yes, I was given several weeks' time to prepare to come here. The library in our court is immeasurable."

"You have books on how we dance?"

"We have books on everything. Every world and their cities and people and customs… Most of it is handwritten notes by other scholars, bound into books. Our primary reason for existing is to learn about the Multiverse and its inhabitants. You can think of us as cosmic librarians."

"And when you go back, will you write about your time here?"

She nodded. "I will make updates into our already-written books about the Nehel. And also the angels, whatever their fate may be."

Our conversation paused as I dipped her.

"Funny," I said. "I thought a race like yours who's seen countless worlds would use something a little more advanced to keep their records in."

Leid laughed. "Our books are not like yours."

"What are they?"

"I probably shouldn't say anything else," she whispered. "We aren't allowed to talk about our practices."

"Who would I tell? I'm the only one who knows your secret other than the council and my family."

"Your family knows?"

"They know you aren't one of us. Come on, Leid; it's pretty impossible to cover that up when you *live* with them."

"Have you told them what I am?"

"No, they haven't asked. I think they know the matter is a secret. I trust you, and that's good enough for them."

"You trust me?" she repeated, looking at me with sullen eyes.

"Why wouldn't I?"

Leid leaned in and rested her cheek against the center of my chest. "Thank you."

A camera flashed from somewhere above. A journalist had probably been waiting for that moment. We were going to make headlines tomorrow. Oh well.

All I did was wrap my arms around her. We were hugging more than dancing now. Ara and Tae were smiling at us from the refreshments table, making remarks to each other that I couldn't hear.

The song ended and we broke away. Leid gave me her signature smile. "Thank you for the—" But then her face changed and she looked behind me, searching the crowd. Her eyes rose, and then widened.

Before I could ask what was going on, she whirred in front of me with her arms out.

Gunshots thundered through the theater. All three of them hit Leid. One in the chest, one in the arm and one in the head.

She collapsed at my feet, looking up at me with a smoking hole in the center of her forehead, blood trickling down the bridge of her nose.

As the crowd screamed and scattered for the exits, all I did was stare at Leid. Everything in me went completely numb.

But then she *blinked*.

"Qaira," she slurred, blood seeping from her lips, *"run."*

My despair turned to horror in an instant. *How…?*

When I didn't move, she struggled to get back on her feet. Her back arched inhumanly, movements stiff and disjointed. It was like she was an animated doll, obeying the whims of an invisible puppeteer.

She grabbed the gun on my belt as shots rang out again. Leid returned fire, aiming somewhere above. A figure fell from the north-tier balcony, hitting the dance floor with a thud. The assailant's wig slipped off when he fell, a mop of black hair now lying beside him. An angel in disguise.

Angels.

More shots. One whirred by my head, hitting a woman behind me as she attempted to flee for the lobby. I couldn't tell how many gunmen were above us, but I knew there were a lot more than I could take alone. They were picking off the crowd at random.

No, not at random.

Ara was knelt at the refreshments table, hugging Ceram. She was covered in blood and her eyes were closed. My brother ignored the spray of bullets that hit our guests around him, face contorted in a confused wince.

"Go!" Leid was screaming. "Help your people!"

When I looked at her again, the bullet wound was gone. All that remained was a smear of drying blood on her forehead.

"I'm not leaving you here!" I shouted.

"I can handle myself, don't worry. Get your family to safety."

She was telling the truth. I darted for Ara, ducking bullets on the way. He still hadn't moved.

"Come on!" I shouted, trying to pull him to his feet. "We need to go!"

"I-I can't!" he cried, not letting go of his fiancée, who was clearly dead. "We need to get her to a hospital! S-She's—"

"Ara, she's dead! And you'll be too if you don't move! Help me find Tae!"

He didn't answer me so I yanked him to his feet with all the force I could gather. He dropped Ceram and we fought all the way to the exit.

"No!" he screamed. *"No! I can't leave her there! Don't make me abandon her!"*

I smacked him across the face, snapping him out of it. *"She's fucking dead!* Are you going to leave her unavenged?"

The pain in Ara's eyes waned, giving way to darkness. That was exactly what I wanted to see.

"Come on, I need you."

As we hurried into the lobby, I looked back at Leid. She was still in the middle of the dance floor, her beautiful white dress drenched with blood. Half a dozen bodies scattered the floor around her, and she wasn't finished. My scholar would be just fine.

But my city was burning.

When we reached the rooftop port, pillars of smoke slithered over the night sky, illuminated by the flames that birthed them. Entire blocks were lit up like torches, and we gazed across the cityscape in horrified awe. The hum of Enforcer crafts was carried over the roaring fires and explosions, and I grabbed my radio.

Then, I remembered Raith's call.

* * *

Bullets.

Fire.

Explosions.

Screams.

Fuck the council's rules; I was balls deep in the chaos.

"Get back, get back!"

I dove from behind a ruined craft as it erupted into chunks of smoldering metal. My men scattered behind other debris, returning fire at the angel gunmen. One of them had grenades, but we couldn't tell who. It was kind of scary; the smoke and cinders made it near impossible to see our enemy until they fired.

We had pushed the angel rebels out of Upper Sanctum for over an hour, having finally surrounded the handful that was left on Main Street.

"Clear!" shouted Lt. Fedaz.

I waved the men behind us forward, and we weaved through the wreckage. It was hard to focus because I was worried about my sister. I hadn't seen her since the rebels attacked the theater. I also couldn't stop thinking about the state of ruin that Sanctum was in; the body count would be horrifying.

My mask felt constrictive, but I wouldn't dare take it off. I'd already figured out why the angels had come here tonight. A failed assassination attempt.

Tink-ta-tink.

A little metal sphere rolled along the left side of the street, giving off strange blue light.

"Grenade!" someone shouted, and again we dove for cover.

Angels did not use typical grenades; we only called them that for lack of a better term. When they detonated, a flash of blinding blue light disintegrated anything it came into contact with. This time, another ruined craft exploded. Some of my men had been hiding behind it and they were torn to shreds by the blast. Blood and body parts rained on us.

A charred, severed arm fell into my lap. I recognized the ring on its thumb. It belonged to Garan Geiss.

I tossed it away, bile rising in my throat.

"Qaira, we need to get on the roof!" Ara screamed beside me. Another spray of bullets hit our cover. "They're slaughtering us!"

I surveyed the street. There was an alleyway about ten feet from us, but taking a step out into the open was certain death.

"Have teams three and four cover me," I ordered. "Everyone start shooting. I'm going to ascend."

"Wait, no," Ara said, grabbing my arm. "You're the Regent now. Let me do it."

"I'm the only one who can kill them," I argued. "If you keep them occupied they won't even see me."

More bullets. Our cover was on fire.

"Ara, tell me you'll do that!" I screamed. "It's our only chance!"

With a reluctant nod, my brother grabbed his radio and commanded a full out assault. As our teams stood and began firing at the rooftops, I darted into the street.

No one had seen me.

My wings released and I rose into the black, reloading on the way.

I had a clearer picture from above. There were three teams scattered over the Agora roofs, all preoccupied by my men. I kept rising, until I was well over a hundred feet above them.

And then I dove for the closest team.

The whistle of my wings cautioned them to turn around, but it was too late. I landed right in the middle of them and closed my eyes. Blood splattered across the inside of their visors, and they collapsed simultaneously.

I took off again, diving for the next team. It was very important that Ara and his men kept their attentions to the street. The noise of gunfire muffled the sound of my approach, but if I was spotted prematurely then they would shoot me down. My life was in my brother's hands, and for the first time, I trusted him with it.

Smoke and the night sky shrouded my armor; the whites didn't see me until I dove between them. The second team fell as easily as the first.

One more.

My head was pounding. I hadn't ever used my ability so fiercely. For the first time in my life, I was thankful to have it.

But the last team saw me coming, and sprayed bullets into the sky. I rolled mid-air, feeling a hot sting in my shoulder. I was hit.

The pain was nothing to my adrenaline, and I landed ten feet away. The moment I hit the ground, I sprinted toward them with my rifle raised, blade gleaming red in the rising cinders. The angels were still reloading. Two soldiers forfeited their lives to jump in front to protect the scrambling gunmen. One swung a blade they'd unsheathed from their belt, and I ducked, plunging my own through their stomach. I speared him all the way through, lifting him off the ground. With a snarl, I threw him from the rooftop.

The other turned to run while the gunmen pointed their weapons at me. I could see their faces through the translucent screens of their visors. They knew how hopeless it was.

And then they all fell, blood and brain matter leaking from their helmets and onto the ground.

"Clear," I announced into my radio.

As my men cheered below, I winced and sank to my knees, clutching my wounded shoulder.

"Sanctum Militia, report."

"This is Sgt. Kros, sir. The Agora has been stabilized. All clear, Regent."

I breathed a sigh. Ara commanded our teams to do a final sweep of the area, and I stared woefully at my burning city.

Crafts descended through the smoke to collect our troops. One hovered above the rooftop, and the door slid open. Leid sat on the cabin bench, staring at me.

She was covered in blood, and I couldn't help but stare back.

When I entered the craft, she tossed me my gun. "You're hurt."

"I'm fine," I said. "Just a graze. Have you seen my sister?"

"Yes. She's with the council at Parliament. We took her there because I didn't know how safe Eroqam was. We're picking her up now."

I nodded, sitting next to her as our pilot flew over the carnage. "So, you can survive bullets."

"Yes," she said, looking away.

"Can anything kill you?"

"Yes," she said again. "But not easily."

"You violated your contract again."

"Depends."

"On?"

"Harm's way doesn't include bullets; you just said that yourself."

"I don't think that clause was based on a technicality."

Leid smiled, but it didn't reach her eyes. "Ceram is dead. I saw her body—"

"Yes, I know. Garan is dead, too."

We sat in silence after that. The silence allowed my thoughts to roar. After a minute or two, I stood from the bench, narrowing my eyes at our pilot. "Take us to Eroqam."

"Not Parliament, sir?"

"No, we'll have another craft pick my sister up."

"Sir."

"Qaira?" Leid called, giving me a confused look.

"I'm done," I said, staring out the window. "I'm done playing games, Leid. I'm going to find out who that insurgent is *tonight*."

167

XVIII
THE ULTIMATUM

"QAIRA, LET'S TALK ABOUT THIS," Leid begged, hurrying after me as I stormed through the Commons.

I said nothing, trying to ignore her. As I reached the door to Yahweh's room, she moved to block me, covering the lock with her body. "Don't do this," she said. "*Please*, don't do this. There has to be another way!"

"Leid, step aside," I warned, quietly. She didn't move. "I'm not saying it again."

Still, she didn't move.

I grabbed her neck, flinging her aside. And for some reason, she let me. Before she could try to talk me down anymore, I barged into the kid's room.

It was dark and he was asleep, but the light from the hallway shined on his face and he stirred. His eyes opened and he saw me approaching him, covered in blood with a crazy look in my eyes.

"Q-Qaira...?" he stammered, still drunk from sleep.

I snatched him by the collar and yanked him out of bed. He yelped, falling to the floor and I dragged him halfway across the room until he finally got to his feet.

As we emerged from the room, Leid grabbed my arm. I looked down at her.

"He didn't do this," she said. "Don't hurt him."

"He is my *only* leverage!" I shouted. "After everyone who died tonight, you're still going to fight me on this? Ceram, Garan, *all* of those guests! Whose side are you on?"

She stared up at me, silent and stoic. Then, Leid stepped out of my way.

Yahweh kept quiet the entire time. He had a faraway look in eyes, like he knew the end was near. He didn't even struggle as I led him toward the communications room. When I opened the door, he whispered, "Are you going to kill me?"

"That all depends on your father."

* * *

As the projection screen connected, Commander Raith's eyes settled on his son. More specifically, on the knife that I held to his neck.

Then, he looked at me. His expression told me that he already knew where this was going.

"Apparently I didn't make myself clear the first time," I said. "We agreed that—"

"I tried to warn you, *Regent*, but you wouldn't take my call."

"A message would have sufficed."

"I don't know how many of your soldiers have been compromised, Qaira. Leaving a message might have proven worthless."

"The angel rebels were able to sneak through our airspace borders without detection. I find that odd, considering there were over a hundred of them. I know you know who the Sanctum informant is. This is your only chance to tell me."

Raith's eyes narrowed. He said nothing.

I grabbed Yahweh's hair and wrenched back his head, pressing the knife harder against the soft tissue of his throat. He yelped, shutting his eyes.

"Again, *who* is the insurgent?"

"Put the knife down, Qaira."

"The next thing that comes out of your mouth better be the answer to my question, or your son will die."

Lucifer's façade broke. Desperation flooded across his face. "I don't know. They're anonymous, even to me. I can't identify which one it is."

"Which one? Which one of *what?*"

Again, Lucifer said nothing. I could tell he was really fighting himself on this one. It was time to add some incentive.

I raked the knife across Yahweh's face, slicing through his cheek. Blood trickled from the thin red slit now marring his perfect white skin. He screamed, clutching his face. The kid tried to break free but I was too strong.

"No!" screamed Raith, reaching for the screen. *"Don't hurt him!"*

"Tell me who the insurgent is!" I screamed back, holding the knife to Yahweh's eye. *"Don't make me do this, Raith!"*

"Qaira!" Yahweh sobbed, unable to take his terrified gaze from the knife that grazed his eyelashes. Tears streamed down his face, mingling with blood from his gash. He was crying pink. *"Please! Please, I beg you!"*

"Don't make me do this!" I screamed again, a tinge of a plea in my voice.

The fight on Lucifer's face disappeared. He hung his head in tired defeat. "The Eye of Akul."

I stared at him, unable to believe my ears. I almost dropped the knife. "Say that again. I don't think I heard you correctly."

"Your council. Someone in your council has been giving our base ship information in order to sabotage your reign. They wanted your people to lose hope in you so they could usurp your throne. When that didn't happen, they planned your assassination. Your brother's too. They want to rid Sanctum of the Eltruan family."

"Who is it?"

"I don't know. I said that already. They correspond with our base ship using a voice modulator and keep their messages brief. Coordinates, routes of safe passage through Sanctum; those sorts of things."

"And what do the angels get out of this?"

"If the Eye of Akul claimed Sanctum, they would let us stay."

171

At this point, I had to try really hard to keep from falling. My legs felt like rubber and my stomach was knotting up. I knew that the council and I had issues, but I never thought they wanted me dead.

I looked away, letting everything sink in. Raith wasn't lying— the moment he explained it, it all made sense. Shock had numbed me to the core, leaving no room for anger. Not yet.

My grip on Yahweh released and he scrambled to the other side of the room, hiding under a desk. Lucifer's stare burned on me, and I returned his gaze with equal fire.

"I told you, and now you must promise not to hurt my son."

I reached for the switchboard, my index finger hovering over the CUT FEED button. "If the Eye of Akul catches wind that I know about this, the next time you see me I'll be waving your son's head around on a fucking pike. Sleep tight."

I pressed the button. The screen went black.

For a second I stared at the blackness, recalling memories of the council in our home, with my father, at our family gatherings… All this time, and they would kill me? They would kill my brother and sister, too?

'They're upset because you aren't as easy to manipulate as your father was.'

Leid was right. She was *always* right.

And the council had left my ceremony early. They'd known what was going to happen. But who was it? Isa? Kanar? Shev? *All* of them?

The shock finally receded, anger filling up the empty space. I searched for Yahweh, finding him cowering beneath a desk nearest the door. I reached under and dragged him out, and he pressed his back to the wall. His face was still bleeding. My anger waned.

"Come on," I said, guilt clenching at my insides. "It's over."

The kid didn't budge. My eyes trailed to his pants. There was a wet stain over his crotch, leading down his legs. I looked away, disgusted. Scaring children wasn't usually my thing, white or not.

Although I got what I had wanted, I wasn't proud of how I'd done it.

"Don't make me say it again," I muttered, heading for the door. He followed at a safe distance.

I found two soldiers in the hall and ordered them to take Yahweh to the shower rooms so he could clean up. As they walked away, the kid didn't even look at me. His head was down, eyes cast to the floor, shame marking his face. I watched them until they disappeared around the corner, and then I radioed for my brother to meet me in the conference room.

He was going to *love* the news I had for him.

* * *

"Hello, Isa."

"Qaira, is your family alright?"

"Yes, we're fine. I was calling Parliament to verify that you and the others are safe?"

"Yes, we're all at Parliament trying to stave off media and the officials. It'll be a long night for us."

"I'd like to hold a meeting with the council tomorrow morning, if that's alright with you? Every one of you must attend, as I think I've found a way to stop the Archaeans once and for all."

"Oh?" Isa sounded surprised; I could have sworn I'd heard disappointment in her voice. But that could have just been my paranoia. "What do you have planned?"

"I don't have time to explain. I should be with my family."

"I understand. Does seven-thirty work for you?"

"Yes, it does. I'll see you and the Eye of Akul bright and early."

"Goodnight, Regent."

On our televised screen, news reports played footage of me leaping across rooftops and slaughtering the angel gunmen on loop. The headline read: SANCTUM'S SAVIOR. The media loved me or hated me, all depending on the day. But then they showed a crowd of spectators chanting *'Savior'* over and over again as the

173

enforcers fought the fires on Main Street. My sister sat on the couch, watching, glass-eyed and crestfallen.

"Tae, are you alright?"

"So much death," she whispered, wincing as fresh tears fell from her eyes. "I can't take it anymore, Qaira."

I leaned her into me and she rested her head on my shoulder, sniffling. "It'll be over soon," I promised, eyes on the screen. I didn't have the heart to tell her what I'd found out tonight. She couldn't handle it. Not yet.

When Tae retreated to bed, I searched for Leid. I hadn't seen her since the Commons.

I was exhausted but couldn't go to sleep knowing she was angry at me. She had every right to be, but I at least wanted her to know that I didn't break our oath. She wasn't in her room or the research laboratory; there was only one other place that she could be.

Sure enough, the mournful sound of her cello floated from the music room and through the hallway of my estate. The song was sad. Leid never played any other kind.

I approached the music room slowly, trying to give myself some time to think of a good way to apologize. Ideally, my apology wouldn't be an actual apology. *I'm sorry* wasn't an easy thing to say. For me, at least. But I owed her something.

The music faded as I reached the doorway. I paused in the threshold, my expression falling to confusion. Leid sat there with her head hung, bow drooped at her side. The cello rested crookedly between her legs, its neck across her knee.

A minute passed. She didn't move.

"Leid?" I called, cautious.

Nothing.

I took a step into the room. Something didn't feel right. The air was weird; like the gravity had shifted and its weight made my legs heavier than usual. *"Leid."*

The silence broke when she started to sing. The sound of her voice startled me, and I jumped.

'On the edge of love and death, count to ten and hold your breath,
The Ocean of Maghir is calling, so place your courage to the test'

A hymn of Moritoria. Even the beauty of her voice couldn't mask the song's morbidity. I took another step into the room, even though instinct was telling me to run.

"Approach, approach, approach…"

Another step. Now I was within arm's reach of her.

"Leid," I whispered. "Stop playing around."

She lifted her head, hair sliding from her face. Grey veins wriggled beneath her skin like animated roots. Her eyes were pitch black, and she smiled at me from ear to ear.

I recoiled, tripping over my own feet and crashing into a collection of wind instruments. Leid collapsed from the chair, my mother's cello slamming into the floor beside her. She clutched her throat, coughing violently.

I watched from where I'd fallen, too frightened to move. When her coughing didn't let up, concern smothered that fear.

"Leid!" I shouted, battling the pile of instruments around me. "Are you hurt?"

She curled in response; forehead against the ground, arms tucked into her chest.

"Are you hurt!?" I shouted again.

I broke free, crawling to her. She collapsed into my arms and when I looked at her face, it was normal again. Her violet eyes were wild and frightened, chest heaving as she tried to catch her breath.

I didn't know what else to do, so I held her as tightly as I could. Eventually her breathing slowed and her body relaxed.

"Are you alright?" I asked.

"Yes," she said, weakly.

"What happened?"

"I… I don't know."

I wanted to ask her about her face, but I wasn't sure if that had been real.

Leid pulled away from me and smoothed her hair. Her face was flushed with stress and shame. She averted my eyes for a few minutes, collecting the cello and placing it back into its case. When she latched it shut, she murmured, "It happens sometimes."

"What happens?"

"Panic attacks."

I stared, incredulous. "Your panic attacks are a lot different than anyone else's."

She smiled, looking down. "I am not like anyone else."

True enough. "Was it because of me? Of what happened in the Commons?"

"I… don't know, really. That could be it, but sometimes they happen for no reason at all."

"I came here to apologize. I'm sorry for the way that I treated you. You didn't deserve that. I was angry."

Leid hung her head. She said nothing.

"I didn't hurt him. Well, not badly. I had to take some measures to get Raith to talk, but I did it, Leid. I found out who the insurgent—"

And then I realized she was crying.

At first all I did was stare as Leid sobbed quietly into her hands, my face twisting with confusion. This wasn't the worst fight we'd ever had; something else was going on. Something I didn't know about.

I knelt beside her and scooped her up, catching a brief glimpse of her face. I tried to hide my shock. Leid's tears were crimson colored. Scholars cried *blood*. I didn't say anything and let her sob on my shoulder. I'd have to burn my shirt later.

As sad and confusing as all this was, a small part of me was happy for it. Leid had seen the worst side of me, and now here she was, letting me know that there was something dark and painful beneath her surface, too. Even if she never told me what it was, I was just satisfied knowing she felt safe enough to fall apart on me.

"Did you feel guilt?" she whispered.

"What?"

She pulled her face away from my shoulder and looked up at me. Her eyes and cheeks were smeared with blood. It was kind of horrifying, but I couldn't take my gaze off her. "When you hurt Yahweh, did you feel any guilt?"

"Yeah," I sighed.

She smiled, cupping my face. "That's good. You need to embrace your guilt. Revel in it."

"Nehel are taught that guilt is weakness."

"You're wrong. Guilt is the marker between man and monster."

"Which do you think I am?"

"Which do *you* think you are?"

My eyes left hers and I gazed at the floor, letting that question hang.

XIX
CRUELTY AND COMPASSION

At seven thirty sharp, an anthem of marching boots stormed through the Parliament lobby. Officials and workers moved aside as fifty enforcers made their way to the second floor, led by Commandant Ara Eltruan.

Crowds of employees observed them with curious frowns, whispering amongst each other. The Sanctum guards standing watch by the doors did nothing to stop Ara's men. They would never dare to question Special Forces.

This was not a typical day for anyone. Enforcers specialized in apprehending Archaeans; but today, their targets were Nehelians.

My ears caught sound of their approach before I saw them. I was waiting in front of the Council Room, keeping the secretary in his seat by a firm grip on his shoulder. My eyes darted to each and every soldier as they passed, marching through the double doors and disappearing into the shadows. When the thunder of feet ceased, I let go of the secretary and headed for the door.

"If you're not here when I get back," I said over my shoulder, "my men will gun you down."

The secretary only sat there, glaring at me.

I walked through the cool, dimly-lit hall of the Council Room—the throne room, where the Eye of Akul worked their deadliest machinations. Was it here where they'd planned our assassinations? Was it here where they'd communicated with Commander Raith? Everything had happened right under my nose. Thinking about it made me sick.

And thinking about what I had to do made me even sicker.

179

But I hid it well, sliding from the shadows of the line of enforcers, emerging front and center. The Eye of Akul were standing behind their podiums, looking over the soldiers with confusion in their eyes.

"Regent, what is the meaning of this?" demanded Isa.

"I thank you all for being so punctual," I said, completely ignoring her. "There isn't much time, so I'll just dive right in."

I cleared my throat, sliding a folded piece of paper out of my breast pocket. "The Regent of Sanctum stands as a symbol of our honor, strength and courage. He represents the Nehelian torch— our flame against the darkness of The Atrium. The Regent is Moritoria reincarnate, the blessed Kings of Maghir, attesting to the ever-prevalent nature of our race."

The council stared at me, their confusion waning. I was reading the speech that Isa had given at the ceremony last night, two hours before it had turned into a slaughter. I imagined their brains as gears, clicking chaotically as they realized where this was all going.

"Sanctum, the Regent is our shield, protecting us from the dangers of ourselves and enemies. It is his duty to exterminate those intending us harm, those committing *treason*—"

"Qaira," Kanar interjected, "whatever it is that you think we've—"

"The next person to interrupt me will get a bullet in his head." I waited, looking over all seven of their worry-creased faces. No one made a sound. "Now, where was I? Oh. Therefore, we place down our lives, ourselves, to uphold the safety and integrity of our people. For Sanctum." I crumpled the piece of paper in my fist, throwing it over my shoulder. *"Di Sanctum,"* I said again, lip curling with indignance.

The council looked at each other.

"I'm about to put your claim of loyalty and selflessness to the test. I ask that the insurgent make his or herself known to me. If no one steps forward, I'll be forced to assume that *all* of you are insurgents. Surely a selfless person wouldn't condemn six innocent people to die."

Silence.

"Either way, you're going to die. You might as well come forward and spare your partners' lives."

"We don't know what you're talking about, Qaira," Kanar said, his voice a shaking whisper. "On what grounds can you accuse us of treason?"

"Commander Raith gave you up, sorry to say. He doesn't know which one of you it is, but fortunately that means *shit* to me. I'll kill every single one of you without batting an eye."

Still, nothing. Isa sank to her seat, sobbing into her hands. Kanar and Shev glared at me, shock and disgust taking turns with their expressions. Everyone else began to plead, begging me to let them go. They weren't the insurgents, they said. They didn't know anything about anything.

"I'm going to give you thirty seconds," I announced, glancing at my watch. My enforcers raised their rifles in unison, pointing them at the council.

The crowd went wild.

"Qaira, listen to me!" shouted Kanar. "How could you even think that I would betray you? I was there the day that you were born! I've been your father's friend for *thousands* of years!"

"Twenty seconds."

There was a moment when I'd noticed a change in Shev's expression—a faint glimmer of recognition. We shared a look, and *I knew.*

But he didn't say anything.

"Times up," I announced, tapping my watch. With those words, the shouts faded. "This morning you all have proven your worthlessness to Sanctum and its people." I tossed Ara a sidelong glance, but he didn't return it. He was too busy seething at the council. "As you know, my brother lost someone very special to him last night, and I'm sure there are a few things he'd like to say. Or, maybe not. Nevertheless, I'll leave him to it."

Silence.

"I thank you all for your years of service to us." I turned, heading for the door. "Unfortunately, Sanctum has outgrown you."

The screams erupted again, and now they were belligerent. I caught 'monster' and 'disgrace' several times before Ara shouted, *"Aim!"*

As the doors closed behind me, gunshots erupted through the council room. The screams peaked, and then all was silent once again.

Like an obedient pet, the secretary hadn't moved. He stared up at me with wide, horror-stricken eyes as I came around his desk and patted him once on the shoulder.

"You're fired."

* * *

"This is Ysana Lima with Sanctum Public Broadcast. Our station interrupts your regularly scheduled program to announce some shocking news.

"This morning at approximately eight o'clock, an enforcer strike team marched on Parliament, led by Commandant Ara Eltruan under the instruction of Regent Qaira Eltruan, and executed all seven members of the Eye of Akul. Digital Forensic Investigations has announced that the Eye of Akul was found guilty of treason, providing the Archaean rebel forces with information that aided in over a dozen acts of violent war crimes. Last night's Archaean strike on Upper Sanctum's 8th District left over two hundred Nehelians dead, along with three Sanctum officials in critical condition at Eroqam Medical Facility.

"Investigations are still pending, but it is already confirmed that military files containing hundreds of facility access codes have been compromised. Eroqam database forensics has discovered evidence linking the Eye of Akul to over twelve terrorist attacks over the past year.

"Although our Regent has declined to speak in front of the camera, he made this statement to the press:

'My heart goes out to all of those who lost someone yesterday night, and I only wish I'd found the perpetrators sooner. The Eye of Akul fooled us all, and Eroqam shares your shock. I will be doing everything that I can to right the wrongs caused by my ignorance, and I ask that you once again put your faith in me. I still promise you prosperity, council or no council.'

"Regent Qaira Eltruan led our defending forces to victory last night against impossible odds. I think it's safe to say that Sanctum truly has a savior."

I shut the screen off, massaging my head.

My sister sat beside me, hands clasped over her mouth. She was going to see it sooner or later; might as well be sooner.

"Why... why didn't you tell me?"

"I didn't know how to. You were a wreck last night."

"I can't believe it," she breathed. "I...can't."

"Yeah," I said quietly.

"They tried to kill you, Qaira."

"I know. I was there."

"They tried to kill Ara."

I leaned forward, elbows propped on my knees. "They're gone. Don't worry."

Tae stood, pacing the living room. I watched her, concerned.

"Is *everyone* in Sanctum trying to kill us?"

"No."

"Am I even safe to leave our house?"

"Yes, Tae. Calm down. The threat has been taken care of."

"How can you be so sure? Kanar was like a second father to us, and he tried to have you *killed!* If we can't even trust our own family—"

"The only people you should trust are me and Ara."

"Gee, thanks," Leid muttered from the dining room. I'd forgotten she was here.

"And Leid," I fumbled, wincing in error.

Tae retreated to the kitchen for a stiff drink, and I stared at our blank televised screen. I thought about the look Shev had given me. Although I wasn't certain that he'd acted alone, it was quite possible that I had murdered six innocent people today. No, not just people. The Eye of Akul; the council that had served as my leash.

But now the shackles were off. I had total control of Sanctum. There was nothing stopping me from complete annihilation of the Archaean race. That execution had been a means to an end; for the ultimate good.

That was what I kept telling myself.

* * *

The digital lock beeped, followed by a *click*.

I opened the door to Yahweh's room, finding him on his bed, scribbling something down in a notebook. As he wrote, he glanced at another book that Lucifer had given him. He ignored me, but I knew he'd heard the lock disengage.

"What are you doing?" I asked.

"Nothing," he muttered, closing the notebook. I'd caught a glimpse of strange symbols that weren't in Archaean, framed with calculations across each page. The book from which he read was a biomedical dictionary.

It was late in the evening now and due to the recent events, we had cancelled our plans to work on the prototype. I placed his dinner on the desk while he stared at his lap, scratching the bandage on his cheek. It was clear that he didn't want to talk to me, and I didn't blame him.

Testing his will, I pulled up a chair and sat in front of his bed.

"What do you want?" he demanded not a minute later.

"How would you like to punch me in the face?"

Yahweh looked at me, the animosity in his eyes fading to confusion.

"I'm serious," I said, grinning. "I'll give you a free shot."

"That's how Nehelians solve their problems, not angels."

"Oh come on, I know you want to."

He only looked back at his book, ignoring me.

I sighed. "I wouldn't have done it, you know."

"Done what?" he murmured, turning a page.

"I… wouldn't have killed you. You're too important to us."

"You cut my face and pulled my hair so hard that I still have a headache. The level of disgrace I was subjected to yesterday night made me *hope* that you'd kill me. Your confession is invalid."

Alright, I'd tried. "This doesn't change anything. We're still coming for you tomorrow—"

"I wouldn't expect anything else. Please leave."

Nodding, I headed for the door. As I grabbed the handle, he added, "And I think you should stop visiting me unless it pertains to our project. We can sit here and play chess all day long, but in the end I'm an angel and you're a Nehelian. I can't be kind to someone who might barge into my room in the middle of the night and torture me again."

I kept my back to him, feeling the sting of his words like little daggers. "That's perfectly fine with me, *white*."

I left his room without looking back.

XX
FRAIL

"NO, STOP," sighed Leid. "Your fingers are too tense."

Playing the violin was a lot harder than firing a gun. "I thought it sounded fine."

"Of course you did. You're a novice."

I chose to keep my mouth shut. It was ten thirty at night and I'd agreed to practice in hope of easing my stress. Big mistake. I had only been playing the violin for a little over a month, and thought I was doing pretty well given the amount of time. But not Leid. She rode my ass like I was the laziest piece of shit ever.

"You need to make your fingers looser. Let them glide over the strings."

"I don't have dainty little girl fingers like you."

Leid giggled. "Dainty girl fingers? Is that what you call them?"

"Yes."

She stood and placed her cello aside, leaning over me. "Here," she murmured, "like this." Her hand encased mine and she guided my fingers across the board. Each time my knuckles tensed she lifted them, until they bent impossibly. "You need to make them elastic. Loose fingers allow for better gliding."

I tried to grab her but she slipped away, scowling.

"Take this seriously."

"This isn't helping my stress, but I have another idea," I said with a grin.

She ignored me, moving to her satchel. I'd bought her one a couple of days ago so she'd stop carrying around my briefcase. I hadn't seen her without it since. She turned around and smiled, holding up a bunch of sheets.

"What is that?" I asked.

"A song I've been writing."

"Really?"

Leid nodded, placing it on my music stand. I looked it over. "Think my stiff fingers can handle it?"

"Maybe."

"Play it for me."

She retreated to the stool, not even bothering to take her sheets. Tucking the cello between her legs, Leid began to play.

The song was sad; beautiful, but sad. The despondence floated around the room, painting everything in shades of grey. I watched her, discomforted by how much the music moved me.

When she stopped, I asked, "What is that song about?"

"Us."

Us? A song that sad was about us?

She caught the look on my face, her brows creasing with worry. "You don't like it?"

"What do you want me to do?"

That question caught her off guard. She only stared at me.

"How can I make you happier? If that song is about us, then I'm concerned."

Leid glanced away, sullen. "I'm sorry. I'll write us a better song."

"It's *not* the song!" I rasped. "It's you! It's that storm cloud you carry over your head! Have I done something?"

"It's not you," she almost whispered. "It's never been you. Please, don't think that."

I sighed and got to my feet, turning from her. Running a hand through my hair, I tried to think of a way to get her to tell me what was wrong. I couldn't think of anything. I wasn't good at this kind of shit.

And then Leid hugged me from behind, arms curling across my stomach. I felt the warmth of her cheek as she laid it against my back. "I didn't mean to upset you."

My frustration faded. "I'm not upset."

"Yes, you are."

"No, I'm not." I just wanted to know about her. "I need to go."

"Where?"

"I forgot about an errand. Can you wait in my room until I get there? I should only be a couple of minutes."

She nodded.

I squeezed her hand and then departed for the hall, heading in the direction of the Commons.

***

The angels were familiar with the Court of Enigmus, and on more than one occasion Yahweh had hinted that he knew about Leid in ways that I didn't. It was time for him to shed some light on the subject. After our last chat, I was pretty sure that he wasn't going to talk, but I was prepared to do some heavy stepping.

As his room came into view, I spotted Lt. Narish Ketar pacing in front of it. It was long past the end of his shift, and my suspicion spiked ten-fold when our eyes met and his face twisted with fear. He stopped pacing, now still as a statue.

"What are you doing here, Lieutenant?"

As he fumbled with a response, I glanced at Yahweh's door. Lt. Ketar was one of the few enforcers who knew the access code to the electronic lock, as he was tasked with bringing the kid meals every other day. The lock was deactivated.

"Wait," Ketar gasped. "Wait, *sir*, before you—"

I threw open the door.

The room was decorated in blood splatter; across the walls, the bed sheets, the torn pages of books scattered along the floor. Yahweh lay in the middle of the room, curled into a fetal position as two enforcers stomped him to death. I couldn't tell if he was conscious.

I lunged into the fray and shoved them off. They staggered back, shocked at the sight of me. I punched the closest soldier in the face, and several teeth flew from his mouth as he hit the ground. The other tried to run, but I ripped out my gun and shot him in the back of the head before he could make it to the hall. He collapsed in the doorway, bleeding out.

Lt. Ketar was still right where I'd left him, staring numbly at his comrade's body. I stepped over it, gun shaking at my side.

"Did you let them in?"

Ketar backed up, raising his hands. "Sir, I—"

"That was a yes or no question, Lieutenant."

"They lost their families at the ceremony!" he shouted.

"DID *YOU* LET THEM IN?!"

Ketar's back was to the wall. "*Yes!* Yes, I let them in! I'm sorry! *Sir, I'm sorry!*"

With a snarl, I grabbed his coat and pulled him inches from my face. His eyes widened and his mouth contorted into a scream. But before he could make a sound, his head erupted. Chunks of bloody brain matter painted the hall.

I released Ketar and returned to Yahweh's room, kneeling at his side. He was face-down and static. I reached toward him with a shaking hand, afraid to see the damage. But then he coughed.

I rolled him over and put a hand over my mouth. His face was unrecognizable, swollen and battered. Yahweh's nose was crushed, and both of his ears were bleeding. His eyes were welted shut by massive bruising, and many of his fingers were broken, pointing in impossible directions.

Nausea exploded up my throat, but I staved it back.

"Kid," I whispered. "Can you hear me?"

He didn't respond and only struggled to breathe. Each breath was a haggard, wet gasp. His head rolled to the side, resting against my knee.

"Leid!" I screamed to the vacant hall, hoping that she'd somehow hear me. *"Leid, Leid, LEID!"*

Coming to my senses, I reached for the radio on the dead enforcer's belt. "Eroqam Communications, come in. This is Regent

Qaira Eltruan, requesting *immediate* medical support in the Commons, room 24E."

"We are contacting Eroqam Medical Facility, sir. Stand by."

Leid appeared in the doorway, looking around the room and then out into the hall. Her face was blank with surprise, like she couldn't believe what she was seeing. Her gaze stopped on the corpse at her feet. "What happened?"

"What does it look like?!" I exclaimed. "You need to help him! He's dying!"

Leid knelt beside me, gently placing her hands on Yahweh's chest. "A few of his ribs are broken. I can feel them rattling." She leaned down and put an ear over his mouth, dread filling up her eyes when she heard the gurgling. "He has massive internal bleeding. He's drowning in his own blood."

"Eroqam, I need that medical support *yesterday!*"

"A team has just been dispatched and is on the way, sir."

I tossed the radio on the bed as Leid rolled Yahweh onto his side. "That should help him breathe easier," she said.

I paced in front of them, muttering obscenities.

"Qaira, I don't think there's anything we can do. There's too much trauma. This is really, really bad."

"You have to fix him," I ordered through my teeth.

"How? I can't—"

"FIX HIM!"

Leid jumped, looking up at me with a desperate wince. Then, her face calmed with revelation. "Give me a pen."

I had no idea why she wanted a pen, but I slipped one from my breast pocket and Leid snatched it from my hand. She disassembled it, all the way down to the hollow tube. And then to my horror, she plunged it into Yahweh's neck, right between his clavicles.

Blood spurted out of it, splashing all over her dress. The kid's chest heaved and he gasped for air.

As I stood there, stunned, she reached for me again. "I need another pen."

I cringed. "What are you going to do with—"

191

"Qaira, no time. You wanted me to help so I'm helping. Now give me another fucking pen, *please*."

Reluctantly, I handed her another. This time she plunged it into his back, between his shoulder blades. More blood, but Yahweh's breathing stabilized despite the quickly expanding pool of blood beneath him.

"Is... is he okay?" I stammered.

"He can breathe, but now he's bleeding to death."

"Where the fuck is that medical team?!" I screamed at no one.

"Yahweh will need a transfusion."

"What, blood? We don't have any other angels to donate!"

Leid said nothing, staring sadly at the boy. I sank to his bed, holding my face.

"I have to tell Raith. He's the only one who can save him."

"No," she snapped. "You're not telling him anything."

"But how else are we supposed to—?"

"Get to the Communications room and jam Crylle lines. Send for that other physician, Namah Ipsin. Tell him to bring lots and lots of Archaean blood."

I bolted from the room, sprinting through the Commons. I was thankful that Leid had a plan, because if Yahweh Telei died, everything was over. I burst through the Northern Wing, feet pounding across the empty hall—;

And then I realized that I had never told her Namah's full name.

XXI
BLOOD TIES

NAMAH FILLED A SYRINGE WITH PAIN medication, glancing at Yahweh laid out on the hospital bed. I'd expected the angel doctor to be horrified by the sight of him, but he didn't even bat an eye. As he administered the syringe into the IV, he shot me a disdainful look. It was the most expression that I'd seen on him all morning.

"How skilled are your surgeons?" he asked. "I'm going to have to get inside and stop the bleeding soon."

"I don't know. I'm not a surgeon so I can't make a comparison."

Namah didn't respond, watching Yahweh stir. The kid was pale(r) and his face was still lumpy, but at least the staff had cleaned up all the blood. "Regent, I'm going to do everything that I can for him, but I'd like you to know that there's a very good chance he won't survive this."

I glanced at my feet, saying nothing.

"How sad you look," he said, a little surprised. "I don't understand why. Yahweh Telei is the son of your arch enemy. He's just another *white*, isn't he?"

My jaw clenched. "Keep talking and you'll be lying right next to him."

"Did you do it?"

"Of course not."

Namah smiled, thinly. "Then I'll consider your threat empty."

Wow, this guy had a lot of nerve. Maybe I should have told him what I'd done to Yahweh's assaulters. But that would be gloating, and killing my own men wasn't something to gloat about.

"Let's talk about the problem," he began, taking a seat in a chair across the room. He was looking through a collection of files that one of our doctors had given him. "All the blood I've brought doesn't match Yahweh's type."

"Meaning?"

"I can't use any of it for a transfusion. It will induce an immune response that'll kill him."

"You brought several types with you. *None* of them match his?"

"His type is rare. Only two percent of us carry it. And I'm sure the number is smaller now that there are hardly any of us left." Another thin smile. Dr. Ipsin's jabs were calculated.

"What about his family? They'd have the same blood as him, right?"

"Not necessarily, and Commander Raith isn't—"

"I know."

Namah arched his brows. "He told you?"

"He never stops talking."

The angel physician glanced at Yahweh. "Interesting. His biological father is a general. Sending for him would alert Lucifer, and I'm sure you don't want that."

"Siblings?"

Namah hesitated. "His brother is no longer with us. At this point I can only make Yahweh comfortable."

I hung my head. "Then go ahead and tell Lucifer that—"

"No," said a voice from the door. *Leid.* "There's another way."

"I told you not to come here," I whispered, glancing at Namah.

Neither of them looked at me. They were too busy looking at each other. After what seemed like eternity, the angel said, "Suddenly everything makes sense. I wasn't aware that the Court of Enigmus held stock in The Atrium. I'm sure Lucifer would find that *very* fascinating."

Leid smiled. "Lucifer Raith won't find out, if you value your head."

Namah crossed his arms. "How is Ixiah?"

"Can't say. You'd have to ask his noble." Before this confusing exchange could continue, Leid said, "Test Yahweh's blood against Qaira's."

The angel tilted his head. "You want me to run a cross match between an Archaean and Nehelian? Must I explain immunology to *you*, too?"

"Nehelian and Archaean genomes differ by one percent. Nehelian blood contains a mutagen factor that might be undetectable during a transfusion."

"… And you know that how?"

"Because I'm a scholar."

Meanwhile I just sat there, blinking at them.

"Ah, I forgot all about Vel'Haru arrogance."

"Test the blood."

Namah pricked my finger, collecting several droplets of blood into a tiny vial. Without another word, he vacated the room.

"You two know each other," I said.

"Not really. He knows another scholar. I know *of* him, and he of me."

I frowned. "If the Court of Enigmus is so friendly with the angels, why did they send you to help us fight them?"

"Not all of us are friendly with the angels. It's hard to explain, but we uphold the discipline of neutral conduct. Our feelings are removed from our jobs."

"Are they?" I asked, and she looked at me knowingly.

Then, she smiled. "How are you feeling? You look tired."

Boy, was that an understatement. My exhausted gaze settled on Yahweh's vital machine. Judging by the readings, his pulse was getting weaker by the minute. The repetitive *beep beep beep* and flashing lights hypnotized me, and it was a long time before I said, "I'm fine."

Which was a lie, considering it was five in the morning and I hadn't gotten *any* sleep. In an hour and a half I was expected to meet with the Board of Commerce.

"I'm going to get some coffee," Leid announced, heading for the door. "Would you like any?"

"Yeah, thanks."

Right before she left, I grabbed her arm. She froze.

"How do you know about our genome?" I asked.

"I've been doing a lot of reading, if you haven't noticed."

I had. There was always a science periodical at the dinner table with her.

"Scholars are scientists. Many of us have fields in which we specialize."

"I thought you were a war tactician."

"I am, but my scientific field is biochemistry. Coffee, remember?"

I let go of her, and Leid disappeared into the hall.

… A biochemist war tactician. Fun.

No longer able to keep my eyes open, I closed them and reclined in the chair. I must have fallen asleep for a second, because the next thing I knew Namah was exclaiming, *"I don't believe this!"*

Startled, I nearly fell out of my seat. "W-What?"

He held the report up to my face, pointing at it. "You're a match!"

Namah almost sounded angry.

Suddenly, a white cup floated in front of my face. Leid was holding the steaming coffee over my head and I took it, nodding thanks.

Namah shook the report at Leid. "How is this possible?"

"Qaira's blood is composed of the same percentage of formed elements, plasma and serum," she explained, not needing a recap of the events in her absence. "The only difference between them is their antibodies. Nehelians don't have any."

He blinked. "No antibodies? How do they fight disease?"

"They have antibodies, but their conformation is alien. Nehelian antibodies aren't as specific, either. Their self-recognition is determined by factors other than cell wall antigens."

196

I had completely zoned out, allowing them to have their hardcore scientific discussion in private.

Namah glanced at the report again, brows furrowing. "Well, it did something to Yahweh's blood."

"What do you mean?"

"Yahweh's antibody concentration doubled after I mixed their blood."

"No immune response?"

"No, just more antibodies. None of them attacked."

Leid tapped a finger against her chin. "May I see your report?"

He gave it to her. After reading it over, Leid shook her head. "I don't know why that happened. Nonetheless it might *help* Yahweh, so let's proceed."

Namah retreated to his medical supply bag, retrieving a syringe and two large canisters. "Please roll up your sleeve, Regent. I'll need at least two liters."

Two liters. I should have eaten something.

The angel doctor hesitated as he saw my track marks. "How long has it been since you used?"

My lip curled. "What business is that of yours?"

"Your blood is going into Yahweh. Mixing surgical anesthesia with malay could be deadly."

"I've been sober for two months."

"Congratulations," Namah muttered, slipping the needle into my arm.

***

Leid drove me to Parliament because I could barely see straight after donating all that blood. She kept asking if I was sure that I wanted to go to work, but I had too many meetings to stay home. There was only one Regent now.

Then she'd offered to take over my duties for the day, but I wanted her to stay at the medical facility in case something happened.

Walking in a zig-zag to my office, I was expecting half a dozen voicemails, piles of past-due paperwork, and perhaps several disapproving glances from my secretaries who were waiting on me. But those expectations faded when I saw my brother standing right outside my door, arms crossed.

I froze halfway in the hall. He glared at me.

"You kill *three* of our men?" demanded Ara.

I sighed, pushing by him to unlock the door. "They almost killed my hostage."

"We kill angels all the time. You chose an angel over three of your own?"

"Ara, enough. I'm not feeling well."

"I don't fucking care. Do you have any idea how this looks?"

"Close the door."

He stepped inside, doing as I instructed.

"How *does* it look?" I said. "That kid is vital for our project and your men risked everything for a little revenge."

"But did you really have to kill them?"

No, I didn't really have to kill them, but seeing Yahweh on the floor like that had sparked something in me that I wasn't able to describe. Ara wouldn't understand. "They acted against my orders. I didn't have a choice. I've killed many, *many* people who have gotten in my way; this isn't any different, Ara."

"This *is* different, Qaira," Ara said with narrowed eyes, leaning over my desk. "That attack at the ceremony has gotten everyone riled. When word gets out that you killed three enforcers to save a little angel boy, it will cause an outrage. You could lose all credibility!"

"You're the Commandant now. Cover it up."

"The soldiers already know. I can't cover that up; you left their bodies in the Commons for everyone to see!"

I looked away, too tired to talk anymore. "Whatever. I have to get to work."

He ignored my want of silence. "All three of those men lost their families in the attack. The soldier whose head you exploded all over the Commons lost is wife and son."

"And you lost Ceram," I said. "But you weren't there with them, beating a helpless kid to death in some pointless form of absolution. We will have our revenge, but not like this. If Yahweh dies, we have no chance of exterminating the angels."

Ara's face changed. "I've heard rumors of you visiting that kid every day for hours. That true?"

"What I do is none of your business."

"So it *is* true. You like that white kid. You killed our men out of sentiment."

I slammed my fist on the desk, snarling. "Get out of my office, Ara, before I *throw* you out!"

Surprisingly, Ara didn't even flinch. Instead he smiled. "You really think you can?"

His challenge might have been amusing, had I not donated nearly half my blood supply an hour ago. But it was then when I noticed the state of decline Ara was in; his pale skin, blood shot eyes framed by dark bags, and when he got close enough I caught the faint aroma of stale booze and body odor. Ceram's death had destroyed him.

"You look like shit," I said. "Cool it with the drinking. You're acting insane."

"I'm acting like you."

"I don't waste my money on cheap whores and liquor every night. What would Ceram think if she saw you now?"

And that had done it. My brother lunged across the desk and punched me in the face. It came as a surprise, even more so as my chair flew backward with me in it, and I slammed my head on the window sill.

"Don't try to change the subject, you fucking white sympathizer!" he screamed.

I stumbled to my feet, throwing the chair aside. Blood trickled down the corner of my mouth and I wiped it away. "You *fucking—*"

Ara grabbed my desk lamp and swung it at me. I ducked, kicking the desk outward and it slammed him in the groin. He fell forward and I grabbed his collar, tossing him sideways. He slid across my desk and hit the floor next to Leid's armchair.

We became entwined like a ball, rolling along the floor exchanging punches. I snuck my knee in between us and heaved him over me. Ara was sent head first into the wall. He stayed down.

I sat up with a wince, finding my brother crumpled in the corner. He lay on his side holding his face, *sobbing*.

My anger faded. "Ara?"

"She's gone!" he cried. *"But I still see her everywhere! I can't sleep because I relive that night in my dreams! I... I don't know if I can live without her!"*

I glanced at the door. A group of personnel had gathered around the window, watching us with looks of terrified awe. They dispersed the moment I spotted them.

"Ara, stop crying."

He didn't, curling tighter in the corner.

I leaned against the armchair, watching my brother fall apart. It took me back to the night of my father's death. "It's supposed to feel like this," I said. "It gets better."

"How would you know?" he exclaimed. "You've never lost someone who—" His mouth stopped abruptly, revelation filling up his eyes. Ara looked at the ground, ashamed. "Oh."

Even though that had hurt, it stopped his crying.

Silence. We just sat there.

"I don't even remember our mother," Ara whispered, wiping his eyes.

I didn't respond.

"Do you?" he asked.

"A little," I mumbled. "Bits and pieces."

".. Do you remember doing it?"

I shook my head, but that was a lie. It was still as clear as yesterday. "You need to stop drinking and get back to your routine. It's the only path to recovery."

Ara looked at the ground again. "I didn't mean to call you a white sympathizer."

"I know."

My office was trashed. Files scattered everywhere, a tipped cabinet, and my desk chair was upside down with a wheel spinning. Both of our noses were bleeding and I grabbed a box of tissues that had fallen off my desk. I handed one to him.

As we wiped our noses, we began to laugh. This wasn't the first time that we'd scrapped. Probably wasn't the last, either. "Remember when I held you down in the yard at school and shoved dirt in your mouth?"

"Yes," he said. "I came home and threw a door handle at your head."

"How did you get that door handle?"

"You locked me out of my room and I pulled it off trying to break in."

"Oh, yeah."

"I missed you and made a hole in the wall. Dad was pissed."

"That was the first time he swore at us."

"He called us shit birds."

We laughed again.

I glanced at my watch. "Fuck."

"What?"

"The Board of Commerce will be here in fifteen minutes. Help me clean up, and *fast*."

XXII
CLARITY

THE SURGERY WAS A SUCCESS.

Namah, Leid, along with a team of six Nehelian surgeons managed to stop the internal bleeding, and Yahweh was announced stable after an eight hour procedure. He was moved out of the critical care ward and to the recovery ward, and although he was still unconscious, I was told that he would recover very quickly. Without me, Yahweh would have died from blood loss during the surgery.

I had saved the life of an Archaean by giving him half of my blood. Never saw that one coming.

I never saw *any* of this coming, actually. What would my year-ago self think if someone told him that his first serious relationship would be with an alien librarian who could beat him in an arm wrestle, and a favorite past time would become playing chess with an endearing angel kid?

Leid had fallen asleep on me half an hour ago. She had been sitting on my lap explaining everything that had happened while I was at work, but she—like me—hadn't gotten any sleep in over twenty-four hours. It wasn't long before she'd cozied up on my chest and dozed off. My arm was going numb, but I let her sleep. One of us had to, at least.

I waited for Namah to return with an update, Leid's shallow breaths grazing my ear.

After several minutes the angel physician returned, glancing over Yahweh's chart. He noticed us sitting there and gave me an awkward look. "Still stable. His pulse is getting stronger and I predict he'll wake up sometime tomorrow. You might as well go home."

"In a little while," I said.

Nodding, Namah sat in the chair on the other side of Yahweh's bed. He looked tired, too. There was a moment of silence as he watched Leid sleep, before he said, "She seems to like you."

"Yeah," I said, resisting a shrug.

"Yahweh seems to like you as well. I'm still trying to understand the appeal."

I gave him an unamused look, but Namah was smiling.

"You called Leid something earlier today," I began, and he tilted his head. "Something other than a scholar."

"Vel'Haru?"

"Yeah. What is that?"

"That's the name of their race. They call themselves scholars to try to cover up their stained reputation. Scholar is just a title."

"Stained reputation?" I whispered, fearing she might hear us.

"We aren't supposed to talk about it. Let's just say that their previous endeavors weren't quite as diplomatic."

"What's their purpose? Leid said it was to learn of the Multiverse."

"That's kind of true, but that's more of an umbrella reasoning. They stake claim in worlds that could benefit their own. They offer their services in exchange for things they need."

"What kind of things?"

"Food, drink, a lot of chemical substances—depending on the world and how skilled its inhabitants are at making them— literature, fossil resources, stuff like that. What did your scholar ask for?"

"I don't know. Her deal was with the Eye of Akul, and they're dead."

"Well I'd be careful, considering she's taken a fancy to you."

My stare hardened. "Meaning?"

"You might be the bargaining chip."

I didn't reply, confused.

"Yahweh's brother isn't with us anymore because he was taken by one of them five hundred years ago, just a little while before Felor collapsed. The scholar who was contracted to help our leaders negotiated for the general's oldest son."

"What did he do with him?"

"Turned him, made him into a slave."

"Turned?"

Namah smiled. "The Vel'Haru have their nobles and then they have their slaves, which they call guardians. The nobles are true Vel'Haru, but they have the power to assimilate other races into their own. They become a weaker version of the nobles, sworn to protect and serve them until the day they die."

"What is his brother's name?"

"Ixiah Telei. His noble is Calenus Karim."

My confusion melted away. Now everything made sense. Leid didn't want me to hurt Yahweh because he was *related* to another scholar. I could only imagine how much trouble she'd get into if Ixiah found out she had imprisoned his little brother. "Is Leid a noble?"

"No."

"How do you know?"

"Because they have a certain look, and she doesn't."

"So she has a noble, too?"

"She does, yes. But if what Ixiah told me is true, her noble is dead."

Leid stirred, and our conversation ended. She didn't wake up, but that had been a reminder that talking about these things in the presence of a scholar could prove dangerous.

***

We made it home a little while later, passing on dinner because we were too tired to eat. All either of us wanted to do was sleep forever.

Once in bed, we got a second wind and had sex, but it was clumsy and rushed. Leid fell asleep on my shoulder soon after and even though I was exhausted, I just laid there and stared at the ceiling. My conversation with Namah came to mind.

He'd implied that her kind weren't what she said they were, not entirely. I didn't know how much I could trust his word, considering he was an enemy and might be trying to plant a seed of doubt. And even *if* they were barbaric monsters who used people's lives as bargaining chips, she wasn't like that. She couldn't be. I didn't know the whole picture so I wouldn't cast any judgment. Not like I was the shining paradigm of kindness anyway.

Leid slept in my room more often than not these days. We no longer tried to hide our relationship from my family and at times even slipped in public without giving it much thought. We were getting serious. I'd never been in a serious relationship until now, and I liked it. I liked being with her. More than liked. I'd never told her I loved her—I just wasn't that kind of guy—but I was starting to think that I did.

And that was a problem, because Leid wasn't here to stay. We had nine years and four months left together—maybe less than that if we won the war, and then she would leave. I would never see her again.

Kill Lucifer Raith or keep Leid Koseling.

I never thought I'd be at this crossroad.

XXIII
INFLUENCE

IT WAS ONE O'CLOCK AND I WAS SITTING WITH two representatives from the Sanctum Education Division. They were looking at me like I was the biggest asshole ever because I just told them they weren't allowed to hold their annual fundraiser. That was how most of my days were spent; people looking at me like I was an asshole. All part of the job.

"With all due respect, Regent," the one on the right began, "we've held this fundraiser every year."

"It's not a fundraiser. It's public disturbances and absolute mayhem."

Every year the universities across Sanctum held fundraising festivals, where students entertained the public with terrible theatre acts and musical performances. The problems lay with the fact that they sold alcohol at these fundraisers, which resulted in drunken fights fueled by school rivalries. Sanctum police were called down *every* time they were held.

Not to mention we had to shut down five blocks on Main Street, causing horrendous traffic and equally angry drivers who wanted to go home for the weekend. And the trash that was left all over the streets after these events made Upper Sanctum look post-apocalyptic.

"What do you want us to do?" the one on the left asked. "Our schools need money, and since you refused our tax cuts—"

"Instead of holding all your fundraisers in the same few days, why don't you arrange for an entire month of fundraising, held each weekend at Fadja Memorial Park?"

The representatives blinked at me.

"If we don't do it all at once, the event loses its momentum. People will stop coming by the second week," argued the one on the right.

"I'm not letting you do it all at once. It's a disaster every time."

"It's not a disaster! We raised three hundred thousand usos last year!"

"And we probably *spent* that much cleaning up the mess you left!"

They fell silent, knowing that when I raised my voice it was best to keep their mouths shut. My eyes wandered to the door. Where was Leid? She was better at handling this kind of shit than I was. "Four weeks of fundraising at the Memorial Park. Bring your best acts and you'll pull in a crowd. That's my *only* offer."

Thankfully, my phone rang before they could protest. "I need to take this," I lied. "I'll have the Engagements Committee contact you first thing tomorrow."

They shuffled out, crestfallen and muttering. I picked up the receiver.

"Yes?"

"Is this Regent Qaira Eltruan?"

"Well, you called his private office number so I'd hope so."

"This is Dr. Sterin Razh from Eroqam Medical Facility. I was told to call this number if there were any changes in Yahweh Telei's condition."

"Correct."

"Yahweh Telei is awake and has been asking for you."

I was already reaching for my briefcase. Luckily I didn't have any other appointments this afternoon. "Thank you. I'll be there in twenty minutes."

On cue Leid emerged through the door, a cup of coffee in each hand. I snatched one on my way out.

"Where are we going?" she asked.

"Eroqam," I called, already halfway down the hall. "The kid's awake."

***

Yahweh was seated in bed, covered in bandages. His only visible eye lit up at the sight of us. He placed his chart in his lap, and with a grimace, tucked his hands at his sides. They were covered in bandages, too.

"Hello, Qaira," he murmured, looking toward my scholar with a polite nod. "Leid."

As Dr. Razh turned to leave, I held out a business card. "Take this and contact Eroqam Communications. Tell them to notify Dr. Namah Ipsin that his patient is awake."

I sent Namah back to Crylle several days ago, since a prolonged absence would warrant suspicion. At his reluctance to leave, I promised that I'd notify him when Yahweh woke, and I always kept my promises.

Once we were alone, Leid sat on the chair beside Yahweh's bed. "How are you feeling?"

"Like excrement. How long have I been here?"

"Five days," I said.

"Your hospital food is terrible," he muttered. "I wish they'd given me a feeding tube." When neither of us commented, Yahweh looked at Leid. "Can Qaira and I have a moment alone? If you don't mind, that is?"

"Certainly," she said. "I'll get some coffee. Qaira, would you like any?"

"Any more coffee and I'll have a seizure."

"I'd like some coffee," said the kid.

Leid frowned. "You of all people should know that mixing stimulants with your regimen of medications could be harmful."

"Actually, it would counteract the sedatives they keep forcing me to take."

Leid shook her head and vacated the room. I watched her leave, smirking.

Neither of us said a thing at first, and I watched the compressor in the vitals machine rise and fall with a steady *hiss*. I'd never liked hospitals, and judging by Yahweh's fidgeting, neither did he. Ironically enough.

"They came after dinner," he whispered. "At first I thought it was the guard returning to collect my tray, but then I saw that there were two of them."

My attention left the vitals machine and rested on him as he traced the edges of the chart with a finger. "I tried to be like you and fight back. Didn't work out so well."

"You're not even half my size. Why would you ever want to be like me?"

He gave me a half-smile. "The strength and aggression you carry is desirable to weaklings like me. We all want to be alpha males."

"Coming from an angel, that's surprising."

"Is it? It's the nature of dominance."

"You don't want to be like me, Yahweh."

"Why not?"

"Because you aren't me. Your strength lies in your intelligence. It's clear that your brain is a far more dangerous weapon than any punch I could ever throw."

"Yet I'm sitting in a hospital bed with a trillion broken bones."

"That was out of your control."

"What happened to those soldiers?"

"They're dead."

"... You killed them?"

I looked away, saying nothing.

"I'm sure that sat well with your brother."

"I handled it."

"Thank you, nonetheless."

Silence, again. This was getting kind of awkward.

"What are you going to do about the simulator construction?" asked the kid. "Judging from my chart, I won't be out of here for at least another week."

"Leid's been picking up your slack. We've already finished the prototype and it'll be tested tomorrow."

Yahweh tilted his head. I noticed Archaeans made that gesture often. "I thought Leid wasn't allowed to help in that fashion?"

"Leid also wasn't allowed to endanger the family member of another scholar, so that ship has sailed."

He looked down, ashamedly. "You know about Ixiah."

"Namah told me."

"I didn't tell you because it wouldn't have helped my situation any. It was obvious that you knew nothing of the Court of Enigmus."

"I still don't, really."

"That's probably for the best."

I glanced at my watch. It was two thirty. Leid and I still had to grab an early dinner because we were spending all night at the research lab. "Times up. Namah will be in here shortly to keep you company. Welcome back, kid. I'm glad you're not dead."

I was on my way out when he said, "I'd like to play chess with you again."

"I'll bring it tomorrow."

He smiled, but it was sad. "I'm sorry that we had to meet under these circumstances, Qaira."

"Yeah? Why's that?"

"I think we could have been friends."

I lingered in the doorway, looking out into the hall. All this touchy-feely crap was making me uncomfortable. But I was happy to see that he wasn't angry anymore. The price of winning back his affection had been two liters of blood. "And I'm sorry that I have to kill your father. Really, I am."

"I know."

With a nod in goodbye, I left the room.

XXIV
FLIGHT TRAINING

FOR THE FIFTEENTH TIME TODAY, I WATCHED with tribulation as my simulated craft hit the corner of a building and went down in flames. This was so hopeless.

"YOU ARE DEAD," mocked the simulator, the words displayed in big white text across the screen.

My first impulse was to punch it, but then I remembered how long it had taken to build the simulator. Instead I ripped the headset off and stormed out of the pod. Ara was snickering and Leid was trying not to smile.

"I think it's broken," I said.

"Or you suck," said Ara.

"Says the twat who doesn't even know how to fly our *own* crafts."

"Boys, please," sighed Leid.

"Tell Ara to wipe that stupid smile off his face."

"Well it wouldn't be as funny if you didn't have a massive tantrum every time you crashed."

"You're supposed to be leading Drill in half an hour. Shouldn't you be on your way to the Commons?"

"Thanks for the advice, but I'm the Commandant. I'll go when I'm ready."

"*I'm* the Regent, and I'm ordering you to go now."

Ara glared at me. Then he stalked off, muttering under his breath.

Leid watched his dramatic exit. "Ladies and gentlemen, your world leaders."

I shot her an unamused look and headed back inside the pod. She grabbed my arm, stopping me.

"No," she said. "We need to check on how the other pilots are faring."

Sulking, I followed her into the inner lab.

Over the past few days, we'd produced a dozen simulators that were being tested by selected pilots. They underwent rigorous training from six to ten, while our engineers continued to work on the real thing. So far we'd made fifty crafts. Two hundred more to go.

"I hope they're faring better than me."

"Cheer up, will you? We still have a ton of time to prepare. Just because you weren't amazing at your first go of it doesn't mean you should spend the rest of the day moping around."

My eyes trailed to her lack of skirt. "Well how about we head to the conference room for a few minutes and you can help replenish my self-esteem by screaming out what an amazing fuck I am?"

"… You're unbelievable."

I laughed.

The inner lab was crowded with engineers, craft shell parts and simulators. Within the simulation pods, pilots screamed obscenities as the YOU ARE DEAD announcement flashed across their screens. Their profanities were louder than the drills and hydraulic lifts combined. Flight training wasn't going so well for them either.

Lakash emerged from a pod in the center aisle, red-faced and furious. "Sir, if *that* is how those crafts fly," he pointed viciously at the YOU ARE DEAD message on his screen, "then we are monumentally fucked. We might as well surrender now."

I couldn't stop the grin that spread across my lips. I was kind of happy to know that I wasn't the only one sucking. Lakash was our best pilot, too. "Keep at it, Lieutenant."

"The steer is too sensitive. If I so much as *sneeze* on it, my craft barrels into a bridge!"

Laugher crept up my throat, but I choked it down. "I don't want to hear your complaints. Man up and get the fuck back into that pod. I want you doing figure-eights by next week, got it?"

"Sir," he mumbled, retreating into the simulator with a hopeless look on his face.

Leid was on the other side of the lab, at Station Four, talking to the group of engineers constructing the *Cloak*. The cloak was the craft that looked identical to the one I'd brought in after the attack on Eroqam. The other crafts were designed as military upgrades, yet clearly distinguishable between the enemy vessels.

The Cloak's purpose was to get a team past enemy lines and onto the Archaean base ship. When that time came, I would be its pilot. The Eye of Akul weren't around to tell me that I couldn't risk my life on the front lines anymore. I had made a promise to Sanctum and its people that I would fight, and like I'd said before, I always kept my promises. Sanctum's Savior wouldn't sit behind a desk and let his men die for him.

As the engineers dispersed, Leid sat at the table and watched them work. I sat beside her. "We're not going to be ready for at least another two months," I said, grimly. "And we're already a month behind schedule. My pilots are going to kill themselves if they're given any less time."

"Patience is a virtue, Qaira. Commander Raith isn't going anywhere, so there's no rush."

"And what happens after we win?" I asked.

"...A party? Lots of wine?"

"No, I mean what happens between us?"

Leid looked at me, conflicted. After a moment of silence she glanced at her lap. "I don't know."

"You're not actually planning to leave, are you? After everything that's happened?"

Her gaze stayed on her lap.

"Are you?"

"I've helped dozens of people with their wars, Qaira," she whispered. "I stood by their sides for years and years. Sometimes bonds were formed. It broke my heart to leave, but I always had to."

My heart sank into my stomach. A part of me always knew she'd leave, but lately I had entertained the fantasy that she would quit her job and stay here. Yet it wasn't the knowledge of her leaving that had stung. It was her explanation for it.

"Is that all I am to you? Just another bond to be broken?"

"That isn't what I meant."

"How many others have there been?"

"Others?"

"How many poor idiots like me have you seduced and then dumped after your job was done?"

Leid's eyes narrowed. "That's enough."

"No, it's *not* enough," I said, getting to my feet. "I realize now that I'm just your plaything—a stiff dick to pass the time."

All she did was glare at me.

I walked out of the inner lab and headed for the simulator. Lakash was on his way to Drill.

"Have fun, sir," he said with a crooked grin.

"Believe me, *I will*," I muttered, stepping inside.

'WELCOME TO FLIGHT SIMULATOR Z09. PLEASE WAIT FOR THE GREEN LIGHT ABOVE THE MONITOR TO PROCEED.'

***

Yahweh was still awake when I visited his hospital room, even though it was after midnight. I was planning on tip-toeing in and dropping off some clothes for his release tomorrow, but he got excited at the sight of me and I knew I'd have to stay a while to chat. That was fine, since as of earlier tonight I was avoiding Leid and the dreaded *talk* we would inevitably have later.

"Why don't you take me now?" he asked, hope glittering his eyes. Some of the bandages had come off, though the one around his nose was still on. They'd had to completely reconstruct it.

"I can't," I said. "You haven't had your exit examination."

He sighed. "I hate this place."

"It's almost over. Here are your clothes." I dropped the bag next to his bed and glanced around. "Where's Dr. Ipsin?"

"He's working on my discharge papers."

I took a seat, waiting for him.

Yahweh's face was still riddled with bruises, but there was hardly any swelling and he looked semi-normal. He'd been in Eroqam Medical Facility for nearly three weeks, and I could tell he was itching to escape. I could only imagine how lying in bed all day could drive a person nuts. Especially him, since he was such a twitchy kid.

Yahweh had strange organizational habits, too. One night when I'd delivered his dinner, I found him arranging his books by alphabetical order, all of his clothes by color, and all of his furniture by size and functionality.

"Qaira?"

"Yes?"

"Could you please move my lamp away from the window?" he asked.

I blinked, following his hand as he pointed at it. "Why?"

"It's driving me insane. Placing a lamp next to a window; what a redundant act."

"So what? You're not even using it."

"*Please*? I'd do it myself but I can't leave this bed without Namah chewing me out."

Shaking my head, I walked across the room, unplugged the stupid lamp and set it on the desk beside him. He sighed with relief, like I'd just snatched him from a pit of poisonous snakes.

"Thank you."

"You're so weird."

"There's nothing weird about the adulation of efficiency."

"There's definitely something weird about a kid your age saying *adulation*."

Yahweh grinned, and so did I.

Namah entered then, holding a stack of files. He nodded in greeting and handed Yahweh his discharge papers. "Everything looks great so far. After your final examination tomorrow, you should be good to go."

Yahweh hugged his papers like they were a teddy bear.

I headed for the door. "Namah, a word?"

He followed me into the hall. It was dim and quiet, as it was well after visiting hours. "Listen," I began, "I'm going to give you the benefit of the doubt and allow you to return to Crylle, no strings attached."

"Don't worry," he said. "I won't be telling anyone what happened."

I hesitated, caught off guard by his quick compliance. "Can I ask why?"

"I haven't said anything yet, have I? Your scholar made the repercussions very clear."

"I see."

"That's not all," he sighed. "I'll admit that in the time I've spent with you, I know you aren't the homicidal maniac my people think you are. In fact I have come to respect the Nehel and wish them well."

I said nothing, stunned.

"I've been a doctor for two centuries," he continued, "and am condemned to neutral ground by default. You are our enemy, but we are also your enemy. You kill us, but we kill you. We showed up here and demanded to move in, and although I think there are much better methods of resolution to this conflict than war, it isn't my place to say anything because I'm not a soldier, or a leader, or anything like that.

"And whether you deny it or not, I know you care about Yahweh. The only thing that upsets me is the fact that I've been condemned to working in that *hole* because you kidnapped the only doctor who'd volunteered for Crylle."

"Sorry."

Namah held out his hand. "Whatever the future may bring," he said, "it was an honor meeting you, Regent."

I found myself shaking it. Our grip was firm, our eyes locked.

"Thank you for your cooperation, Dr. Ipsin."

After a moment of awkward silence we departed in opposite directions; neither of us looked back.

***

I returned home at two in the morning, now on the fence about sleeping at all. Either way I was going to be exhausted. Might as well get some work done before that happened.

I took a detour to Yahweh's room, making sure Ara's men had cleaned it up like I'd ordered. It was tidy, but they had stacked his torn, bloody books on his desk—probably unsure of whether to discard them or not. The sight took me back to the night of his attack, and I re-envisioned the scene with growing trepidation.

I couldn't ensure Yahweh's safety here any longer. My trust in our military was waning as their hatred for the angels rose. A year ago I would have loved to see that, but now... not so much. As Sanctum's want of war intensified, Yahweh's fate dangled on a thread.

Reaching for my radio, I pressed the receiver button and dialed Ara's frequency. "Are you awake?"

"Yeah, what is it?"

"... Why aren't you asleep?"

"You called me to ask why I'm not asleep?"

"Come down to the Commons; bring a few guards."

"Why?"

"I need to move some stuff."

"Move what?"

I wanted to tell him face to face. He wasn't going to like my idea. "Just get down here and see for yourself."

"... Fine."

XXV
SIMPLE CHARITIES

I TOOK AN EARLY LUNCH SO I COULD drive to Eroqam Medical Facility for Yahweh's discharge. To my dismay, Leid tagged along even though I'd wanted her to stay in my office in case it blew up or something.

Now I had to deal with midday traffic to a soundtrack of a blaring orchestra that *literally* shook the windows. For someone who supposedly had exceptional hearing, Leid listened to music like she was deaf.

Surprisingly our argument in the research lab yesterday never came up. Maybe she didn't want to talk about it, either. I felt bad for what I'd said, especially since she had been so honest with me.

I saw her lips moving in the corner of my eye. "What?" I shouted over wailing trumpets and crashing drums.

More lip movement.

I turned the volume down. *"What?"*

"Have you told your sister about the sudden change of plans?"

"No. I was more worried about Ara's reaction, so at least the worst is over."

"I'm surprised he put up so little of a fight."

"Me too."

"You're doing a good thing, Qaira."

I shrugged, saying nothing.

We reached the medical facility a few minutes later and I parked in the vacant lot at the west side of the building. Before I could even pull my keys from the ignition, Leid crawled into my lap and started kissing my neck.

"W-What are you—?"

Her tongue traced a warm, wet line along my jaw. My body was already responding and she reached between my legs, kneading the bulge of my crotch. I surveyed the lot with a desperate wince, making sure we were out of public sight.

This was unlike her. She was spontaneous, but never *this* spontaneous.

I pulled her hand away from my groin. She looked down at me, confused.

"You don't want to?"

"I'm trying to figure out what you're doing," I said, breathily. Even though I wanted nothing more than to fuck her senseless, the thought of our fight last night was like a mental chastity belt.

Leid understood my meaning and looked away, shame marking her face. "Qaira, please. Not again."

"Yeah, let's just keep fucking like it never happened."

"You mean more than the others," she murmured. "Is that what you want me to say? Do you want me to tell you that I'll cry for years after I leave?"

I stared at her.

"The life of a scholar is lonely and loveless," she whispered, blood tears brimming her eyes. "Can't I just enjoy being with you now, without delving into a discussion about how I'll never seen you again?"

"Do you want to stay here?"

"It doesn't matter what I want."

"Do you *want* to stay here?" I repeated, sternly.

"More than anything."

"Then what's stopping you? Tell your Court to fuck off."

She laughed, sadly. "There are rules, Qaira. I can't leave the Court of Enigmus. They'd come for me and that would place you and your world in danger."

"Can't you fight them? I've watched you lift a couch over your head."

"I might be strong compared to you, but not to my own."

"Because you're a guardian."

Leid's eyes widened. "How do you know about that?"

"Namah told me."

"Then you understand."

"I do, but I'm not going to give you up that easily."

Leid wiped her eyes and looked at the clock on the dash. "We're late."

"I can't walk into Eroqam Medical with an erection."

She arched a brow, and I grinned.

"Care to help me out? This is all your fault."

***

Almost half an hour later we barged into Yahweh's room, smoothing our hair and clothes. The kid jumped at our entrance, already clutching his bag.

"Thank goodness. I thought something terrible happened to you."

"Traffic," I said, clearing my throat. Leid and I shared a look. "You ready to go?"

"I've been ready for weeks."

I stepped aside, gesturing to the open doorway. Yahweh marched through it, smiling brightly.

When we reached Eroqam, I deliberately walked him through the Commons and the boy slowed as we approached his old room. Placing a hand on his shoulder, I gave him a gentle shove. "Keep going."

He shot me a quizzical glance over his shoulder and pressed on. Those glances continued until we reached the door to my estate. He stood back with Leid as I punched in the code.

"I don't understand," mumbled the boy.

"This is the safest it's going to get," I said as the door slid open. "Make yourself at home."

Yahweh's large, child-like eyes shined with gratitude. "I... don't know what to say."

"Don't say anything, just come inside. I should have been back at the office ten minutes ago."

Leid stayed at the door. "I'll meet you at the port, Qaira."

I waved without looking back, and the kid and I trudged up the stairs. As I led him into the dining room, past the kitchen and through the hall toward the bedrooms, Yahweh marveled at every little detail. All he'd ever seen of Eroqam was the Commons and the research lab.

With my father gone, our home had a spare room. Last night Ara and his team had helped me move Yahweh's furniture and other belongings into it.

My sister caught us on the second floor. She was clutching several bags with Opalla logos on them, dressed in a red skirt suit and black high-heels. Another long, hard day of shopping.

I couldn't be too hard on her. Tae deserved some fun after ten years of being my father's nursemaid.

"Qaira, what are you doing home?" she asked. "Did something happ—" Her mouth stopped moving when she noticed Yahweh peeking out from behind me. "... An angel."

"An angel," I repeated, amused.

"Why is there a little angel boy in our house? What have you done?" demanded Tae.

"This is Yahweh Telei," I said. "He is the only son of Commander Lucifer Raith."

Tae's eyes nearly popped out of her head.

"He's an ally."

"Hostage," Yahweh corrected me.

"What did he just say?" she asked. Tae didn't speak Archaean.

"Nothing. He's helping me with some work and will be staying in our home. It's not safe in the Commons anymore."

"... You're keeping an angel safe from harm," she summarized, incredulous. Even *she* knew that protecting an angel wasn't something I'd normally do.

"Yes."

Tae looked at the boy again. She didn't move.

I rolled my eyes. "He isn't going to bite you." And then to Yahweh, I whispered, "Say something."

"Hello," he said in Nehelian. "I am a friendly person."

224

"H-Hello," she stammered.

"Can you get him settled in? He's staying in Dad's old room. I have to get back to work before I'm impeached."

Before she could reply I crammed his bag in her hands and headed for the stairs. As I hurried down the first floor hall, I heard my sister ask:

"So, Yahweh, how old are you?"

XXVI
PROGRESS

"COME ON, COME ON!" screamed Ara. "He's two seconds behind you!"

I ignored him to my best ability, swerving around the side of a simulated high-rise. Simulated enemy crafts popped up on the screen and I fired, taking them down.

Lakash and I were facing off, our simulators side-by-side. We had practiced every day for two weeks, and although the other selected pilots were doing really well, he and I were the best. As expected.

A crowd had gathered around us—even the engineers had stopped their work to watch the match. Cheers erupted every time either of us shot down an enemy, and to be honest it was killing my concentration.

As I bit down on my lip, four enemy crafts emerged from either side of the street in a pincer-attack. I rolled mid-air, firing at two that flew in front of me.

But now Lakash had pulled ahead of me, having ignored the enemies head on and instead goaded them to take chase. They crashed into an Aero-way bridge. Show off.

'OBJECTIVE COMPLETE. TIME OF COMPLETION:
THREE MINUTES, THIRTY-FIVE SECONDS. NEW
RECORD.'

Lakash had won. As everyone celebrated his victory by patting him on the back and telling him how amazing he was, Ara stood beside my simulator, scolding me.

"You should have kept going! Why didn't you do what he did?"

"You're more upset about this than I am."

"Because I *know* you can beat him!"

"Your pilot just cleared a forty-five enemy round in under four minutes. What's there to be angry about?"

Ara fell silent, looking away sheepishly. "True."

"But," I said, loud enough to alert Lakash and the crowd, "in real life I would prefer you not to make the angels crash into our buildings. That would be expensive, not to mention dangerous."

"Of course, sir," said Lakash, grinning. "I was just showing off. Rematch?"

"No thanks. I think I'll tuck my tail between my legs and head over to the Cloak station. Good job, Lieutenant."

Yahweh and Leid were huddled around the electrical plans that were spread across the table. Neither of them had been watching the contest.

"Those simulators are an *exact* replica of our craft interiors, right?" I asked them.

Yahweh nodded. "I made sure of it. I wouldn't have your pilots getting used to something different. That would be counter-productive."

"How's the Cloak coming along?"

"All we have left to do is install the control system," said Leid. "It should be finished tomorrow night; we're just waiting for a systems engineer to hardwire it."

I nodded, looking over our nearly-finished product. They'd done an excellent job—I couldn't distinguish it from the one I'd found at Yema Theater. I ran my hand across its smooth metal surface. It felt the same, too.

This was our ticket in. Not even the whites would be able to tell it from their own.

Leid started to roll up the plans. "That's it for tonight. Qaira, are you done flight training?"

"Yeah."

"Yahweh?"

Silence. The kid was studying something on a clipboard, muttering calculations under his breath.

"Yahweh?" Leid repeated.

"Yes?"

"Are you done?"

"Oh, yes. For the most part, anyway. I think I can let the engineers finish the shifter torque. But thank goodness I found that miscalculation or else the crafts would have exploded before they'd taken off."

My eyebrows arched. "You miscalculated something?"

He pointed his pen at Leid. "She did."

"Sorry," she muttered.

"Wow, minus ten for confidence."

***

Hours later, well after midnight, Leid and I were still catching up on work. Lying across my bed on opposite ends, I reviewed the key topics for our meeting tomorrow, while Leid read another periodical about new discoveries of gene loci in water-dwelling bacteria, or something.

And she was distracting me. Lying on her stomach, each time she idly kicked her legs I caught a glimpse of the revealing black panties she wore beneath her nightgown—which was actually one of my shirts that she'd stolen. I gave up on reading, eyes glued to her ass. Leid knew exactly what she was doing and kept giving me smug little grins from over her shoulder.

She was irresistible in that way; my body still craved her. Prior to Leid, women tended to get boring after the third encounter. None of them were able to keep my interest long enough to spark a true relationship. Then again, I might have chosen the wrong women. She was exactly the opposite of my usual type, all the way down to her endearing sense of dominance.

Leid liked to lead in bed, and more often than not I let her. There was one occasion where she'd tied me down and rode me for three hours straight, being careful not to let me climax. It was the most painful and euphoric three hours of my life, and although I'd deny that it had ever happened, I'd probably do it again if she asked.

Her foot slid between my legs, pressing lightly on my groin. I was already hard, and she knew it.

"I'm going to get up there tomorrow without a clue of what to say," I said, trying to sound annoyed.

"Oh, stop. You'll be brilliant as always."

"Flattery will get you nowhere."

"Won't it?" she asked, smiling coyly.

I threw my notes aside, inviting her onto my lap. She took the invitation with a smirk, already fumbling with my belt.

***

An hour later, Leid was passed out in my bed and I still couldn't sleep. Deciding to grab a glass of water, I headed to the kitchen and found Tae and Yahweh sitting at the dining room table, chatting over tea.

"What are you doing up so late?" asked my sister.

"Funny, I was about to ask you the same thing."

"Tae and I were discussing herbal tea recipes," said Yahweh. "Some of them sound delicious."

Arching a brow, I walked into the kitchen. "Sounds like a riveting conversation. Don't let me stop you."

Yahweh was almost a part of the family. He joined us for two of our three daily meals, and was free to roam our estate during the day while I was at work. Although Tae had mentioned numerous times that it'd be nice if she had some company on her shopping endeavors, he wasn't allowed to leave without my supervision.

But Tae seemed happier with him around, and I was glad they'd hit it off so well. My sister had been very lonely since Dad died. All of her friends were married and busy starting families— no doubt that would happen to her soon as well—but in the meantime Yahweh made an excellent substitute. Likewise, the kid didn't seem so bored.

Glass of water in hand, I returned to the dining room, knocking on the back of Yahweh's seat. "Come on, it's bed time."

Yahweh glowered at me. "Stop treating me like a child."

"But you are a child."

"I'm not tired."

"You're going to be tomorrow. We have half a day of Cloak wiring ahead of us. I don't want you too tired to work."

"I'm *never* too tired to work."

"Bed time."

With a sigh, Yahweh slid from his seat. "Thank you for the tea, Tae."

My sister smiled. "Goodnight Yahweh, I'll see you at breakfast."

I walked him back to his room and he huffed the whole way down the hall. He kept insisting that I treat him like an adult, but it was hard. When we reached his door, he stopped. Just as I raised the glass of water to my lips, I heard him say:

"I don't think you're allowed to have sexual relations with your scholar."

I froze, mid-sip.

"You're having sex with Leid, aren't you?" he pressed.

"Mind your own business, white."

"Why won't you answer me?" he said, unfazed.

"Because you haven't even reached puberty yet."

Yahweh sighed, again. "I have a doctorate in medicine, electrical engineering and molecular biology. It's safe to say I've already taken sex education."

"Yeah, I'm fucking Leid, and thanks for your advice."

"Do you love her?"

I hesitated, staring at him. "What's it to you?"

"Nothing, really," Yahweh said, shrugging. "I've just seen it all before."

"Stop stalling and go to bed."

"I am a genius who is handing you your victory on a silver platter. I don't need to be told to go to bed."

"Go to bed."

"I wonder if once I reach adulthood I'll become as narrow-minded and ignorant as you."

"Good one. I'll see you tomorrow, *genius*."

As Yahweh opened the door, I remembered something I'd wanted to ask him. "Hey, what happened to your real parents?"

He paused in the doorway, partially concealed by shadows. "Pardon me?"

"Where are your parents?"

"On the Ark."

"The what?"

"Our base ship."

"No, I mean *where* are they? Aren't they concerned for your safety at all?"

Yahweh looked away, uncomfortable. "My father and I have never seen eye-to-eye. My mother is mentally ill."

"Your father's a general for Raith, right?"

"Yes, his First General. Lucifer offered to take care of me when I finished school, and my father seemed pleased to get me out of his hair. He told me it is an honor to be mentored by our leader, and I suppose it is."

"Do you love Commander Raith?"

"Very much."

Yet he was working for me with minimal reluctance. Interesting.

"Goodnight, Qaira," murmured Yahweh, slipping into his unlit room and shutting the door.

I headed down the hall, battling my conscience. The kid didn't know what I had planned for him, and now I felt guilty about it. I'd made the plan several months ago, before he'd coerced me into liking him. But it was too late. I'd come too far and there was no turning back.

Leid had said that guilt was what separates man from monster, but she was wrong.

Guilt did not distinguish whether you were a man or monster; it made you *aware* that you were a monster.

And somehow, you had to live with it.

XXVII
MONSTERS AND METHODOLOGY

"WHEN THE ARK BREACHES OUR AEROSPACE, four teams of fifty crafts will attack it from here," I pointed my laser at the west border of Upper Sanctum, "here," now the east, "here," now the north, "and on the southern border of Lower Sanctum, here. Attacking from these points simultaneously will give us the element of surprise."

I paused, allowing questions.

Uless raised his hand, like clockwork.

"Lt. Fedaz."

"What about the rest of Lower Sanctum?"

"We're trying not to take the fight to Lower Sanctum, since that's where civilian evacuations are to be held. Keep the angels *away* from there."

Garan raised his hand, also like clockwork.

"Lt. Geiss."

"Why Lower Sanctum? Shouldn't we be making it a priority to protect Upper Sanctum?"

"From an economic standpoint, yes," I said. "But assuming the angels will think that as well, Upper Sanctum is the most likely place for a first attack. I don't want any civilians caught in crossfire so we'll be taking them all to the Aeroway shores, underneath Crylle. It is unlikely that the whites will try to damage their own refugee camp."

When no one said anything else, I continued, "Sanctum Forces will be stationed along the Agora and Main Street in our outdated crafts. I want the Ark to see them first, so they'll expect run-of-the-mill artillery. Let me stress again that we are not trying to win the battle, we are trying to keep them occupied. Our objective is to get the Cloak behind enemy lines and onto the Ark without any detection.

"The Cloak will be stationed here," I said, pointing my laser at the port between Eroqam's north and west spires. "We'll look identical to the angel crafts, but I'll be relaying a signal that tells *your* crafts our location until we clear dark water. For the love of Sanctum, do *not* shoot at us." I paused. "Any more questions?"

Lakash raised his hand.

"Lt. Perma."

"What happens when the Cloak reaches the Ark?"

"I was getting to that. The Cloak will hold twelve enforcers, including myself, charged with infiltrating the Archaean base ship and executing Commander Lucifer Raith and all of his generals."

"Only twelve of us, sir?"

"If our plan goes accordingly, there won't be many angels left to defend their ship. We need to hit them hard so they'll send everything they've got. I have a feeling the whites are arrogant enough to leave their ship minimally guarded."

Lakash nodded, settling back into his seat.

Siri raised his hand.

"Last question, Lt. Samay."

"How are we getting the Ark to cross our aerospace borders?"

I smiled. "Just leave that to me. I've said my piece, and now your Commandant will give a detailed briefing of your positions around Sanctum. Ara, you're up." As he ascended the stage, I descended, giving him an encouraging squeeze on his shoulder. "Good luck."

"Thank you, Regent."

I walked up the center aisle of the conference room and exited through the back doors. I didn't need to stay to listen to Ara's briefing because we'd gone over it the night before. There were more important things to do.

Leid was in the communications room, surveying the angel's military frequencies we planned to hijack tomorrow. Yahweh had given us a list that he'd memorized, and now Sanctum IS was confirming their authenticity.

"All of them look good," she said when I walked in.

"What about Sanctum PB?"

"Public broadcast is a go. Our evacuation message will be up and running at noon tomorrow."

"Have you heard about the final flight diagnostics from Yahweh?"

"No, not yet."

"Are you done here?"

"Pretty much."

"Then let's go."

***

When we reached the lab, Yahweh met us with an irritated frown.

"What is it?" I asked. I had to shout because the room was filled with the sound of drills as final touches were being put on a line of crafts.

"Nothing," he grumbled. "One of the engines won't start."

"That's not nothing," I said. "We need every single one of those jets."

"It's fine," he interjected, looking even more irritated. "Your engineers are working on it now. It wasn't an error on my part, which means it's fixable. Probably a wiring issue."

The defective craft wasn't hard to spot. It had over thirty engineers buzzing around it, making hand gestures and pointing to a cluster of exposed cables. And then I noticed Leid had left my side and was making her way over there, finger tapping her chin.

She spoke to the engineers, and they to her. Leid glanced at the cables and then got on her knees, crawling underneath the craft. She dug through the wires and then raised her thumb to the engineers, telling them to try again.

"Oh for goodness sake," muttered Yahweh.

The engine started. Everyone clapped. Leid curtseyed, her pretty blue dress stained with oil.

"I don't even know why I'm still here," sighed the kid.

I patted him on the shoulder. "Don't be too hard on yourself. No one expects you to compete with a scholar."

Yahweh crossed his arms. "Scholar my left foot."

All I did was scoff.

Leid returned, trying to wipe the oil off her dress to no avail. "Was that the only problem?"

"Yes," he huffed.

Leid blinked. "Is there something wrong?"

"He's upset that you're smarter than him," I teased.

"I am not!"

She tugged on my arm. "Let's go. We need our rest, and so does Yahweh. We have a big day ahead of us."

***

"You should talk to your sister," murmured Leid, dipping her pen into the ink jar. "She seems frightened."

I didn't provide a response, wincing as the pen scraped across my arm. Rarely did I care about a fill, but tomorrow every soldier would be wearing their ink. I wasn't one for superstition, yet I didn't want to take any chances. Not tomorrow.

"Qaira, are you listening?"

"Yes, fine."

I didn't know what I'd say to Tae. She was frightened for a good reason.

"You seem awfully calm about everything," she noted.

"Calm?"

No response. The ink pen dug deeper into my skin, and I hissed. After another minute I turned to look at her. She was frowning, eyes on her art.

"What's wrong?"

"Nothing. Hold still, I'm almost done."

"You never wear a face like that for nothing."

Leid didn't answer me. I gave up and lay back down. I'd almost forgotten the conversation entirely when she said, "I don't think you should go on the Cloak."

"Why not?"

"You're the Regent."

"You sound like the Eye of Akul. I need to be there when Lucifer Raith is executed. I need to be the one who does it."

"So you'd place your personal vendetta over the safety of your own people?"

"Hey," I warned, "I'm doing this for Sanctum. I need to be there to make sure everything goes according to plan. I don't trust my men to it. As a matter of fact, I'm placing the lives of my people before my own."

"And what if you die?" she asked, her voice almost a whisper.

"Ara and I have already discussed that. If anything happens to me, he'll be Regent in my place."

"Your brother is not ready to be Regent. He's barely grasped being Commandant."

"Leid, *why* are you doing this now? An hour ago you were all for my plan. What changed?"

And then I saw the look in her eyes, the frustration on my face receding. "You won't lose me. I promise."

"You can't promise something like that," she said, glancing away. "You can't possibly know if—"

"I love you."

Leid stared at me, abashed. I'd never said that to anyone—not even my own family—and was certain she'd never expected to hear it.

As the seconds ticked away, I rolled my eyes. "Don't leave me hanging here."

"I love you, too."

"I won't die, okay?"

Again, her eyes left mine.

"Okay?" I repeated.

"Okay."

Then we shared an awkward moment of silence. Leid capped the pen and crossed her legs as I settled back onto the bed.

"Go and talk to your sister," she nagged, twisting the lid on the ink jar.

"Fine," I muttered, throwing on a shirt. My arms were sore, and they probably would be for several hours. "You better be here when I get back."

Leid smiled. "I will."

***

Long after everyone was asleep, I sat in the observation room of the vacant Drill arena. I wasn't tired, as always, but tonight there was a good reason. Tomorrow brought the possibility of never seeing this place again—or my family, or Sanctum. My plan was a solid one, but the chances of a loss were still pretty significant.

And even if we won, Leid would go home, and...

The door to the observation room opened. A second later, Ara joined me.

"Can't sleep either?" he asked.

I didn't respond.

"Are you going to be able to do it?"

Again, I didn't respond. Not at first. Instead I sighed and rubbed my forehead. When I closed my eyes they stung—a telltale sign that I was *exhausted*, but what Ara was alluding to was that my conscience wasn't letting me sleep. And it was true.

"I don't have a choice," I muttered. "We never had a back-up plan."

"Leid knows?"

"No."

"Qaira, if it's too morally-taxing, then I can do it for you."

"Raith has to watch *me* do it. I need him berserk enough to lose all focus."

Ara didn't say anything for a while, watching the empty arena with a troubled frown. Then he shook his head, laughing sadly. "I feel bad about doing this. Who knew the thought of killing a white would actually upset me one day?"

"Yeah," I sighed.

"And what about Leid? What will she do?"

I didn't want to think about that. There was no better way to make Raith charge us than killing his son. Taunts wouldn't bait him. Perhaps genocide in Crylle might, but that seemed like too much effort and would leave too much room for the angels to prepare. The plan from day one had been to use Yahweh to upgrade our crafts and then execute him on the televised screen, in front of his father. I wasn't that kind of man anymore, but we were in too deep. I couldn't stop everything to spare the life of an angel. Sanctum would throw me from my throne.

As for Leid—well, I would just have to deal with the fall-out later. One war at a time.

"We'll cross that bridge when we get to it," was all I said.

Ara got to his feet, placing a hand on my shoulder. "I'm going to try to get some rest. So should you."

"Maybe."

Ara vacated the observation room, and I was left to stew in my guilt. But if I sat here long enough, another idea might present itself. So far I hadn't thought of anything, though.

Exhaustion slowly crept in, smothering all the guilt and worry, dipping me in lucid dream. I imagined that I was watching Drill; shadows of men moved across the arena to the sound of faint gunfire. Red paint splattered across the walls, and I thought of how much it looked like blood—;

My eyes widened. Eureka shook me from that dream.

I had another plan.

XXVIII
THE EXECUTION

"THE EVACUATION NOTICE IS LIVE, SIR."

"Good, wait for my call and then have your teams get into position. We need an evacuation team at the Agora in ten minutes. Assemble that one first."

"Yes, Regent," said my brother, severing the line.

Lowering the radio from my mouth, I leaned against the wall and closed my eyes. A long, steady exhale of anticipation and fear deflated my chest. I'd taken a moment to walk the halls and collect my wits, pacing between the empty research lab and communications room. My suit was gone, replaced by my old enforcer uniform, military tags jingling on my neck at each step.

"Regent," announced my radio, *"civilians have started making their way to the Agora."*

"Thank you, Lt. Samay." I hung up and dialed my brother back. "Commandant, have you assembled that team?"

"Just finished, sir."

"Dispatch them to the Agora and start leading the civilians to the Aeroway."

"Sir."

Somewhere in that crowd was my sister. I had sent her away before the notice went live, instructing a few of my men to guard her personally. I wasn't sure if the angels knew about her, but Tae would be leverage if caught. Leverage we couldn't afford.

The communications room was dark and nearly empty. All but two analysts had evacuated. They'd volunteered to keep the feed rolling.

Leid sat in the center row of empty computer terminals, watching the evacuation message flash across a dozen screens at the front of the room. It was on loop, and would be for half an hour. That was how long we had to evacuate Upper Sanctum.

"How long?" she asked, the screens' luminescence casting an eerie blue glow across her face.

"Half an hour."

"Is that enough time?"

"Probably not, but it's all the time that we can afford." I looked around. "Where's the kid?"

"Yahweh is waiting in the lab."

"I'll send for him."

As I radioed for one of our guards to bring him in, Leid's eyes left the screens and settled on me. "What now?"

"Now we get the Ark to come on down."

"You never told me how you plan to accomplish that."

"You'll see for yourself very soon. *Lights.*"

The analyst closest to the switchboard activated the lights. My eyes had grown accustomed to the darkness and the glare made me squint for a second or two. The door slid open and Yahweh emerged with a guard. He stepped in, and the guard retreated to the hall. He was carrying a notebook—the same notebook I'd seen him writing in numerous times. Whenever I'd caught a glimpse inside, none of it was legible. Just a bunch of calculations and molecular diagrams.

"What now?" he asked, looking at the screens.

"Now we wait," I said, gesturing to an empty seat. He sat, hugging the notebook to his chest.

I glanced at my watch; another twelve minutes before the evacuation was complete. Another twelve minutes of playing it cool. A rifle was strapped to my back, but it was protocol for Enforcers to be armed at all times. Neither Leid nor Yahweh found my weapon suspicious.

"How do the angels determine their leaders?" I asked.

Yahweh tilted his head. "What do you mean?"

"If Commander Raith dies, how do they determine who's next in line?"

"They go by militia rank. If Commander Raith... dies, then his First General would be Commander in his place."

I took notice of the fear in Yahweh's eyes. It was clear that his true father wouldn't make a good leader. "What if his generals die, too?"

"Then... I don't know."

"You're Raith's adopted son, and also the biological son of his First General. Wouldn't leadership fall to you?"

Yahweh blinked. "Me? I couldn't lead us."

"Why not?"

He didn't respond and cast his gaze to the ground, seeming troubled. Perhaps he'd finally realized what I was planning to do.

"You should give yourself more credit," I said. "I think you'd make a good leader."

"Leaders are strong."

"You are strong. Maybe not physically, but you're strong in *here*." I placed a hand over my heart. "And that's more important than brute strength."

The troubled look on Yahweh's face intensified. "I don't want to talk about this."

Before I could respond, my radio said, *"Evacuation is complete, Regent."*

Five minutes early. Impressive. "Good job, Commandant. Move Sanctum Forces into position along Main Street."

"Sir."

A tingle of dread shuddered down my spine. I didn't want any part of what came next, but it had to happen. "CA Tren, send a televised transmission request to the Ark."

Communication Analyst Tren returned to his computer and began to type, his fingers hitting the keys so hard that I could hear each stroke. "Calling now, sir."

The dread spread from my spine, shooting cold sparks across my arms and legs. Getting to my feet was a difficult task. I had to force my hand to grab Yahweh and yank him from his seat. He lurched forward, nearly dropping his notebook. As I pulled him in front of the screen, he looked up at me, confused and frightened.

From across the room, Leid watched us with a measure of concern. "Qaira, what are you doing?"

She was about to get up from her seat but Commander Raith appeared on screen, forcing her to stay out of sight.

Lucifer did not say hello, already sensing something was amiss. "Regent, has there been another attack?"

"No, you've kept your lackeys in check."

Commander Raith's eyes lowered to his son, mirroring his fear. "Then what is this about?"

"This is about how you never should have trusted me." I forced a smile, removing the rifle from my back.

Leid was livid, having realized my plan. She leaned forward in her seat, eyes darting between me and Commander Raith, debating whether or not to expose herself. Yahweh trembled, looking back at me with a wince.

"I don't understand," he stammered. "What have I done?"

The smile on my face waned as I met his gaze. "I'm sorry," I whispered.

"Don't," warned Lucifer. "Please, whatever it is that you want, I will give it to you. What do you want?"

"It's too late for negotiations, Raith."

"Do you want us to leave? We will leave. I give you my word that we will depart from The Atrium the moment Yahweh is returned."

I didn't answer, shoving the kid forward and taking a step back. I raised the rifle to his back. Yahweh burst into tears.

"I'm sorry!" he screamed at the screen. *"Father, I'm sorry! Please forgive me for what I've done!"*

"Qaira!" shouted Lucifer, his perfect face marred with desperation. "If you do this, Sanctum will be a smoking crater within the hour. That is a *promise!*"

Leid watched us, hands across her mouth. Blood tears brimmed her eyes, but she stayed loyal to me and didn't move an inch. How I loved her for it.

246

"I'm counting on that," I said, and fired.

Yahweh cried out as the bullet hit the center of his back, red smearing across his shirt. He looked back at me with wide eyes, that same fear and confusion ablaze. And then they rolled into his head and he collapsed.

Leid turned away, sobbing quietly.

Raith stared at his dead son, wordless. Then his eyes rose, burning on me. Blue fires raged behind glassy films. I was expecting a threat, but he said nothing. A second later the screen went black.

The moment it did, Leid tackled me with a snarl. I didn't even hit the ground before she started whaling on me. Her belligerence was almost incoherent. All I heard was 'monster' between a chorus of profanity. And I just laid there and took it.

Ten punches later, the kid stirred. Leid's fist hovered mid-air as she noticed him.

Yahweh got to his feet, looking himself over. He swept his hands across his back, searching for a bullet wound. But he wouldn't find one because I'd used an ink gun. Lucky for me he'd fainted. When he realized he wasn't mortally wounded, Yahweh stared at me.

Leid was staring at me, too.

"I had to make sure it looked real," I explained. My words were slurred and I leaned to the side, spitting blood. Her fists had felt like cast-iron.

She slid off me. "That... was probably the cleverest thing you've ever done."

Yahweh said nothing, still in shock. He collapsed into the closest chair, evidently torn between relief and shame.

"Commandant," I called into my radio, "get your jets into position. We're heading to the Cloak." Raith hadn't officially declared war, but his look had been evidence enough. I didn't know how much time we had but was hoping for at least twenty minutes.

"Already on that, sir."

As Leid spoke to the analysts, I nodded to the notebook in the kid's hands. "That all you're going to bring with you?"

"It's all I need," Yahweh said quietly, not looking at me.

"Come on; I'm taking you home."

He got up and followed me into the hall.

"Qaira, wait," said Leid.

I paused as she chased after me. As I turned she reached for my neck and pulled me down into a vicious kiss. Yahweh rolled his eyes, looking away.

"Be careful," she whispered against my lips. *"Please."*

"I will. Where are you going to be?"

"I'm staying here with the analysts. Ara has asked me to delegate between teams on the telecomm."

I wasn't really thrilled with that idea, since Eroqam would be a hotspot—but if anyone was likely to survive a bomb, it was Leid. All I did was nod and cup her face, looking her over one more time. My thumb grazed her bottom lip before I pulled back and headed down the hall, Yahweh close behind. I could feel her eyes on me the entire way.

As we reached the port, Yahweh said, "Don't do this, Qaira."

"It has to happen," I said, gesturing for him to enter first. "I'm sorry; I really am."

He paused in the entrance, absolution in his gaze. "It won't end well for you."

I smirked. "Nothing ever ends well for anyone."

After a second of hesitation, Yahweh was swallowed by the shadows of the hangar deck. I slipped on my mask and followed.

XXIX
FALLING SKIES

It was midday, and Sanctum was dead silent.

Aero-crafts lay abandoned, scattered chaotically in the streets. High-rises were inactive, advertisement billboards still tuned to the evacuation warning, looping silently.

Above the city, the sky was getting darker. The wind picked up—small gusts at first, amassing into violent torrents that threatened to bend street lamps and rip store signs from the Agora.

The gravity changed; a slight shift that left a ring in my ears. The sky was growing darker still, but now the darkness was centralized, like mass drifting slowly to an ocean surface. A whistle broke through the wind, and a bright sphere emerged through encircling green and black clouds. It was the size of Sanctum—maybe even larger, shining red light through its porous surface.

All Eroqam lines were static. The Ark's appearance had snatched the breath from our lungs. From the Cloak, my men and I watched the angel's descent in horrified awe. Without my plan, there was no way we could have won. And as certain death grew closer still, the possibility of victory shriveled until I could barely see it anymore.

The light around the Ark was getting even brighter. The whistle turned into a roar, and then a deafening screech. A symphony of shattering glass occurred around the city as the noise blew out a thousand windows.

The ship appeared to shudder, growing little spines that came loose and fell toward Sanctum like black raindrops. But then the raindrops started to move, soar.

Jets.

Eroqam lines exploded.

"Detection of level three radiation—"

"Sanctum Forces, move to the front of the line!"

"First wave, first wave!"

"Level four radiation, and climbing! That light is toxic!"

"Enforcer jets, hold back," I ordered into the headset coiled around my ear. "Sanctum Forces, move to meet the first wave." *And die.*

The first line roared overhead by the dozens, engines shaking the ground, and the Cloak teetered from their downdraft. They met the Ark's first wave as they prepared for a full-assault on Eroqam—just as I'd expected—and our sky became an ocean of artillery and fire.

Our first line didn't last five minutes, also as I'd expected. But now the angels were cocky and had congregated above Eroqam and the central Agora, ready to blow them to smithereens.

"Ara, give the command!" I shouted.

"Enforcer jets, move out! Keep those whites occupied!"

From around the city our jets rose like hornets at supersonic speed, surrounding the group over Eroqam and executing them in one fell swoop. The artillery and fire intensified, the air filling up with bullet tailsparks and smoke. An enemy jet crashed into Eroqam's western spire, and giant chunks of coua rained on the port where my team and I waited. A chunk fell dangerously close, rolling several feet away.

We all were quiet, watching the battle ensue. Except for Yahweh, who shrieked at *every* explosion and cowered further into the corner. He was seated on the bench with knees drawn to his chest, hands over his ears. Poor kid.

"Enforcer jets, engage the base ship," Leid ordered over the command line. *"Attack the thin metal cylinders on the underside of the Ark; we need to take out their communication satellites."*

"Sanctum Forces," my brother ordered not a second later, *"keep the angels busy and cover those Enforcer jets!"*

"Sanctum Forces, bring the fight a little closer to us," I said, adding my two cents.

Once the sky was a complete cluster-fuck, I started the engine. Yahweh moaned behind me as we slowly left the port.

"The Cloak is in the air," I announced. "Coordinates are 58, 32, 156. Do *not* attack us."

"Your flight coordinates are tracked, Regent," said Leid. *"The Cloak is safe to go."*

"Get me off!" Yahweh cried, clawing at the walls. "We're going to die!"

"Someone shut him up," I ordered.

Lt. Geiss forced him back on the bench with a mean look.

"Keep screaming like that and we *will* die," I said. "I need to concentrate."

I weaved through the battle, tailing several enemy jets on my way up.   As I fired aimlessly at Enforcer jets—missing intentionally—my team assembled their weapons and tugged on their masks. *Clicks* of knife and scope attachments and *clinks* of bullets hitting chambers filled the cabin. As we cleared dark water, I switched our feed to enemy lines. Nehelian turned into Archaean as soldiers screamed commands at each other. They sounded scared, and that made me smile.

Commander Raith's voice, ever-calm and authoritative, broke through the hysteria. "Front-line units, cease attack on Eroqam and fall back. A Nehelian fleet is attacking our satellites. *Crush them.*"

Soon, I thought. *Very soon.*

I hadn't realized how close I was to achieving my goal until now. We were almost at the Ark, the pores along its surface near enough to recognize them as jet docks. The amount of Enforcer jets had already been cut in half. Pretty soon they would all be gone, and then the angels would decimate Sanctum. I had to kill Raith before any of that happened.

I flew the Cloak into a dock, continuing down a port tunnel into a dark, terrifying unknown. Tiny white lights guided our path through a narrow cavern of metal beams.

We were in.

We were *in!*

I had to keep myself from laughing. My team crowded around the pilot seat, watching the alien scenery blur by the windshield. The tunnel opened into a loading dock. I parked the craft between two larger ones—probably carrier units. A crew of angels carried metal crates into one of them. They didn't even notice us pulling in.

I turned off the engine and opened the hatch. The ramp descended slowly, creating a bridge to the dock. As I left the pilot seat and moved to the exit, my team awaiting orders, I pointed at Yahweh, still curled on the bench.

"Stay here."

He didn't reply but he didn't budge either, so I assumed he got the message. I motioned for my team to follow behind me in single file, and together we marched down the ramp.

The angels noticed us, finally. But it was far too late for them now.

Two of them dropped their crates and made a break for the door. Lt. Geiss and Samay shot them and they fell simultaneously with oozing holes in their heads.

Two more had the courage to reach for their side arms. They, too, fell a second later.

All that was left was a lone angel, backing away over a growing pool of his comrades' blood, holding up his hands in surrender.

My team stayed at the dock's edge as I followed the angel through the blood and bodies, leaving crimson footprints across the cement. He tried to run but I snatched him by the uniform and lifted him off his feet by his neck. He was young—maybe a little older than Yahweh. That was unfortunate.

"Where can I find Commander Raith?" I asked, pulling him inches from my mask—so close that the red light of my eyes cast a glow across his terrified face.

"The command station," he stammered, choking.

When I didn't respond, the angel pointed to the door on the right side of the loading dock. "D-Down a mile, then a left. T-There's an elevator that w-will lead you to the Aerial deck."

"Thank you," I said.

The boy's eyes widened and he opened his mouth to scream. Before he could, his head exploded all over me. I wiped brain and bone fragments from my mask, throwing the corpse aside. I hadn't wanted to kill that angel but I couldn't risk him alerting the soldiers. Instead I'd given him an instant, painless death. For the most part.

I returned to the Cloak and dialed Eroqam a final time.

"Advisor Koseling, this is Regent Qaira Eltruan." I was being so formal because there were other CAs in the communications room who might have been listening in. "We are on the Ark. This will be the last transmission you will receive, as my team and I are leaving the Cloak and will not attempt to contact you again in fear of alerting enemy satellites of our location."

"Will you contact us after you've executed Commander Raith?"

"Yes. Until then, make sure my brother and our forces hit the angels with everything they've got. We need to keep them distracted."

"Three of their satellites have been taken out, so we've bought ourselves some time. Be careful, Regent."

"I will, over."

I severed the call and turned to the kid. He was staring at all the blood on my suit. "Let's go."

Yahweh got to his feet and I ushered him down the dock. He froze on the deck, looking over the bodies. A pool of blood almost touched his shoes, and he stumbled backward into me.

I shoved him forward. "Go on."

"Where?"

"Wherever. This is the end of the line."

"You…you're just going to let me go?"

"I'm going to count to thirty. If you're still here I'm going to shoot you, and it won't be with an ink bullet this time."

Yahweh took another step, wearing an incredulous frown. "Aren't you worried that I'll alert my father?"

"If you alert your father, I'm going to die. If you don't alert your father, he's going to die. I know I've put you in a tough situation, but that's how it has to be."

He looked away, conflicted.

"But if you alert Commander Raith, a lot more people are going to die than him. I'll have to kill everyone that gets in my way, and you would be responsible for that."

"Can you promise that no harm will come to any of our unarmed civilians?"

"I can't promise that, no. But I can definitely *try* not to harm them. When or *if* you claim any sort of power, you need to convince your people to leave The Atrium."

After a moment of hesitation, he nodded. "Fine."

"Now get out of here. Thirty, twenty-nine, twenty-eight…"

I raised my rifle and Yahweh bolted for the door on the left— the one that led away from the command station. I stopped counting when he disappeared. Lowering my rifle, I whispered, "Goodbye."

And then my men surrounded me. I nodded to the door on the right.

"Let's go. Keep a twelve-foot distance behind me at all times."

XXX
SYMPHONY OF MACHINES

WE REACHED THE ELEVATOR, FIFTY soldiers later. Luckily for us most of them had been taken by surprise and were dead before they could return fire. The ones who had heard the rifles weren't as surprised to see us, but we'd handled them too. My team had left most of them to me since we had to move as quietly and quickly as possible.

I fumbled with the elevator keypad, leaving red smears across the buttons. My suit was covered in blood and gore. I'd lost two of my men already, whom had caught bullets in crossfire. I was also pretty sure a bullet had grazed my right arm, because it was kind of sore. There was no blood that I could tell, so it wasn't serious.

The elevator flashed a red light every time I pressed a button, and a message on the screen above the doors asked for a card key. I didn't have a card key.

"Fuck," I muttered, retracing my steps.

"What's wrong, sir?" asked Lt. Fedaz.

"We need a card to open that door. Cover me; I need to check some of those bodies."

I could feel my heart in my ears as the element of time slipped from my grasp. We had to hurry. Eventually someone would alert Raith and then we would be trapped down here. I wasn't panicking yet, but my body was certainly gearing up for it.

I returned to the bloodbath of twelve headless angels in the east corridor, rifling through their suits in hope that they had a card. My men knelt and covered me from both directions, guns pointed at each tunnel bend should an enemy try to surprise us.

And then I found the card. It was around a soldier's neck, held by a chain and drenched in blood. Hopefully it wasn't ruined.

We returned to the elevator and I swiped the card through a thin rectangular slot. Another red light flashed above it and a message appeared on the screen again:

PLEASE SLIDE CARD OTHER WAY

"Oh for fuck's sake," I breathed, flipping it around. A green light and awful bell-like music filled the hallway and we spun, pointing our guns down it. The doors slid open and we backed into the elevator. I pressed another button and the door closed.

Ding.

Next stop, the bridge.

***

My men and I weaved through a maze of glass hallways—empty, thankfully—which gave us a scenic view of all the lower and upper floors, wrapping around the Ark like rings on a planet. As much as I hated the angels, I couldn't deny the stunning quality of their technology. The hallways led upward, like a ramp. Faint alarms blared from somewhere, and automated voice messages ordering soldiers to report to the hangar played on loop. My plan had worked; they were too busy vacating their ship to *protect* it.

The sound of voices made us back up a step. Someone was coming down the ramp. We receded to the closest bend, and I motioned for my men to back away as far as they could. The voices grew louder.

Female. *Laughter.*

I could see them through the wall. Two angel girls dressed in cadet uniforms, chatting informally like a war *wasn't* going on. Even though I was in clear sight, they didn't even notice me, too busy discussing rumors about a boy in Aviations.

Their stupid conversation came to a halt when they rounded the bend and their heads exploded simultaneously, splattering the glass with pink and red mist. We all took a moment to look at them, and then pressed on.

I'd found that display to be a little insulting—that was how serious they were about this war. That was how serious they were about *us*.

But that all would change very soon.

The glass hallways came to a very abrupt end at a narrow corridor, guarded by two Archaean soldiers. Their uniforms were different than the others—these ones had rank. White and navy painted plate, visors hiding their faces. Undoubtedly, they were the only things between me and the command station.

They saw us and pulled out their guns, aiming them at me. I froze and held up my hands. I was smiling, but they couldn't see that.

The one on the left reached for their radio, but Lt. Geiss shot it out of their hand. They'd only seen me first, as my men had yet to leave the glass hall. Now there were twelve of us, and those angels weren't so brave anymore.

With our weapons pointed back at them, the one on the left shoved the one on the right behind him in a protective stance. Judging by their heights alone, the one in front was male, while the one behind was female.

I took another step across the bridge. The male shook his gun at me.

"Move another inch and I'll blow your head off," he warned.

"If you kill me, you and your partner will be next to die," I said, gesturing to my men.

After a calculated moment of silence, the male said, "Cereli, get out of here."

"I'm not leaving you," said the female.

"I said get out of here!"

"I won't!"

I watched their exchange with an arched brow. "How about I let you both walk away if you give me the card to open that door?"

They said nothing at first, looking me over. How horrifying I was—covered in the entrails of their friends, red lights beaming viciously from the eyes of my mask. "Do you know who I am?" I asked.

"Yes," said the male, gun still pointed at me.

"Then you should also know how pointless your resistance is." I waved to my men. "Put your guns down."

They did so, reluctantly.

"See?" I said. "You two can just walk right by, I promise. All I want is your card."

After another moment of silence, the female leaned in to her partner. "Seyestin, give him the card."

"I'm no traitor," he snarled.

"No one called you a traitor. I've given you a choice between life and death. You can either give me the card willingly or I'll take it from your corpse. Don't be a hero."

I could tell my men were wondering what the fuck I was doing. Yes, I'd admit that this wasn't typical behavior of me, but a gunfight in front of the command station *couldn't* happen. Raith would definitely hear it.

Finally the angel soldier, *Seyestin,* reached a free hand into his coat pocket. He dropped the card on the floor and kicked it toward me. It slid across the tile, stopping in front of my boots.

I picked it up and stepped aside, gesturing for them to pass. They inched by, Seyestin holding Cereli behind him, gun waving chaotically in our faces. When they cleared our group, they took off in a sprint down the bridge.

"Why did you do that?" asked Lt. Geiss. "They're going to alert the soldiers."

True, I could have exploded their heads once they'd been in range, but I always kept my promises, and I'd promised to let them go. A man was only as honorable as his word. "It doesn't matter anymore," I said, looking at the unguarded door. "We're at the end of the road."

Card in hand, I moved toward the command station door. My men followed close behind, guns raised once again.

***

Commander Lucifer Raith stood at the navigation desk, a digital map of Sanctum and all of its activity flashing on a screen. He had both of his hands on the desk, a fierce look in his pale, blue eyes as he watched it.

"General Arahman, place our primary strike force out of defense. We're resuming our attack on Eroqam."

Silence.

Lucifer turned to General Arahman's podium, finding him sprawled over it, *dead*. Blood trickled down the crystal surface—everything on the Ark was glass or crystal—and then his eyes rose to *me*, standing in the doorway.

Before anyone else could react, I stepped inside and my men came through the door behind me, executing everyone except for Raith.

Stunned, the Angel Commander looked over the bodies at his feet, and then back at me.

My grin faltered for just a minute when I realized how tall he really was—easily six and a half feet. "Hi," I said. "You didn't want to come to me, so I thought I'd come to you. Nice place you got here. Very shiny."

Lucifer said nothing, staring daggers.

I removed my mask and inhaled, thankful for some fresh air. Then I nodded to the communications panel that General Arahman was bleeding all over. "Order your troops to retreat from Sanctum."

Raith's gaze slid to the panel, but he didn't budge.

"Really?!" I screamed, waving my gun in his face. *"Do I need to show you that I've never been more dead-fucking-serious in my entire life?!"*

He moved to the panel and radioed for his troops. "This is your Commander. Cease all attacks on Sanctum. I repeat, cease all attacks on Sanctum and return to the Ark." He let the radio slip from his hands. "And what do you plan to do now, Qaira? Over four thousand soldiers are about to return to the very ship that you're on. I doubt you and your handful of enforcers could fight your way through all of us."

"I know how your wars work," I said. "If your leader is killed, the war is over. Until a new one is assigned, soldiers won't fight. Isn't that right?"

"Yahweh has told you much about us."

I smiled.

He tilted his head. "Then why am I not dead yet?"

Before I could respond, Lucifer's hand shot toward the side of his desk, mashing a button. The door behind me slid shut, sealing us off from my men. An alarm shrieked, and the room lit up in flashing light, casting both of us in red iridescence.

We were alone.

Lucifer disappeared from view, the flashing lights making it difficult to see. I caught a blur on my right and felt his fist against the side of my face. The force of his punch sent me staggering into the wall. I dropped my gun, and it slid across the room, disappearing underneath the navigation desk. Before I could recover, he grabbed my coat and flung me headfirst into a panel of computers.

He was stronger than I'd anticipated. Taller and stronger. I didn't want to use my ability. *Not on him.* Tearing Lucifer to pieces bare-handedly would feel much more satisfying, but he was making that ambition very difficult.

I feigned injury and he grabbed me again. My forehead collided with his nose, and it crunched against the blow. Lucifer stumbled and I tackled him, pummeling his face as we hit the floor.

A gun barrel gleamed in the light, just before it cracked me upside the jaw. My vision blurred and Lucifer shoved me off. I rolled behind the navigation desk as he opened fire, missing me on all accounts.

When he ran out of bullets I sprang from the desk, a computer screen held over my head. It caught him square in the chest, wires and microchips exploding everywhere. Lucifer was down again and I lunged at him, ready to end this.

He kicked a rolling chair into my path and I tripped, landing hard on my hands and knees. When I looked up, I caught a glimpse of his shadow fleeing through a door at the back of the room. Commander Raith was running.

Running from *me*.

Gunfire and screams erupted from the hall; the angels had found my men. I wanted to search for the button that unsealed the door, but Raith was getting away and I couldn't even afford a second to think. The door from which he fled led into another portion of the command station, sealed off by a glass wall. My wings released and I dove through it, sliding to a stop in an explosion of crystal shards, cutting him off.

Lucifer crashed into me and we rolled along the floor, exchanging blows. Eventually he stopped moving and I got to my feet, heavy breathed. The gunfire had intensified and I couldn't hear my men anymore. An organic kill was no longer an option.

My eyes narrowed; Lucifer held his head, screaming.

I upped the severity, inch by inch. Blood trickled from his nose, ears and eyes. Pretty soon he was reduced to a shriveled, moaning mess. It was the most beautiful thing I'd ever seen.

"Here we are," I whispered, kneeling at his side. "Just how I always knew it would end. All you had to do was leave and this could have been avoided."

Raith looked up at me, blood streaming down his face, mouth contorted into a furious snarl. "I'll *kill* you—"

I kicked him in the stomach and he curled. "Yes, I can really see that being a possibility here."

A *pinch* on the back of my neck.

My smile faded as I felt for the source. My fingers grazed something cold and metallic protruding from the base of my neck. I pulled it out.

A dart.

Chills plummeted down my spine. My body felt heavy; pinpricks bit at my arms. I turned, and then my eyes widened.

Yahweh Telei stood with his back to the wall, a gun clutched in his trembling hand. At first I couldn't believe my eyes, considering my vision was tunneling and I had to squint to see him properly. *"...You."*

The kid said nothing, staring up at me in terror.

"What have you done?" I shouted, advancing on him. "Tell me what you've done!"

Yahweh tried to run but I caught him and slammed him back against the wall by his neck. I found it hard to even curl my hand at this point. The room was swaying and nausea crept up my throat. All I wanted to do was sleep.

"I-I'm sorry..." he choked, loose tears falling from his eyes. *"I'm sorry, Qaira! I can't let you kill my father!"*

I shouldn't have let him go. I shouldn't have kept him alive, but when I tried to correct that mistake, nothing happened. Three times I tried to explode his head to no avail. *"What was in that dart?!"* I screamed. *"What was in it, you fucking white?!"*

The fear on Yahweh's face vanished. "I told you this wouldn't end well for you. Do you remember?"

I could barely hear him. All of my senses were shutting down. There was movement in my *very* limited peripherals and I spun to find Lucifer right behind me. Everything was a blur. In an instant I hit the ground, feeling his fist against my face, the coppery taste of blood invading my mouth.

And then I felt nothing; tasted nothing.

Everything went black.

XXXI
SUBJUGATION

FRESH PAIN RIPPLED ACROSS MY FACE; light shined behind my eyelids.

The pain forced a cringe across my dry, blood-caked lips, which brought forth even more pain. But the pain was second to my surprise that I was awake. I was *alive*.

My eyes opened like tiny slits and I saw a white room bereft of any furniture, save for a stretcher across the room. I tried to move but realized that I was bound by straps around my neck and wrists, keeping my arms twisted to a boiler pipe. I tried to break the straps by force several times, but failed. I was too weak, or they were too strong. Probably both.

Whatever Yahweh had shot me with was still in effect. I felt drunk and tired, tingles ran up and down my spine and through my extremities.

I couldn't stop wondering why Raith had kept me alive.

The door opened at the far side of the room, near the stretcher, and two guards entered first. Behind them, Lucifer and Yahweh appeared side by side, looking solemn.

Anger filled my chest like steaming water would a mug, but all I had the strength to do was stare. Yahweh broke through the guards and approached me. Lucifer hung back, looking at me in a way that I'd never seen. One of surprise and slight regret—as if to say *'I can't believe you spared him.'*

Surely Yahweh had told him everything that had happened, and the thought of Lucifer knowing about my mercy for the kid brought a rush of heat to my cheeks. Shame was too weak a word. I'd been fooled by a child.

Without a word, Yahweh knelt in front of me, syringe in hand. I knew what he meant to do and inched away futilely, deeper into the corner, shutting my eyes. He tilted back my head and injected the syringe into my neck. Gravity flattened my body then, pushing me to the floor as my eyes rolled into my head and I battled seizure.

Yahweh watched me writhe, sadness in his eyes. "I'm sorry, Qaira," he whispered.

I heard the words but could barely make sense of them. I wouldn't have responded either way.

"Get him up," ordered Raith, and rough hands fumbled with my restraints and forced me to my feet. My knees buckled several times on the way to the door, and the guards dropped me once, one of them muttering, "He's heavy."

I was slammed into a chair at a long metal table and a guard fastened the chain around my neck to one of its legs. I leaned back and tried to focus on the ceiling, which spun violently and I had to close my eyes or else I would vomit.

Lucifer placed a glass of water in front of me. "The sedative has dehydrated you. Part of what you're feeling is water-loss. Drink, or you'll die."

He didn't need to tell me. I grabbed the glass with shaking hands and downed it in four gulps, gasping as the water punched my gut from the inside. Raith looked at Yahweh, who had lingered in the doorway.

"Is it safe to be alone with him?"

"It should be. That sedative should stay in his bloodstream for a couple of hours."

Raith nodded. "Thank you, Yahweh. You may leave us."

The door closed, and then there was silence.

Lucifer looked over my wounds, indecisiveness behind his gaze. The water had helped my concentration a little, and I stared back, glassy-eyes filled with contempt.

He probably looked as bad as me, maybe even worse. One of his eyes was welted shut and blood caked the side of his face, tinting his hairline pink.

"You're clever," he said, sighing. "I'll give you that much. But your intelligence ends where you thought my son would actually *help* you kill me and destroy his own people."

"What was in that dart?" I demanded, slurring.

"A drug that reduces parietal-lobe activity, from which Yahweh theorized your ability stems. He showed me his notebook and told me that he'd been working on it in captivity."

That notebook. The kid had been conspiring against me the *whole* time. How could I have been so stupid as to not be suspicious of that notebook? All I did was hang my head.

"And my men?" I asked, this time much more quietly.

"Unfortunately they were killed by my men outside of the command station."

I was waiting for him to bring up Leid and the Court of Enigmus, but he never did. Yahweh hadn't told him that part, which came as a surprise. And a relief.

"The inhibitor effects aren't permanent," he assured me, "but necessary for us to have a civil conversation. I imagine you'd be quite belligerent otherwise."

"Civil conversation." I forced a laugh. "Why haven't you killed me?"

"Yahweh argued for your life," said Lucifer, reclining in his seat. "Make no mistake I was ready to shoot you in the head, but then he told me about your act of mercy after your men brutalized him."

Ugh.

"He also told me that you are worth more alive than dead, and after some thought, I agree."

"Well, you might as well kill me," I said. "I'm not negotiating with you."

Lucifer smiled, showing me a row of blood-stained teeth. "I don't expect you to. Not *you*, anyway."

The guards had re-emerged through the door and he nodded to them. "Take him to the communications bridge. I'll be there shortly."

***

I was slammed into another chair—this one with some padding, at least.

That didn't stop the hot white pain that shot from my tailbone as the guards threw me down without any regard. But I was too drugged to care.

Screens flickered in front of me, foreign in appearance from the ones at Eroqam, made of flat, almost fluid-looking surfaces framed by blue crystal. The screens flashed, casting a glow across my face and I squinted. Its light burned my eyes.

There were other angels in the room. *Analysts.* I could feel their condemning stares on my back. I ignored them, squinting at the screen.

The weight of the chair shifted, and in my peripherals two hands rested on either side of me. Large hands; long, strong fingers, white skin.

"Connect to Eroqam," said the owner of those hands. Lucifer Raith.

"Sir," said a voice far away, "who do you wish to speak to?"

"Ah, right. Normally I would ask for Qaira, but I suppose now I'll seek his next in charge." Raith paused, looking down at me. His eyes shined with antipathy. "That would be your brother, yes? What's his name again—Ara?"

No.

No, he couldn't see me like this.

I clenched my jaw, saying nothing.

That had been confirmation enough. "Request the audience of Commandant Ara Eltruan over the televised line."

A moment of silence.

"We're on standby while they locate him, sir."

"Thank you." Those hands tapped their fingers on the chair-back, goading me to break them. "You could save yourself the humiliation and surrender now, you know."

"Get fucked, you Archaean piece of shit."

"… Very well."

The screen flashed and a light below it blinked green. The image of my brother melded into view. At first Ara looked angry, but then he saw me, and the anger faded into surprise. Then, *dread.*

"I have bad news, Commandant," announced Lucifer. "Although you can see that for yourself."

Ara said nothing, staring at me. I couldn't bear his look and cast my eyes down. He looked worried and scared, two things that my brother should have never felt. *Not for me.*

Somewhere in the communications room, Leid was watching, too. This I knew, and it only made the shame even worse.

"Here are the terms," said Raith, delving right in. "I'm willing to hand over the Regent in exchange for your surrender." Ara opened his mouth, but Raith interjected, "We don't want Sanctum. You can keep it. All I want is for you to command your army to lay down their weapons and allow the Ark into The Atrium."

Ara hesitated, shifting his gaze between Lucifer and I. The fear in his eyes waned—indecisiveness, *conflict.*

"Don't," I said.

"If you reject my terms, Qaira will stay with us. Indefinitely. I'm sure more than a few angels here would like to meet him."

Ara looked at me again. *Fear, desperation.*

"Commandant, as your Regent, I order you *not* to surrender," I said, but it was more a plea than a command.

"Qaira, I can't let you—"

"Don't surrender!"

Ara glanced off screen, looking at someone.

Looking at *her.*

"I'm a patient man, Commandant," pressed Raith. "But lately my patience has worn thin. What will it be?"

Ara kept looking off-screen. He shook his head, communicating.

No. No, don't look at her. Don't let them know she's there.

But Commander Raith had already picked up on the unseen presence. "Who else is in that room with you, Commandant?"

Ara darted off-screen, whispering, *"No!"*

Arguing. Muffled, incoherent, but it was clear that the other person was female.

Again, Ara. "No, you can't! *Stop!*"

And then, Leid. Center screen, violet eyes ablaze with enmity. She stared at Raith like one might a maggot, a chagrined smile painted across her lips.

No.

No, no, no…

"No!" I screamed, unable to hold in that thought anymore. *"What are you doing?!"*

But Leid ignored me, her eyes never leaving Raith. She gave him a long hard minute to take her in, but he hadn't needed that much time to finally understand the situation. In fact, now he looked as horrified as me.

"A contract with a scholar," he said, his words barely anything more than breath. *"Well,* isn't this something?"

"So you know what I am."

"I do."

"Then I don't need to explain why you'll release the Regent immediately."

"I'm not so sure about that," he said, crossing his arms. "I might contact the Court of Enigmus and inform them that one of their scholars has violated her contract."

Ferocity wicked across Leid's face. It was a look I'd never seen on her, not even in her angriest moment. "I suppose that's another option, but let me stress the fact that should you do that, the Ark will be a ball of smoking scrap metal within the hour."

Was she really capable of destroying the Ark? *By herself?*

"You'd actually commit genocide?"

An eerie, beautiful smile. "It wouldn't be the first time, Commander Raith."

The confidence on his face bled out. "Yahweh didn't tell me about you. Why?"

"I'm not sure. Maybe you should ask him. Do you believe my threat?"

The entire bridge was silent. All eyes were on the screen.

Lucifer hung his head, sighing heavily. "Yes, I believe it."

Her fury dimmed, like a slow-dying flame. "Good. I'll be there in half an hour to take the Regent back to his city. I'd prefer him in one piece. Is that fine with you?"

"It's fine."

"If you contact the Court of Enigmus, I'll know, and our meeting won't be a pleasant one."

Before he could respond, she cut the call and the screen switched to static. The moment Leid was gone, Raith kicked over the vacant chair beside me. But he didn't scream. He didn't make a single sound. All he did was glare at me with rage far beyond what words could measure. His desire to kill me was as palpable as my rapid-fire pulse. But he didn't. He *couldn't*.

He couldn't because that scholar was in love with me.

"Take the Regent back into holding," he muttered.

As his guards approached, Raith stormed from the bridge without another word.

XXXII
VENGEANCE

THE BOILER PIPE WAS WEDGED BETWEEN MY shoulder blades, its cold metal biting through my suit. The guards had tied me a lot tighter this time.

My discomfort wasn't much of a concern. All I could think about was how Leid had just thrown herself to the wolves in order to save me. Surely she knew that after I returned to Sanctum, Lucifer would call her people and they'd come here to…

What would they even do? Punish her? Punish *us?*

The minutes ticked away as I faded in and out of coherency, slipping between lucid dream and painful reality. The relief of rescue had been snatched away by the knowledge of subsequential consequence.

And then I thought of Lucifer Raith—of his vainglorious air and snide demeanor. I had failed to kill him, and in turn the war was left unfinished, stale-mated yet again. But now I stood to lose a lot more than my world.

I would lose Leid.

And then I would lose everything else.

The door opened and Yahweh appeared, dragging along a vitals machine, stethoscope swaying on his lithe, boyish neck.

He reached into the pocket of his white physician's coat, retrieving another syringe. I cringed, but didn't cower this time.

"I'm here to make sure you're okay," he said in an assuring voice. "I haven't confirmed the inhibitor's safety so I'd like to check your vitals, if you'll let me."

"How could I not? Your cunt of a father saw to it that I can barely move."

Yahweh froze, several feet away. "I won't force you to accept care."

I eyed the syringe. "Like you didn't force that thing into my neck? *Twice?*"

"You act like I had a choice."

I opened my mouth to respond, but then I actually thought about what he'd said. In the split second that it'd taken to exhale, I placed myself in his shoes. He was right. I hadn't given him a choice. I'd forced him to help us execute his father, and I was stupid for believing Yahweh would actually go through with it.

All I did was look away.

Yahweh continued his approach, kneeling beside me. He shined a light in my eyes and I squinted, turning my head.

"Stop," he instructed. "I need to see how dilated your pupils are."

I conceded, only because it would be over sooner this way. Yahweh removed the light and put the stethoscope tips in his ears, sliding the cold metal diaphragm under my suit, against my bare skin. I jumped at the sudden stimulus, and he looked away, concentrating on the sound of my heart.

I didn't like this; I didn't like him touching me. It felt disgusting and awkward.

"Your heartbeat is elevated," he stated. "But I bet you're considerably stressed. Are you still dizzy?"

"A little."

"Can you see me well?"

"Unfortunately."

Yahweh sighed, removing the diaphragm from my chest. Then he shoved something into my mouth, which I immediately spat out. He picked it up, holding it in front of my face. It was a thermometer.

"I need to check your temperature," he said. "Please hold this under your tongue or I'll be forced to put it somewhere else, and I can guarantee you won't like *that*."

Someone kill me.

The underside of my tongue pressed down on the thin cylinder, and Yahweh let go of it. As I held it in my mouth, he sat cross-legged beside me, awaiting the result. He didn't look at me, and instead cast his sad gaze at the floor. "I know you won't believe it, but I didn't want any of this to happen."

I didn't respond, since the thermometer was still in my mouth.

"I created the inhibitor as a failsafe, in case everything turned out like... well, like *this*."

The thermometer beeped and he took it from me.

"Are you done?" I muttered.

"Almost."

"What else?"

"It wasn't a lie, Qaira," he whispered. "I didn't pretend to like you. I like you very much. I respect you, and I wish you felt for Lucifer as you do for me. We're not that different."

"We are very different," I said coldly, gazing away. "And I feel nothing for you. Not anymore. Not after what you did. I should have let you die."

Yahweh recoiled, as if he'd been slapped. The hurt on his face was hard to ignore, but I did it anyway. He gathered up his equipment with eyes trained on the floor, hands shaking as they worked. "Malice is an ingredient for destruction," he said. "Malice saves nothing. No one. Maybe one day you'll understand."

And then he shuffled out, closing the door.

My disdain melted away as he left, and I watched the door shut with reluctant guilt. As angry as I was, I had lied to him. I wouldn't have let him die, even now.

And then I realized that I could feel my arms and legs; Yahweh had forgotten to give me that syringe, and the effects of his last dose were fading. The guilt faded with them, replaced by a surge of adrenaline and rage. All hope was not lost.

Yahweh was wrong. Malice *did* save something.

It saved me.

And now it was the only thing that kept blood pumping through my veins.

***

The external port opened and angels dragged me out, cold wind beating our bodies. It slapped my face like a frozen hand, and even threatened to tear the visors from the guards' heads. Raith led the charge, unflinching, his long red coat whipping like a war flag behind him.

A black smear grew prominent against the canvas of muddy clouds, rising from below until it broke cloud cover and approached the port.

An enforcer carrier-craft.

Everyone was still as it docked and the doors opened. Leid had come alone, which meant she'd known how to fly our crafts all along. My brain started to scream *'How?!'* but then thought such an effort was a waste. It was better not to question these kinds of things when it came to Advisor Koseling.

It was a gallant gesture—coming alone to an alien base ship, surrounded by armed angels, wearing only a thin smile. It was an act of non-provocation yet a display of apex predation, as if to tell her enemies that she needn't any help to kill them.

Wrapped in a white fur coat that touched her knees, she stepped off the craft and rose to face Commander Raith, stopping just feet from him. The difference in their heights was ridiculous. He, six-five and she, five foot nothing. But when it came to Leid, size didn't matter, and Raith knew that all too well.

He looked down at her, mild surprise crossing his face, leading me to believe scholars weren't normally so tiny. And then his eyes settled on hers, softness rounding the hard edges of his frown. He'd noticed her beauty.

"Good evening, Commander Raith," she greeted, studying his wounded face. "The televised screen does you an injustice, I must say."

Lucifer ignored her sarcasm. "Why are you putting your life on the line for Qaira Eltruan?"

She didn't respond, looking at me. "May I have him, please? It seems he needs medical attention."

I kept my head down, feigning sedation. In reality I was eyeing the blade on a soldier's belt.

Lucifer didn't move aside. "You're not a noble."

"Correct."

"Whose guardian are you?"

My attention pricked at the word *guardian*.

"I am the guardian of no one."

"Every noble has a guardian."

"My noble is dead."

He smiled. "Aipocinus' guardian. Ah, if only he could see you now."

"If only," she recited, growing annoyed. "I didn't come here to discuss private Vel'Haru matters with a lesser."

"It's hardly private when you're threatening to kill us for a man who isn't even worth the dirt on my boots."

My jaw clenched.

Leid's smile faded.

He noticed her falter. "You're in love with a genocidal monster, and I'm sure you know that. *Why?*"

"Give me the Regent, Commander Raith. I won't ask you again."

Lucifer sighed. "Release him," he ordered to his men. He stepped aside as the guards ambled me forward, handing me off to Leid. But as soon as they let go of my arms, I broke the chains around my wrists, links flying in every direction. Before anyone could react, I slid the blade from the sheath on the soldier's belt and shoved him off the side of the port.

He fell, too stunned to spread his wings, succumbing to turbulence within seconds.

Lucifer turned at the commotion, just as I lunged at him with the blade raised over my head. He stepped back as I swung. Warm blood hit my face, accompanied by a searing pinch in my gut. I hadn't heard the shot fired, but caught the echo.

A hit.

A hit!

But not a fatal one.

Raith was still alive, pointing a smoking pulse gun at my chest. Blood gushed from the sleeve of his right arm, a severed hand lying between us. Adrenaline had allowed him not to notice it yet, but then he did, and he *screamed*.

And then I realized that he'd hit me, too. He'd hit me *worse*. I held my stomach, dropping the blade. My steps were staggered and I couldn't keep my balance. My body was getting colder by the second.

"Qaira!" Leid screamed, but she sounded distant, far away.

And then my feet ran out of port, and I fell off the Ark, eyes rolling into my head as clouds and darkness coalesced.

***

My body hit the cold, black waves with a *clap*.

The Ocean of Maghir welcomed my arrival with open arms, pulling me under. I sank, watching what little light there was fade with the surface. My eyes stayed open, waves droning in my ears, as objects fell around me. Bodies, all of them. Thousands of bodies—fallen Sanctum soldiers, children—now corpse statues, slaves to Maghir.

I tried to flail, thrash, swim to the surface, but my body was leaden. I was gone. *I was lost*—just another body in the ocean of death. A lost soul in a place I had never believed was real.

"Qaira..."

My eyes fluttered. Black bubbles drew from my lips like crystal oil.

"Qaira..."

Warmth returned to my fingers, and they twitched. I floundered, rising.

"Qaira, please...!"

Leid.

Leid.

I fought for the surface as shadowy hands grabbed at my feet, trying to pull me under again. My lip curled in a snarl, determination moving waves of heat through my body, giving me strength. No, I would not go. *I would not.*

My face broke the surface and I opened my eyes wide, gasping for breath.

And then cold air beat against my face, and I was weightless.

Falling, again.

A hard slap sent my head sideways. Reality exploded back— roaring wind, that searing pain in my stomach, and Leid's screams. *Sobs.*

"Qaira, wake up!" She slapped me again and again, even as I awoke and stared at her, utterly confused. *"Your wings! Use your wings!"*

We were falling from the Ark.

We were falling. Leid had jumped off with me.

I pulled her into me, releasing my wings. But I was too late— the ground was seconds away, and all I could do was cushion the bone-shattering collision that would follow. I turned sideways, shielding her from impact. My back slammed into the tundra in a cloud of debris. Leid was torn out of my arms as we rolled along the ground for what felt like eternity.

I lay on my side, coughing up blood. Leid was strewn only feet from me, but it might as well been miles. I couldn't reach her. I couldn't move.

Blood trickled down my forehead, pooling into my eyes. It stung, and I shut them, unable to lift my hand to wipe the blood away.

She was face down and unmoving, a lithe arm outstretched, scratched and bloody.

"Leid," I whispered.

Nothing. Not a single thing.

No.

No, please.

Gritting my teeth, I forced my arm to move and I reached for her outstretched hand. Our fingertips fell centimeters apart. Too far.

Sight left my eyes like a heavy blanket, and the last thought I had was that I would return to Maghir's Ocean—;

And this time, Leid would sink with me.

TITLES IN THE HYMN OF THE MULTIVERSE:
(THE ANTITHESIS)
1.   INCEPTION
2.   HONOR
3.   FALLEN
4.   WAR
5.   VENGEANCE
(DYSPHORIA)
6.   RISE
7.   PERMANENCE (MAY 2019)

Connect through facebook:
https://www.facebook.com/terrawhitemanscifi/

Sign up for the mailing list for new releases in Hymn of the Multiverse, advanced reading copies, book giveaways and sneak peaks at works in progress: http://eepurl.com/dDFIy5